Mrs. Randall

Mrs. Randall

Christopher T. Leland

1987

BOSTON

Houghton Mifflin Company

Library of Congress Cataloging-in-Publication Data

Leland, Christopher T.
Mrs. Randall.

I. Title.   II. Title: Mistress Randall.
PS3562.E4637M7   1987   813'.54   86-27830
ISBN 0-395-42729-0

Printed in the United States of America

S 10 9 8 7 6 5 4 3 2 1

For my godparents

W. J. FARWELL

&

THELMA W. FARWELL

And for my grandmother,

JULIA F. RUDOLPH,

"The prettiest baby in Lock Haven"

Prologue

1904

HE WATCHED THE LIGHTS fade one by one, smothered quick as kittens, as they turned the wicks down. There amid the bushes, his breath smoky in the dark, he waited unmoving, keeping time by the cheap watch bulging in his breast pocket. He sat two hours and forty-three minutes, through the vague clatter of dishes and pans in the basin; a tune moaning on the pedal organ. The front door opened once, then slammed, the bolt sharp and final in the latch. Between those sounds was silence, when he dared not rustle the branches around him; when he pulled his jacket tighter to him and strained to catch the crack of approaching footsteps or the snuffle of a curious dog.

He saw her for an instant before she closed the curtains, just a shadow against the light. There would be a moment when, hidden, she was naked, before she slipped into the flannel nightgown trimmed at the throat with lace. Then she would turn down the comforter, settle into bed, dim the light, and lie still and alone till sleep came.

His eyes closed. He could see her on her side or back, whiter than she should be for not being in the sun, whiter still for the white of the sheets, for autumn and approaching snow, not yet asleep because she sensed someone was near. But that would pass. As his watch ticked on, she would grow accustomed to the fear, befriend it, and forget it. Then she too would close her eyes.

He stirred stiffly, his knees aching and toes and fingers numb. He crept forward, doubled over as he approached the window. Hugging the deeper shadow beneath the eaves, he took from his pocket the tack and string, then slipped off one cuff link. He looped a knot around it and pressed the tack deep into the wood of the sash, so when she stood there next morning she would see the jewelry dangling, or would awaken before dawn to find it set tapping on the glass by the wind.

He eased back to the bushes; then, the street. In the darkened town, he met only one person, head inclined against the chill, striding quickly down the sidewalk from dark into dark.

At the boarding house, the landlady told him she did not approve of boys who kept late hours.

She awoke when it strove inside her, pressing tentatively just as the sun came up, and she lay expectant, hoping it would move again. Feeling it there did not shame her as it had at first, swelling each day a little larger. Her humiliation had transformed itself like the season, till in the deceptive stillness of that October morning, she waited with anticipation and something like pride for the next quiver of that thing alive within her.

The room took shape with the sunlight. The caps of the bedposts changed from silhouettes of candle flames to brass rosebuds; the coat rack from a lurking bandit to a housedress, sweater, and broad-brimmed sunhat. She heard her aunt in the kitchen and felt no more movement there next to her belly. It must be sleeping now. She would have liked to remain, utterly still, till it stirred again. But her condition allowed no shirking. That is what her aunt would call it — "shirking" — if she had to come to rouse her. She pulled herself up and slowly out of bed, wary of dizziness; slipped out of her nightgown and into the housecoat. Feeling clownish, ungainly, she pinned back her hair, which gave her face a severity almost penitential. Before, she had always let it hang free, caught sometimes with a ribbon, but since no one saw her now, it was better to pull it out of the way, so it would not hang in her face as she read or cross-stitched or tatted, pitted cherries or shelled peas, performing whatever minor and sedentary tasks her aunt invented, telling her it was important to keep busy.

She straightened the bedclothes and set the things on the bureau in order: her hairbrush and the picture of her parents and the jewel case with a lock, empty but for a cut-glass pendant and an antique ring. With the room set right, she pulled back the curtains to let in the sun. She did not pause to look, but gathered up the letter she had begun the previous night and was almost to the door before she noticed the shadow, suspended like a faint, gray tear in the frame of the window. She turned, and something caught the light, glistening there beyond the glass. She opened the window and reached out. Teetering on the sill, every moment afraid of falling, she could just grasp it, close her fingers around it, and break the string that held it.

Back inside, she opened her hand and studied the cuff link, its silver plate wearing thin on the back, engraved with the initials CEB.

In the sticky afternoon, she crouched with her cousin and sister, watching them slither and swing to the water. And he above all, shiny and brown with that slash of white from his waist nearly to where she should not have been looking at all.

She hid the cuff link in the jewel box, covering it with the pendant, then locked the lid and pushed the key deep into her pocket, beside the baby not yet born. She pinched her cheeks, thinking she might be pale, and went to joint Aunt Emma for breakfast.

They knew less of her than they did of Emma, and of Emma they knew little at all. Just after Emma had arrived in town ten years before, a neighbor dropped by and asked in a neighborly fashion about her past. Emma replied in a voice like a brandished knife that she had no past, no past worth mentioning, and that was the end of that. A few times, she had taken the train east, perhaps to Pennsylvania, for she corresponded regularly with people who shared her name in a half-dozen places in that state. But she got letters too from New York and Maryland and Knoxville, Tennessee, so it was difficult to tell with certainty where exactly she had come from.

She could be seen downtown on Tuesdays, and every Sunday she occupied a back pew in the Methodist church. Beyond that, she remained at home, supporting herself with her sewing and by drafts drawn on banks in Philadelphia and New York. She had various acquaintances in town, women who commissioned outfits they had seen in magazines or, now and then, a wedding dress. She had no friends. With little use for gossip and a suspicion of idle conversation, she spent her time alone, gardening or indoors, but for her weekly excursions downtown or to church and a trip each spring to the cemetery to decorate the graves in the charity plot. She was flawlessly neat, really rather pretty, cordial but always distant, and maddeningly enigmatic.

When she returned from her last trip east, Emma brought with her a girl — her niece, she said, married and widowed within a month, now expecting a child. That was all she offered, and that only grudgingly to the pastor. Rumors of wealth and position and high living had always swarmed around Emma, and the rumors redoubled with Sara's arrival. They learned her name from a letter she received postmarked Wilkes-Barre soon after her arrival. After that, all mail was addressed to Emma.

During the six months she had been there, Sara herself went to town only once: on a visit to the doctor one Thursday afternoon. Emma stopped there regularly afterward as her niece's time drew near. Dr. Blankenship, when they asked him, said the girl would give birth within a couple months, that during the examination she had answered all questions with either yes or no, and when he asked her if she were a little afraid to have a baby, had not said anything at all.

She looked younger than she ought to, Sara decided, watching Emma at the organ, not quite severe or settled enough for a woman of more than thirty. It was nothing she did to herself: not face creams, the way she dressed, how she wore her hair. She surely lacked the easiness of youth. When she smiled, which was rarely, it was at something more touching than funny, and even then the smile had a reticence, a sadness, which could not be denied.

Sara set down her book and looked closer.

It emerged when Emma left herself unguarded, not when she spoke or prepared to go to town. But in those moments when she did not notice others around her, it rose like the flicker of pride still visible on the face of a saint. Something unfinished, something uncontrollable she would have suppressed if she could, shone through those eyes of a spinster still young but growing older, lonelier, and finally a little mad as she pumped the treadles of the organ and fingered some etude she had learned long before.

The baby moved, and Sara glanced at the clock. The light-headedness that had come and gone sporadically returned, and she touched her palm to her forehead. It was late, and she did not want to leave him too long in the cold. But she could do nothing extraordinary, nothing suspicious. All day she had done her chores deliberately, serenely, though when she thought of the cuff link, she would tremble as with a chill. She had read that afternoon as always, forcing herself to follow the story, and had finished the letter home, re-reading it all to detect any change in tone. She had grown wily as the child grew within her.

The music stopped, and Emma turned on the bench. "Are you tired tonight?"

"No, no, I've been feeling a little dizzy."

"Dizzy?"

Sara nodded; touched her temple. "Yes. You know, like before."

"Is it worse now?"

"A little, I think." Sara shifted in her chair.

"You should sleep."

"Oh, no. No. Play some more. I'll sit up with you."

"No, I'm tired too. We might as well both go to bed." Emma gathered the music off the rack and slipped it into the basket by the organ.

Sara rose and turned down the lamp by the armchair, then waited by the threshold of the hall till her aunt came from locking up. They walked together to the door of her room.

"Good night, Aunt Emma."

"Good night." She brushed her lips across her niece's cheek. "Call me if you need anything in the night."

Sara lit the lamp in her room, waiting for the sound of the latch on Emma's door. Hearing it, she picked up her brush for a moment, then replaced it noisily on the bureau. She slipped a shawl out of one of the drawers and pulled back the covers on her bed. Turning down the wick, she tiptoed as best she could to the straight-back chair in the corner and sat.

She waited there, hands folded, five, ten, twenty minutes, knowing time rushed for her, wanting to be sure her aunt was sleeping. Finally, when she could stand it no longer, she went to the jewel case. She felt the plain, smooth wood of it there in the darkness, like a tiny hope chest in her hands. She found the key in her pocket, opened the box, and took out the cuff link. In the dark, she tried to trace the initials with her fingertip — angry and happy and sad at his coming; hoping he was still there, that he had not left because the lamp was out.

8

In the gloom, she touched it, white and angry yet for all the
years across the brown, hard expanse of him, and he was saying:
". . . and Daddy always called it my dueling scar, 'cause that
sounds a whole lot better than getting caught on a fence, don't
you think so?" He laughed and rolled off the pallet; walked
through the gray-black of the cabin to peek outside.

With him gone from beside her, she could smell the musti-
ness that seeped from the walls and the few sticks of furniture,
there in that place which had once been his family's. She smiled,
stretched contentedly, no more afraid or guilty than the time be-
fore, and watched him flip the half-rotten curtain tentatively
aside.

"It's stopped raining," he said.

She crossed to the window and pushed it open. The night's
chill struck her, pure and sharp.

"Coleman?" she whispered.

She heard a rustling, then saw him take shape out of the
bushes, tangled in the branches, then free of them, moving almost noiseless across the lawn. His clothes were black. She
reached out.

He took her hand, grasping it as if he would pull her to him.
But they remained, after that first touch, frozen, her skin fair on
his as fine paper on rosewood. Her fingers were warm against
him. He strained to see her face.

"Sarie," he said. "Sarie, come outside."

She pulled her hand away. "I can't come outside."

"Should I come in? I want to talk."

"We can't talk, Coleman." She drew her shawl closer. "My
aunt will hear."

"I have to talk to you. Let me come in."

"No!" She pushed him back as he struggled onto the sill. "No,
you mustn't."

"Come outside, then. It'll be all right." He knelt below the
window. "Here, step on my shoulder."

9

She poked her head out, her whisper rising. "I can't climb out, Coleman. I might hurt the baby."

He started at the word, then continued, coaxing. "Step on my shoulder. I'll be careful. Hurry, before someone sees us."

She might have closed the window then, melted back into her room. She hesitated. Then she was struggling over the sill, inch by inch, her feet probing the night, seeking his shoulders. She slipped slowly down his back, till her toes touched ground and she was next to him. He looked at her briefly through the darkness, then kissed her quickly and very hard on the lips.

"This way," he said, taking her hand. "Quiet."

He led her to the arbor at the back of the property, overgrown, almost a ruin. The crossbeams sagged under vines thick as tree limbs, through which the glow of night passed weakly if at all over seasons and seasons of dead leaves, soft and damp in the cold.

Coleman scooped clean a filligreed wooden chair, weathered almost to rotting, incongruous still in the desolation. He motioned for Sara to sit down.

"You shouldn't have come, Coleman . . ." she began.

"I want us to get married."

She could feel his eyes upon her and did not hear his breath. He had not meant to say it then, she could tell. But she knew too why he had, why, unsummoned and near-rebellious, words meant to come after long and often-rehearsed arguments and pleas had lurched forth in a presence whose power he had forgotten, as she thought she had forgotten his.

She shook her head slowly. "No, Coleman." She stood up. He grabbed her shoulder.

"Why? Why not?" He turned her around, standing so close he brushed her belly with his own. He jumped back, as if he had not really noticed till then.

He placed his hand tenuously, gently, on the baby. "When will it come?"

"Soon."

"When?" he insisted.

"In two weeks, maybe." She stepped away. "Help me back through the window now."

"No. Not yet." He stroked her stomach again.

"Stop that!"

His hand leapt as if burnt. "I'm sorry," he stuttered. "Don't go back yet. Don't go back at all. Sit down." He pushed her gently into the chair. "I want us to get married."

His face took shape out of the gloom, wide-eyed with a patchy three-day beard. He might be handsomer now than before, she decided, handsomer than when they were last together in darkness, his looks becoming firmer, riper in the months that had passed, adolescence fading — very slowly, not completely — as he came closer to being a man.

She touched his hand. "I can't marry you now, like I couldn't marry you then."

"But you can!" It was more plea than declaration. "We could go right now to a preacher or a j.p. It'd be done before you know it."

She pursed her lips, superior, feeling much older then. "Do you think someone would marry us, with me like this?" She did not even bother to gesture.

"But sure." He took her shoulders. "Sure. He'd understand then why we were in a hurry."

"We'd need consent, Coleman. Both of us. And you couldn't get it and I couldn't either, not nine months ago and not now." She drew herself up. "And even if we could, I wouldn't marry you."

His hand fell away.

She began to cry.

"Sarie . . ."

"It's all set now." She spoke, breathless, quick, afraid to stop. "It's all set. I'm going away when it's over. Down South. And it will be like it never happened, and no one will know, and things will start fresh and everything will be like before."

He stared at her, bewildered, as if she were talking in another language. "Hey," he whispered, kneeling beside her. "Hey, it can't be like before. You'll have the baby."

She laid her head against him and was silent for a moment. Then she said deliberately, finally:

"No. I won't have the baby."

"You won't . . ."

"I'll leave the baby with Aunt Emma and go away and never come back and no one will know. Coleman. Coleman, it's all planned. It's the best way. It is . . ." She could see he did not believe it, that he did not accept it. "It is." She drew her hand along his stubbly cheek; stroked his hair gently off his face.

"That's a lie!" He threw himself away from her. "It's a lie, a goddamn lie! Do you hear me?" He would have shouted if he had had any breath, but his words came out in a strangled sound, not a whisper but that of a man struck full in the chest. "I didn't rob my own kin in the middle of the night and sneak away and come west five hundred miles for Aunt Emma. And I didn't run around crazy and cry and not tell anybody about it the day I found out you were gone because of Aunt Emma. And . . . and . . ." His voice hissed softly, furiously. "I didn't lie down with Aunt Emma . . . to make a baby."

If she had thought, she would not have said it.

"You didn't mean to make a baby with me."

They stood under the arbor — intimate; alone. The only sound was the rub of Coleman's boot as he ground it slowly into the leaves, as if everything churning inside him were a mechanism for performing that one, simple motion, over and over, passion enough to cry and storm and pull the arbor down around them reduced to that one repetitive act, grinding wet leaves into a mash there in the darkness.

"Do you remember . . . ?" Sara trembled with new cold and steadied herself against one of the posts. She did not look at him. "Do you remember Jeffery McCalister? He was the McCalister's oldest son, Mrs. McCalister who clerked at the dry goods store. Do you remember him?"

She sounded very tired, more tired than she ought to have been. She did not wait for Coleman's reply.

"He left town years ago, before we could really know about it. I think sometimes I recall who he was, seeing him once when I was very little — at a picnic, I think, where someone said his name. But he left town very suddenly and no one was sure why and he never came back, even though he was very young at the time." She cleared her throat and pulled her shawl higher on her neck. "He was very handsome, if I remember him really, a little like you, a very handsome man even though he wasn't quite a man yet when I think I saw him. But he was Aunt Emma's age and he was her beau, I guess you'd say, a lot like you were to me, he was to her then, and . . . and the very same thing that happened to us happened to them . . ."

Coleman did not take his eyes from the lawn. "And she gave her baby away and so now she thinks she . . ."

"When they found out, when the family, my family, found out that Aunt Emma was going to have a baby, my father and my Uncle Edgar and Uncle Jim said they would kill Jeffery McCalister even though he was only sixteen. And they would have done it. If he hadn't run away, they would have done it. And they knew and you know and I know no jury would have ever blamed them, just like if I ever told them this baby was yours they would kill you probably and no one would blame them. But he ran away so they couldn't kill him, and they decided that nobody would ever have to know that he and Aunt Emma had been together if she didn't have the baby. So one night . . ."

She swallowed.

"One night — I remember it was a Sunday night because we had been to church that day and Aunt Emma hadn't gone with us and didn't come to dinner either. I was only four, and they sent me to bed early, I think, but later I got up because I had a dream. I called but nobody came so I got up and went down the hall. And when I got to Aunt Emma's room, I heard noises, the bed creaking and some other sounds like crying. So I went to the door and opened it and even though they saw me I saw them all there first — Mother and Grannie Ada and all my aunts around the bed, holding Aunt Emma on the bed and Mother was holding her mouth and Aunt Edna was kneeling on top of her, on her stomach, pushing her knee into her stomach.

"Then Mother saw me. She took her hand off Aunt Emma's mouth and Aunt Emma started screaming and screaming and I ran back down the hall and I could hear Mother behind me. But she didn't come into my room. She only locked the door.

"And in the morning, when I got up, Dr. McFarland was there. Grannie Ada told me Aunt Emma was very sick, and she stayed sick for a month or two, and then she got better and moved away, came here after she lived down South for a while where we have people. Where I'll go."

She stopped. She was crying.

Coleman drew close behind her and ran his hands up and down her arms. "I'm sorry. I'm sorry they killed her baby." He pulled her to him. "But it isn't our fault. She can't take our baby for what they did to her. She could have married somebody and . . ."

"No! Don't you see, Coleman? After what they did, when they had to call the doctor, it made it so she couldn't have any more. Any more babies. They did something to her insides and Dr. McFarland told them she would never be able to have . . ."

His voice was firmer now. "But that's not our fault. She has no right to take our baby. It's our baby. It's half my baby and —"

"Coleman!" She grasped his collar and twisted suddenly to face him. "Coleman, if it wasn't for her there wouldn't be any baby! They would have done what they did to her to me. Even if they made everything inside all wrong. Even if it made me just like her. If she hadn't been there when we found out and made them let her take me and told them she would never in this life let them do to me what they did to her, they would have done it!"

She bit his shirt to keep from crying aloud, pressing into him as if that recalled threat lurked outside the arbor. He looked away into the darkness, idly petting her hair, on his face the mute incomprehension of a man just shot.

"Take me back now, Coleman. Take me back to the window."

The moon had risen while they talked. They crept back across the lawn through the silver night, and he boosted her gently across the sill. Inside, she turned, framed in the deeper black of her room.

"How did you find me?"

He smiled for the first time since he had come. "Errol, my brother-in-law, you know, he works at the P.O. I help him sometimes, and I saw how many letters came from here, even though the writing wasn't yours. So I stole one once and saw your letter with one from your aunt. So then, about three weeks ago, I decided I ought to come and get you."

"You shouldn't have come."

He laughed softly, bitterly. "Everybody does things they shouldn't, sometimes."

"Yes." She paused. "Coleman . . ."

Before she could say any more, he leapt up to kiss her, holding himself there with his elbows locked and his hands planted on the sill. His arms began to tremble, but still he kissed her till they gave way beneath him and he fell back to earth.

She slipped further into the darkness.

"Good-bye, Coleman. Here."

The cuff link arced through the night, rustled the dry grass. He picked it up.

"Keep it. Please."

"No. Good-bye."

"Sarie."

"Yes."

He put his hands on his hips, looked at his feet; began to back away.

"My room is in the boarding house across the street from the doctor's. I can see him come and go, and who comes for him. So when it's time, I'll know."

"Coleman!"

She leaned far out the window.

He was already gone.

She stepped out of the office into the June near-twilight just before supper, as the heat broke and the guests at the boarding house began to gather on the porch. Fanning themselves with folded newspapers, chatting in that idle and revealing way of strangers, only one or two noticed her at all as she turned down the street, walking with that serenity somehow reminiscent of Emma's frosty dignity. The regulars there — salesmen and circuit riders and rail inspectors — knew her on sight after eight months, the time since she emerged from her aunt's house the mother of a week-old boy. And they, like the townspeople they dealt with, found her as perplexing though less disturbing than Emma; spoke of her — if they did at all — not with malicious curiosity but with the peculiar affection usually reserved for a beautiful object, something delicate and transient like a rose, for there was around Sara an almost tangible air of impermanence, an aura not dreamy but dreamlike, perishable as something glimpsed between sleeping and waking.

And for Sara, gliding down the sidewalk, crepuscular in her

gauzy summer dress through the cool and crepuscular still, it was as if all the buildings beside her were insubstantial as shadows, all the passers-by no more palpable than smoke. In her bag was the ticket to Memphis, thence to Knoxville, and in three days, when she stepped from the vestibule into Cousin Kat's arms, it would be like waking up, like opening her eyes after a year of sleep to find herself again the small-town princess she was meant to be. She would nod at gallantries from Tennessee squires, who would accept her without questions, charmed by her laugh and her carriage and the way she spoke, intrigued by a young lady who knew Buffalo and Philadelphia instead of New Orleans or Atlanta. There would be no expectation of past indiscretions, no one enough uncivil to imagine her loss of that not-even-skin essential for a suitable wife, no inkling that the adopted child of a spinster aunt back North was hers. Even when her hand was asked, there would be no need for confession and recrimination. She had found in Emma's house the morocco-bound volume *Memories of Spain*, written by a man more honest than discreet, who told of Andalusian gypsy girls who, on their wedding nights, carried a secret vial of chicken blood, assuring that the marriage sheets would show the proper stain next morning no matter what the truth.

Yet as she passed, dream within dream down the streets of the town, there was in her tranquility something that gave the lie to the calm of face and gait. Her right hand wound white, her expression so determinedly seraphic it seemed cold and fragile as glass, she felt herself shudder at each second glance from a loitering old man or adolescent, each passing wife or spinster who might understand with the surety of instinct what that mask so carefully fashioned should have hidden.

In the office, they heard the boys playing softball in the park alongside, and she could see herself in the door of the cabinet where he kept the bottle of bourbon and the six battered tum-

blers, the checkers and a deck of cards. Dr. Blankenship, a long, gray man with sad, gray eyes, the faint perfume of whiskey already on his breath though it was not long after four, leaned across the desk saying: "I don't believe you." Not in challenge, almost in apology — "I do not believe you" — as if he were sorry to question her, to call her untruthful. There in that office, with no other sound than the vague cheering, and the slap of the batted ball sharp as her knowledge in that split second that he was sure, that he did not doubt the veracity of anyone, especially of a woman, unless he were certain of the lie. But she could not in that instant accept that, and she grasped the arms of the chair in fear but hoping it looked like rage at the idea her child's paternity should be doubted, saying too loud, somehow with the wrong inflection: "My husband died in a train wreck on the fifteenth of April of last year. In Baltimore."

And the doctor, shaking his head I-do-not-believe-you: "There wasn't a train wreck in Baltimore last year in April, at least, not one where anybody died. The stationmaster says so. He reads all the publications and talks with all the agents. I had him ask. There was no wreck."

She eyed him warily, hoping for some sign that he himself was lying, that for some obscure and unnatural reason he attacked her honor without any foundation. But she could see in his sadness, not just of his eyes but of his whole self — his face and his hands and the way he held his body — that he had grasped some knowledge not yet comprehensible but sound, and that he had set himself to prove it, no matter how hurtful for him or for her.

"Jeffery died . . ."

"If your husband was Jeffery McCalister," he said slowly, "he died in a train wreck over ten years ago, three miles from here, on the line to Williamsfield."

She crossed the street to the other side, which was lonelier, and glanced at the grade crossing two blocks down. She looked away to avoid it, into the dark shop windows, into herself reflected in the gloom.

"He'll ask you about leaving today," Emma said as she diapered the baby. "That's why he wants to see you."

Sara, at the dressing table, wound the ribbon through her hair, which was lush and a little sun-bleached now by the summer. "It wouldn't surprise me," she said quietly. "He's the only one who'll ever have the chance."

"I suppose you're right." Emma took the baby and settled him in the crib, then walked behind Sara and tied the bow. Sara could see her in the mirror, face intent but softer since the baby came.

Emma stepped back. "There. You should wear green more often." She fingered the sleeve of the dress, the color of a lime's flesh. "It sets off your eyes."

The baby stirred — the baby with those same eyes, the burnish of his father's skin — and Emma turned to him.

"Hush now, Jeffery." She stroked his hair. "Hush."

Sara stood and smoothed her skirt. "I should go."

She felt the cloth against her legs, like spiders' webs, like woven dust, soundless as she moved beneath it, cooler than the growing dark. On her skin it was like the past, like a soundless whisper of someone she had hoped to forget, and she cursed herself then for letting her aunt name the baby, and grasped her right hand tighter still.

When the minister said: "Name this child . . ." it was her aunt who said with soft but victorious clarity: "Jeffery Alan McCalister."

She walked, her face set, nodding when a voice disembodied by the gloaming greeted her. "Good evening, Sara."

Just as at the county clerk's, when he asked the father's name, Emma, not Sara, replied, unhesitant: "Jeffery Alan McCalister."

19

And the clerk said: "Spelled like the child's name?"

And Emma responded: "Yes."

And finally: "Where is the father?"

Then Emma, in possession at last of what she had lost to her men's misguided honor and her women's brute incompetence, of the flesh and blood to stand stead for an unborn child and a fleeing lover; Emma, unflinching at last — even if it were half ashes — exultant, said: "He is dead."

And yes, Sara thought at that moment, Coleman Bennett is dead, struck dead by that woman he never laid with to make a baby, dead in the name of a son he had never seen christened for a vanished boy and a snuffed-out bastard.

She hurried a little. There was no one to watch her now, and she had to reach the church before sunset, while there was still light enough to see.

"I shouldn't have understood, Sara," the doctor said as he paced back and forth from the window. "I should not have known because it was all intricate and devious as a Chinese puzzle, but perhaps if it had been simpler I might never have tried. Do you see? I never meant any harm by what I did, discovering things I never expected to find, things I would not, I swear to you, tell to anyone else. But you must help me to understand what has happened, you must do that."

He looked at her with that great, sad face, like a man who discovers someone he knows, perhaps loves, in an act unconscionable and incomprehensible. "What I can tell you is this, that ten years ago the local to Williamsfield was rammed from behind by the two-forty freight, that three people from around here were killed, along with a fellow who nobody knew, who carried a silver-plate pocket watch engraved inside the dust cover with initials. We buried him in the county plot under those initials, which we had to assume were his, like we assumed the watch was really his and not stolen or picked up in a pawnshop somewhere.

20

"About a year later, Emma came to town and took a room at the Dilman House, and one night she came up to me in the dining room, where I used to eat sometimes, and said: 'There's a man buried in the charity plot who was killed in the train wreck here last year. Do you happen to know his name?' And I said that we only knew his initials, or what we thought were them, anyway. And she asked what those might be and I told her and she said she had thought it might have been a friend of her brother's, but that those initials could not be his. She took the house about two weeks after that, and she's lived here ever since."

Nearing the crest of the hill, she could see the spire, like a shaft of pearl in the evening, and she quickened her pace up the deserted street. Faintly, supper noises — muffled voices and the clatter of plates and tinkle of glasses, sometimes a laugh — murmured to her as she passed, drawing closer to the iron-pike fence, forbidding and funereal along the sidewalk, as if to imprison the dead.

"If I tell you, Doctor . . ." She could hardly recognize her voice, there amidst the ruins of a fiction she herself had almost come to believe, staring at that solitary piece of jewelry. *"If I tell you, will you change the records?"*

Sitting now at his desk, his elbows on the wood and fingertips against his chin, still sad but animated — no, exhilarated — before a jumble of confusion that had begun to assume shape, he said: "Legally I would have to, but I won't."

She wrapped her palm around the cool, cheap metal, felt it warm in her grasp. "The 'E' is for Edouard," she found herself saying, "because his mother was French somehow. From the South, I think. He isn't very tall and a little thin, and he has a long scar from getting caught on a fence once, but I think he's the handsomest boy I ever saw. He was just different and better than all the other boys. I let him love me three times, in an empty cabin where he lived once when he was little, and the last time, last winter, we made the baby. My family doesn't know he's the father, and it would do no good to tell them, because my father always thought his people were too dark and too common to be respectable. If Aunt Emma hadn't been there when they found out I was carrying the baby, they would've tried to kill him. They would have pushed on me till I dropped him. She saved Jeffery's life, and it's only right that she should have him."

He averted his eyes and said nothing, but she could see the judgment there, in the very gesture, one not of admiration but of pity. For the first time since she sat with Coleman in the arbor, someone had been privy to that plan so perfectly and Solomonically rational, and turned away not in awe at its biblical justice but in compassion.

Sara realized then that the scheme had failed; failed not because it had been puzzled out by a doctor sad and curious, but because that talisman, that memento intended for her, had fallen into a stranger's hands and set him wondering, had finally filled him with enough knowledge and pain to return it to her and remind her of someone she had half convinced herself she had forgotten, and who now she could never forget.

And the doctor was saying: ". . . but for that, I would have never questioned things. I would have had no call to question things. But the initials reminded me of something. Initials, I kept thinking. And then you or she or whoever named the baby, and it came back to me: 'To J. A. McC./On His 16th/B-day.' That's all it said, no date or year because the watch was small. Then all I could do was suspect, never intending ever to mention anything to anybody, until I found out you were leaving, and I saw that I would never have another chance to be sure." His face was the same, so apologetic and not a little confused, anxious and creased with a great will to understand. "So, tell me something about Jeffery McCalister. Just to help me make sense of this somehow."

She might have told him everything then, all she had heard, gleaned, intuited from conversations and chances and dreams. But there was no point, and she herself was no longer sure that she understood.

"Jeffery McCalister was the son of a lady in the town where I grew up, where Aunt Emma grew up. A clerk lady, his mother. His father was dead, I suppose. I hardly remember him, though I think I saw him once. He was good-looking and seemed very old to me then." She paused, drawing around herself with greatest effort that impenetrability that permitted no challenge, which she had seen her aunt employ so long and well. "He was a beau of Aunt Emma's, and he ran away, and she must have followed him. Perhaps they had planned it. When she found him, even though he was dead, then I suppose she settled down." She smiled, with great naturalness, she thought. "That's all I can tell you."

Her feet on the grass made a sound like whispering, like the speech of the dead, all the breathless murmurings of anonymous dust rising, calling up to her out of the earth, and one among them, indistinguishable but sure, was that of a man of no name but only the initials . . .

"C. E. B.," the doctor had said as he tossed it onto the desk to rattle toward her over the dark, scarred wood.

whose name she knew; whose name was her son's,

"So when I was leaving, I went around the house and saw it . . ."

who fled angry brothers and murder sure as a promise,

"Tacked to the window sash," she finished for him, her thumb polishing the metal, tracing the monogram she had last sought that October night in the dark of her room, half dizzy with confused expectation of she did not know what.

whose love had followed him until she found him to be beside him if only in death.

In the almost dark, she did not need to make out the letters in the stone, flat and soft, already in a decade worn, flush with the earth in the corner of the churchyard; beneath the initials another set of letters, "R.I.P." And yes, she thought, rest now, Jeffery McCalister, who was and then was not and now is, metamorphosed into someone else's bastard; rest for the sake of the living, for the sake of Coleman Bennett who must feel both dead and alive in one body as Jeffery McCalister is both dead and alive in two.

"Do you remember, Sara, that night . . ." The doctor had spoken slowly, sadly, with the pain of already knowing the yes that would verify all that he had guessed and supposed, and she really did not have to listen to capture what he said, because she could recount it herself with the ragged intensity of a torn nerve. "When I held him up by his heels so you could see and gave him the spank, and he began to cry and then . . ."

It had gone on — though she could see the doctor with the baby — that moiling in her belly to cast out now what was useless, as if her body could rid itself of all memory of that nine-month labor of construction, of nourishment and growth, and she heard the dry, sharp sound of the slap and then the breath, the cry of something new alive, which melded, mixed, converged, with another sound . . .

". . . and I could tell you heard it too, because you looked at the window and it was on your face, something unspeakable, and then it ended."

She had seen him then, sure as if she had rushed from the bed and raised the shade, felt the October cold of the glass against her face, as he bit the sleeve of that worn, black coat and ran from under the window away toward nothing, but away, because he had no place anymore and must be anywhere but there and where they made the baby. And she tore her eyes from the window and felt the afterbirth unmoored and turned in her dizzi-

ness and exhaustion to see her aunt raising the baby from the bed in disbelief. In triumph.

There were stars by then, pale but growing brighter in the velvet night, but she did not move, though her aunt would worry and her child of not much longer might crave in some unknowing way her touch. She stood in the green gauziness of a remade virgin, of the very first of spring, beside that marker set sure as a star in the earth's loamy darkness; between her fingers a cuff link, like the tiny tombstone of a man who has lost his name.

Mrs. Randall

1

THEY BURNED HIM on a Friday. I remember it was a Friday because on Fridays we practiced not at school but at the stadium they had built in the hopes the A&M that the legislature was establishing was destined for Franksville. It wasn't. But the stadium gave us, the track team, a place to run unlike any for counties around, but, by some bureaucratic whim, only on Fridays. And on that Friday, I surely ran harder from the stadium to the house than I had run all those laps and dashes since one o'clock; unshowered, barreling past stone arches, down the street, up the hill, mounting the porch to burst through the door, shouting:

"Mrs. Randall! Mrs. Randall! They're going to burn him! They tore up the ties from the spur to the Pritchards' new mill and they're going to burn him!"

She appeared in her dressing gown at the top of the stairs, elegant even then, on a day unspecial, mean. A Friday. Elegant as always, as she should be for being a woman so young, the wife of a man with a son more than half her age. She stood stone still, and her sad dignity melted as utterly as a candle cast in a furnace, making her worthy, in my sixteen-year-old eyes, not of pity but of some hotter and nobler passion as she slumped against the bannister:

"Gams, no! No, they mustn't, Gams. They mustn't!"

*   *   *

29

Mrs. Randall came to live with us when I was twelve. It was not as if I could ever have called her mother. I remembered my own mother too well, and Mrs. Randall as the wife of Mr. Randall. He, since long before I was born, had been state senator from Franksville; had gone to the capital every other year for the Assembly, not to some overpriced hotel they have since torn down, but to a suite in the home of a one-time Princeton classmate, some other lawyer well installed who argued many a case before the state supreme court. For all those many years, Mr. Randall had gone a bachelor, an aging one surely, but one who maintained the looks not only of a sage and prosperous man but also of one perhaps destined for Washington, for a congressional seat or, at least, a call to some undersecretary's desk.

Such a summons would have suited him, and in that he was different from my father — his protégé of sorts, and his wife's second husband. My father, for all his Princeton manners and careful, flawless French, his dashing looks and half-exotic name, had no ambitions outside Franksville. For him, to be a successful small-town lawyer in the place where he grew up represented not a burden but the realization of middling childhood dreams. He had set his sights on conquering a world he knew well and, having done so, had not the slightest inclination toward pursuing some Alexandrian project. There would be no weeping at the Indus. With the certainty and practicality of a child of clerks, he longed for nothing greater than a successful siege of Franksville and, having achieved it before the age of thirty, settled in to enjoy the fruits of his triumph.

My grandparents, on both sides, were long dead by the time I arrived. My mother's parents — my mother who was never well, the incongruous descendant of some hearty seventeenth-century Scotch-Irish renegade, on her face even in childhood photographs the mark of an early death by consumption — my mother's parents were little more than wage slaves, like all those

30

other wage slaves at the mills. In some ways, they were better off. My grandfather was a foreman. My grandmother worked at the company store, serving as agent of indenture for the Pritchards, the last of the great landowning families, enfiefed still on the only facsimile of a plantation Franksville could boast. My grandparents were good Presbyterians. Good Presbyterians with only one daughter who surely even they could see was doomed. So, when the chance came for her marriage with Gambetta Stevenson, they rejoiced, and both died within a year, having completed all their earthly duties, assured that their pale and already dying daughter was well provided for until, too soon, she might join them among those certainly predestined for everlasting bliss.

And my father's people? Grocers who sweated and saved to provide not for their two daughters, who ended first in thrall to the cash register and stockroom and then to their brother's charity, but for that single son, that lonely, golden boy whom they shamed and whipped and guilted through first grade, fifth grade, high school, Princeton. For whom they sacrificed not only daughters but health and wealth and any small, silly pleasures they might have enjoyed, so that son — their Gambetta, marked with that name Italianate and insolite — might catch the eye of Mr. Randall, might apply for and obtain a scholarship there in that North they hated still and had never seen, might return finally to Franksville fit for the bar, with powerful friends throughout the continent and especially throughout the South, indulged by Mr. Randall as the son he had never had and welcomed into any house, even that of the Pritchards — who surely had never before had a second thought about those quiet, gray people at the market on the corner.

My father's first marriage was made and ended young. My mother was neither elegant nor witty, nor did she carry herself right, and I suspected, even as a boy, that he loved her only in that dutiful and desultory way many English princes must have loved those endless German petty duchesses and queens, un-exciting but acceptable in blood and creed. The common view held he might have married up to a landed family, some proud clan retaining Grandpa's sword and an affectionate letter from Robert E. Lee. But my father doubtless knew what he was about, for my mother served in those first years of his career to lend him respectability. Having known New York and Philadelphia, he had grown a little wild, become suspect in the eyes of rich and poor alike for having journeyed beyond the Potomac. He had now to prove his virtue. A moneyed match might have made him seem a parvenue, and a bride educated in the manner of the day could have proved flighty, or worse, ambitious for the social life of the capital. But my mother — sad-eyed and not unattractive — made him somehow humble, unpretentious, even as the brocade of his vests grew more elaborate, his taste in whiskey more refined. And finally, of course, he won the heart of the town when she died, at the funeral with a little boy of six — me — at his side as the casket was trundled into the pit. Grief was the flame of his apotheosis, purifying him of all baser origins, making him once and for all in the public mind an aristocrat, as if Stevenson, like Pritchard or Randall, were a fine old name of the region, worthy of one of those forged genealogies that trace the line back, not to lice-bearded High-landers at Culloden, but to the blue-blooded Royalists of Mars-ton Moor.

Perhaps, if there is a destiny to things, Mrs. Randall came to live in Franksville because of my father, in whose faust astrology there was no place for extended suffering. If the play time missed and the studies done under threat of the strap had made his childhood miserable, he now deserved better than to be a widower at thirty-two. But in Franksville, even in the counties around, there was in that moment no young woman just exactly right, till she came to us quite unexpectedly one autumn out of Knoxville, Tennessee, on the arm of Mr. Randall, whom everyone had long assumed would be a bachelor forever. He might have been her father, even her grandfather, for when she arrived she could have been no more than twenty. There was a stir, of course, intense but short-lived. I was only a boy, but even I was aware of the whisperings and gossiping and looks askance among aunts and neighbor ladies and even the servants. But that lasted only so long as Mrs. Randall remained a rumor: someone glimpsed at the station or seen from a distance on the veranda of her husband's home.

It was not hard to understand why. Even a nine-year-old, sweaty from crack-the-whip in the street, pressed inside by a spinster aunt, annoyed, resentful, could see it — that fragile sadness, that aura glowing from that woman not yet a woman, which told of some unspoken hurt that made her already too wise. I never forgot how she rustled, how she smelled, some vague, feminine, flowery smell that still was different from all the perfumes my friends' mothers wore, different from the gradually dying fragrance of my mother's sachets. She looked down on me tenderly, almost pained, and said:

"Why, he's a beautiful child, Mr. Stevenson, a beautiful one." And then to me: "You are . . ."

"Gams," I said, sullen for having been ripped from the game. "Gams?"

"Gambetta. Like his father," Mr. Randall said. "But they couldn't call him that. It would make things too confusing. And they couldn't call him Betta" — he chuckled and poked at me with his cane, which he always did — "because then the other boys would call him Betty. So they call him Gams."

My father laughed too, and I scowled.

"I think it's a fine name, a very fine name." She put out her hand gravely. "I'm happy to meet you, Gams."

I took her fingers in my palm and barely pressed, as I had been taught, feeling silly to be so formal with the flush of the game hardly off me.

33

"You can run on now, Gams," my father said.

I did, but I did not forget. From that first moment I was moved by Mrs. Randall.

When I was ten years old, we finished building the house on the hill. We did not physically build it, of course, and indeed, much of the work on it was done not by Franksville artisans but by laborers from the capital and even one from Baltimore, a fussy man with a strange accent who supervised the setting of the leaded glass in the entry hall — a varicolored allegory of Justice and Mercy my father apparently thought appropriate for a lawyer. The house sat on what had been Randall property, but was sufficiently distanced from Mr. Randall's home that the two did not crowd each other. Their lawns formed a wide, very gently sloping, and virtually unbroken field, perfect for football and adequate for croquet, a game my father professed to enjoy, though I suspected he did so only because Mr. Randall seemed to find it entertaining and sufficiently untaxing for a man of his age and girth. Our new house sat at the point where the hill began its descent, the foundation abutting the incline on one side. Hence, its front door was actually at a slightly lower level than Mr. Randall's. My father and the architect, however, had apparently conspired so that on the southwest corner of the building, a hexagonal turret thrust a full story above the peaks of the roof, its single, unheated room surrounded by a sort of widow's walk and surmounted by the conical peak of a fairy tale castle, ending in an elaborate iron weather vane, which might, just might, have overreached by inches the highest point of Mr. Randall's more low-slung abode.

This fact was noted below in Franksville, and the ungainly tower itself was the object, I later found out, of some obscene joking among the men of the town. Mr. Randall nonetheless pronounced himself delighted with his new neighbor, as might be expected in that he had suggested the investments that had allowed my father, at so young an age, to afford such an ostentatious project, and had as well picked out the location for it. Mr. Randall and his young wife now socialized almost constantly with his surrogate son, with me, and with my aunts, Lottie and Bea, whose names, tastes, and faces were as plain in Franksville as my father's were exotic.

On my eleventh birthday, Mr. Randall presented me with a very expensive red and gray bicycle and seemed to take great pleasure in watching me career suicidally down the hill or over the lawn. The bravado I demonstrated delighted him almost as much as my imitations of neighbors — Father Finch, Mr. Keller, Mrs. Cash — something my father found perverse in a child so young but which Mr. Randall pronounced a sign of future greatness. He often demanded an exhibition when he visited, before he and my father adjourned to the oak-paneled study to discuss finances and investments over imported Scotch or sherry, puffing Havanas and sometimes laughing at some new and likely marginally legal scheme to increase their profits.

Mrs. Randall would often accompany her husband, though usually she would share dinner or tea with us, then return to her own house while the men repaired to the study. Those times she did stay, she would attempt conversation with my aunts, an effort doomed to fail. Bea and Lottie, in the end, were goodhearted enough, but their sudden ascendance in social position with their brother's meteoric rise in Franksville left them terminally disoriented. Terrified of saying the wrong thing, of betraying the origins that ninety-five percent of the people who passed through the door were perfectly aware of anyway, guests — even ones so frequent as Mrs. Randall — left them tonguetied, reduced to mindless, carefully paced comments about the weather and, from time to time, about me.

"And how is Gams doing?" I would hear Mrs. Randall inquire as I passed through the hall.

"Oh, very well," one aunt would respond.

"Yes, very well."

"He was a bit feverish, I think, the last time I was here."

"Feverish, yes."

"Yes, a cold."

"A cold was what it was."

A stranger would have found it difficult to determine exactly how many people were involved in conversation in the cavernous parlor, which certainly seemed large enough to be plagued by either echoes or ghosts. Neither Bea nor Lottie — who, even as my father toddled, had been sullenly ringing up prices on the cash register in my grandparents' store — ever overcame their discomfort in that house, in the company of those people with whom they had never expected to associate. Draped always in dowdy dresses of the most conservative colors, they were sometimes mistaken for the help by newcomers.

In fact, we had only one servant, Althea, who cooked. Althea, a high yellow who enjoyed considerable status among black people in Franksville, was an altogether different case from my aunts. Unusually tall for a woman of any race, she commanded attention wherever she went, and she ran our kitchen more or less as she pleased. Lottie and Bea were intimidated by her, but my father found her outspokenness amusing and her cooking irresistible. In exchange, she offered him absolute loyalty, something she transferred as well to me: "Little Mister," she called me. I frequently sat on a stool by the counter as she went about her business, baking, roasting, scouring, steaming, all the while entertaining me with stories, admonitions, and reconstructions of events she had never witnessed but which she re-created vividly, effortlessly, while slapping biscuits into shape or expertly butchering a quarter side of beef.

It was from her I learned most about the world beyond the borders of downtown and the respectable white neighborhoods that ringed the hill. She herself lived in Pallister Slough —

Franksville's Niggertown — where the joereaper was called a Lincoln bird because, to black ears, it cried "Freedom, Freedom"; where it flooded at least twice a year; and where the Magic Lady lived. According to Althea, the Magic Lady could work magic in five different languages and often spoke in tongues. She made love potions, told fortunes, predicted the sex of children, and cast spells for luck. She refused, though — ever — to work black magic, though she claimed she once had learned how to conjure devils. Althea believed absolutely in the Magic Lady's works. When I told her, at eleven or so, that I thought the Magic Lady was just a crazy old nigger who tricked the darkies, she opened the oven, checked the potatoes, and said, "You believe what you see fit, Little Mister. But down the road you need a little luck or you got the Devil on your back, don't you come bellyaching to me for no favors from the Magic Lady, hear?"

With time, Mrs. Randall's visits became sufficiently unremarkable that Lottie and Bea no longer felt obliged to keep her company. There would be some obligatory discussion of trivialities, most often the humidity. Then my aunts would withdraw on the pretext of some pressing chore — mending or washing or the upstairs dusting — and Mrs. Randall would either leave or announce she had brought a book. In the latter case, she would settle into one of the wing chairs by the long French windows and while away an hour or two in the silence broken only by the occasional muffled laughter from beneath the closed door of the study.

I would spy on her then. Not always, of course, but often, taking up a vantage point on the stairs or, in summer, outside just beyond the veranda. I did not watch her for long, as I was as incapable of prolonged stillness as any other eleven-year-old. But the fact that I bothered at all — not only bothered but enjoyed it — demonstrates the magic she worked on me even then. There, silent, wrapped in the wing chair in her voluminous dress in those last years of voluminous dresses, she emanated a sweetness, sure as a rose, which left me hopelessly confused. Occasionally a wisp of hair would drift down to her face, and without taking her eyes from the page, she would put it neatly into place. Only later did it occur to me what purposefulness must have gone into developing such nonchalant grace at so early an age, and I wondered what tremendous event had propelled her to that effort.

I even admired the way she read. My father fidgeted with books. The years of scoldings and strappings and mindless parroting of multiplication tables and spelling words, later of Latin declensions and national capitals, of landmark decisions and byzantine laws, had left him no love of learning. Books were the enemy, or at best fickle and demanding friends. Perhaps that explained his growing interest in business, though law in Franksville was rarely too taxing a profession. Investment required slyness, instinct, sociability, and an elaborately maintained series of contacts, but no great expenditure of mental energy. What he lacked in knowledge, he compensated for in common sense and likability, the quality that had allowed him to rise so far, so fast, while evoking so little rancor or envy.

Mrs. Randall did not play with a book. She cradled it in her hand with what, I thought, was remarkable gentleness, the kind one normally reserves for the head of a baby. She remained very still when she read, her eyes moving slowly down the page, hanging on to the final word as she turned the leaf, as if not to break the flow of the phrase. Occasionally a tiny noise would escape her: a sigh, sometimes; others, only a breath accompanied by a languid smile; once or twice, a little hoot of private outrage. I never knew specifically what she read those afternoons, though later, when she came to live with us, she showed a strong preference for Walter Scott and the Brontë sisters, along with some ephemeral figures from the last century whose names I have since forgotten. I don't believe she ever realized how carefully I observed her, and had I mentioned it, she would probably have been surprised and more than a bit embarrassed. Surely I was surprised, even then, at how a child might be so enthralled by the sight of a young woman — even one so pretty and unidentifiably sad as Mrs. Randall — sitting in a wing chair, reading.

Only after many years did I entertain the notion of Mr. Randall as a pandar. I hadn't the cynical wit at the time to consider it, and even much later and with much behind me, the idea struck me as incredibly coarse. Likely some people thought it at the time, particularly that autumn when Mr. Randall undertook his biannual journey to the capital, leaving his new wife behind till the session was nearly ready for recess and the round of pre-Christmas balls provided him a fitting opportunity to show off the greatest prize of his life. Through that progressively drearier fall, Mrs. Randall rattled around in her deserted house, having for company only her husband's increasingly senile servants, loyally retained in spite of their gradually declining efficiency. It was not that they — Eloise, Annie, Dixie, Leon, and John — were unkind to her; indeed, they seemed not even to resent her, as they might be expected to reject this girl who had arrived unexpectedly on the arm of their patron. They simply went about their routines as if she were not there at all. Mr. Randall had been a bachelor all his life, and with the death of his sister years and years before of tetanus, he and the servants had fallen into patterns of activity and mutual tolerance now completely ossified, certainly not alterable by a demure wisp imported from Tennessee.

Mr. Randall's house was, unintentionally but obstreperously, a masculine one. With no woman to smooth, refine, or blend the taste that formed it, it had become a potpourri of Mr. Randall's evolving interests, a showcase of his passing eccentricities. In the parlor alone there were framed and now rather moldy examples of his brief fling with lepidopterology, some oversized pseudoclassical sculptures from the Hellenic period of his thirties, a filthy bearskin rug, and several generations of mismatched furniture retained on the basis of comfort and utility, not aesthetics.

Given all this, along with her newness in Franksville, it should not have surprised anyone that Mrs. Randall spent more and more time at our house. She received occasional invitations to lunch or to tea with what passed in the town for society, but being so young and a stranger, there was little she could do but exchange pleasantries. With us, however, she seemed relaxed, even cheerful. Before dinner, she and my father sat in the parlor, and as I changed upstairs from play clothes to something more appropriate for dinner with company, I sometimes heard her laughter, shimmering up and through the hall. At the table, she always asked after my studies and also my friends, for whose names she had a much better memory than my father or my aunts, and I was properly flattered. After eating, I went about my homework, while my father retired to his study and the women settled around the fire in the parlor, my aunts knitting or tatting and Mrs. Randall reading her book. Sometimes I might ask for help with my lessons, usually from Mrs. Randall, who seemed to know more than Lottie and Bea and was more patient than my father. After I'd gone to bed, he usually joined the ladies by the hearth, and, drifting off to sleep, I would hear again that lambent, crystalline laughter rising from the room below.

I do not know if they had an affair. It did not occur to me at the time, of course, though it was not unlikely — a widower in his thirties, a young and very lovely woman, lonely and married to an absent husband more than twice her age. As far as I know, she never spent a night with us, except once, during a freak November thunderstorm — a spectacular, icy downpour with more terrifying thunder than I have ever heard since — which kept us all up half the night, which kept Althea from going home, and during which, finally, Mrs. Randall retired to the guest room while my father and I remained in the tower, wrapped in overcoats, watching the jagged lightning tear the black night till we were near exhaustion.

When I finally imagined it, I saw them together, the two there in the tower — though that was improbable, of course, both because of the cold and because the room held only a few sticks of furniture. It was more likely, if it happened at all, that my father led her to his study or the guest room, or his own bed.

But still I imagine them in the tower, golden moonlight swirling around them through the French doors, naked, both of them — my father, white but with the black Scotch-Irish hair of his head and body shimmering darkly, making him almost bearlike, but lithe, a black-haired, bearlike litheness possessing that fragile woman on the soft green carpet, her pale smoothness travertine in the wash of moon, that low flame of her eternal sadness momentarily overwhelmed by the brighter fire of her own passion as he pressed his own desiring deep within her.

Most of the details are, of course, my own invention. My father I often saw naked: after his bath, when we swam summer weekends at the reservoir near the Pritchard house. But Mrs. Randall, in all those years, I never saw in less than a lounging dress until the final hours before she died, when her body was wasted nearly beyond all recognizing that it was a body at all. I have tried to create their scene in other places, but the tower is the only one where another face does not appear: Mr. Randall's — looming, leering? — over those two lovers who may not have been so at all till after he was buried and their own vows said, delivering a blessing, whether proud or pornographic, on the woman who was his wife and the man almost his son.

Mrs. Randall returned to the capital with her husband after both came to Thanksgiving dinner at our house. Everything then was as it had been before, with Mr. Randall and my father smoking, drinking, and guffawing in the study as I dawdled with the women in the parlor, too stuffed to move. They were not due back till three days before Christmas, but I somehow knew, when the bells began to toll on a clear but very cold December afternoon, that we would see Mrs. Randall sooner than we had expected. We were called into assembly in the school auditorium, where the principal informed us that Marcus Emerson Randall, state senator, Episcopal vestryman, founder of the Franksville Chamber of Commerce, the Rotary Club, and the Fidelity Savings Bank, outstanding citizen and patron of the Zebulon Vance Elementary School library, had passed into eternal glory three hours before. After several expressions of shock by teachers whose sincerity was always in doubt, a brief prayer, a further impromptu eulogy by Mr. Drindel, and a reading of the Twenty-third Psalm, we were dismissed.

Mr. Randall's funeral train arrived on Saturday, a fact lamented by most of my classmates, who had predicted another half-day's holiday. A viewing had been arranged in the capital, however, so the late senator arrived a day later than expected. The train, a locomotive and three cars, bearing the deceased, the widow, the lieutenant governor, and three associate justices of the state supreme court, chuffed into the Franksville station two hours behind schedule, somberly decked in black crepe. I imagine that, when up to speed, the black engine and dark green cars must have looked like the very chariot of death itself. But now, the bunting fluttered only limply as the train rolled into town. The delay and the bitter wind had thinned the crowd, but there was still what would pass in most small towns for a throng on the platform as the locomotive wheezed a last, mournful whistle.

In the momentary silence, the baggage-car doors slammed open with a sound final as the closing of a coffin lid, revealing Mr. Randall's catafalque, absolutely alone in the wooden emptiness. From the observation platform of the last coach, heavily bundled men with black arm bands — the state officials, honorary pallbearers — lumbered out and stepped solemnly up to where uniformed railroad employees tried, with as much dignity as possible, to maneuver the considerable casket containing Mr. Randall's considerable remains onto the brawny shoulders of six young Episcopalians who would transport it to the waiting hearse. In the midst of this hubbub, a murmur passed through the crowd. On the observation platform, Mrs. Randall appeared.

The governor's wife was at her side, but I know that only from subsequently reading the newspaper. In that instant, I saw only that figure in black, delicate as the plume of a smothered candle, motionless beside the wrought iron gate of the rail car. Her face was lost in fold upon fold of veil, swirling down from a huge dark hat which hid her hair, as her hands were hidden by long gloves, so from a distance there was no sign of flesh at all beneath the layered mourning. She stood, oddly precipitous, for what seemed a very long time. Then, as if at a signal, the crowd parted, and my father's overcoat whooshed in a heap to the ground beside me. He strode toward the train, sleek in his best black wool suit, undaunted by the cold. The conductor, who had been awaiting Mrs. Randall's descent, stepped aside, and at the foot of the steps my father extended his hand upward to meet the offered glove. Then, regally, her wrist resting lightly on his arm, Mrs. Randall made her way after the casket.

Lottie picked up my father's coat, dusting it as best she could. I was almost speechless at his gallantry — a reaction widely shared by the other mourners, which was, I suspect, precisely what my father intended. He guided Mrs. Randall to the funeral parlor's only Packard, and then, after settling her amid the lieutenant governor, the governor's wife, and a few other dignitaries who counted it politic to ride with the widow, he stepped modestly back, moving through the crowd toward us, pausing occasionally to accept the greeting of some fellow citizen whose salutation was a quiet sign of approval.

The hearse lurched forward, and the black cars slowly took their places in the file that would travel to Everhardt's Mortuary, where the body would rest until Monday. Immediately behind the cars came the First Methodist choir in their black robes, their faces blue with cold, chattering out several mournful hymns along the way, including a vocal version of Chopin's Funeral March I have never, gratefully, heard since. My father collected his coat from Aunt Lottie, and we joined the others following the procession on foot for the quarter mile to the funeral parlor. For all the provincial pomp, there was to that day a true and sincere sadness — the attempt of a very small town to muster the appropriate dignities for a man they not only respected but loved. It was the sort of thing not to be seen in Franksville again. But for me, this was surely secondary to the courtship that at least officially began with a dropped overcoat, the love that would flourish till consumed in a fireball one April Friday five years after. But such an event, which would send my own life wheeling in directions then unknown, was unimaginable that last time Mr. Randall arrived from the capital, his destiny fulfilled. He had, after all, done much for that town where he was born, now Rotary Clubbed, stadiumed, and Chamber of Commerced for his efforts. And if, in the end, even he could not deliver that promised A&M, he had imparted to us one final gift. He had brought us Mrs. Randall.

2

THE WEDDING took place in the Episcopal Church, St. Peter and St. James, though my father had been raised Presbyterian and to my recollection had never attended services anywhere else. Mrs. Randall's denominational heritage was as obscure as most information about her past. But Mr. Randall had been a lifelong communicant, and so there was little question on anybody's part that it was appropriate, fifteen months after the requiem for Mr. Randall's mortal remains and immortal soul, that his wife and his protégé should be joined in wedlock before the selfsame altar. Father Finch, more cherubic than usual in his most festive vestments, took the opportunity to stage an extravaganza, combining the wedding ceremony with an interminable sermon and a Eucharist that included incense, though that was irregular in the diocese and evoked some bitter remarks about incipient Romanism from practicants of sparer rituals.

Generally, however, the wedding and the reception that followed on the great lawn separating our house from Mr. Randall's were happy occasions. The spring had come unusually early, and the yellow and white pavilion that had been staked up looked like some vast, exotic flower unexpectedly blossoming among the jonquils and tulips. Despite official prohibitions, there was champagne imported from France, as well as cider for the Baptists in attendance, and an elaborate spread of ham, poultry, and wild fowl, fresh bread, yams, potatoes, home-canned vegetables, and citrus brought at considerable expense from Florida. It was, without question, the most flamboyant spectacle Franksville had ever seen — much more so than anything the Pritchards had ever thrown, and that might have caused some discontent in the town's leading family. My father, however, presiding genially as a young prince over the wedding feast, took pains to flatter Pritchards young and old, an effort whose easy success was perhaps an early sign of that clan's physical and moral destitution.

Mrs. Randall had rejected pure white for her second wedding, eschewing the veil as well. These decisions met with general approbation, in spite of doubts expressed in some quarters that her first marriage had ever been consummated. She wore a cream-colored gown, and her face shone radiant over the stained-glass-light-spangled aisle of St. Peter and St. James. I do think, in that moment before the altar, Mrs. Randall and my father loved each other very much, though within a very few years that would change. The town accepted this as natural, at least at first: my father's early passion burning down to the easy tolerance of a middle-aged man. He was, after all, twelve years her senior, a gap that, in view of her first match, must have seemed to her inconsiderable but, according to the common wisdom, compelled her to accept certain things before her time.

There were certain peculiarities to the wedding ceremony. The parties of the bride and groom sat unsegregated, largely because the former was so small. Mrs. Randall's only relatives in attendance were two robust and very Southern ladies from Knoxville, cousins who resembled her not a whit. They cheerfully confirmed at the slightest prodding the story of Mrs. Randall's past that her late husband had circulated: she was the only child of elderly, very wealthy parents who had made their fortune in the steel boom in Pennsylvania. She had traveled a bit as a girl, then went to live with an aged aunt when both her parents died. After her aunt died as well, she had come to live in Knoxville, where, at the United Daughters of the Confederacy Ball, she had made the acquaintance of Marcus Emerson Randall, a meeting that eventually led her to Franksville and, finally, into the arms of Gambetta Stevenson.

I don't know that anyone believed the tale. I did, of course, as a child, but with the years found it more and more suspect, not so much for any concrete evidence of falsehood as for the aura of Mrs. Randall herself, bespeaking some misfortune more shattering than an orphanhood, which would have been anticipated. She was not melancholic, not a specter mooning about the house like a fugitive from Edgar Allen Poe. Quite the contrary, after she moved across the wide lawn and settled in my father's bed, that rambling lawyer's palace seemed a brighter, airier, and altogether kinder place to be. Yet, even from the first, there was a tenuousness to that cheer, both of the house and of Mrs. Randall herself, which made it seem it might at any moment dissolve easy as a mist. Her mysteriousness, and the power she held over me, grew greater rather than less after she came to live with us, as I saw how, at a word or a sound or a change in weather — or sometimes for no reason at all — she suddenly seemed distracted, even transformed, as if recalling some unshareable moment that would shatter the carefully crafted history her cousins reaffirmed with such smiling vociferousness on her wedding day.

In view of the short time elapsed between Mr. Randall's interment and his wife's remarriage, there was surprisingly little gossip — a raised eyebrow here and there, an occasional reference to feminine ambition, but little more. The goodwill my father had curried over the years, and perhaps that good fortune which seemed to suffuse all he did, smothered any scandal that might have been brewing. Most people agreed that the union was precisely what Mr. Randall would have wanted, and more than once remarks directed to me indicated I should be grateful my father had troubled himself to provide me with a new mother.

That, I have come to realize, had little influence on his decision. Lust played a part, of course. He was still a young man and had taken considerable care to avoid the kind of reputation indiscriminate whoring might have brought him. Six years of such discretion, however, was doubtless beginning to wear, and a new wife would provide him an outlet for his urges as well as the unassailable respectability of wedlock. He required too a helpmate and hostess to maintain his social status, such as one might have in Franksville, and who better for that role than the young and beautiful widow of his patron, exotic in her way as that stained glass paean to his profession in the entry hall. And there was the fortune, of course.

Aside from some cousins here and there, Mr. Randall had left behind no family. The will provided as generously as most of the period for the continued maintenance of the household servants. Such bequests, however, made but a small dent in the real reserves of the estate, a fact my father, having helped draw up the will, was surely aware of. There were a few other minor awards: parcels of land to various friends, papers to the State Historical Society, books to the Zebulon Vance Elementary School library. For the most part, however, all his property, his stocks and bonds, his part of the bank, his mortgages and liens, his holdings in local cotton mills, and all his cash and effects were left in the hands of his "beloved wife," and so, upon her marriage, devolved to Gambetta Stevenson.

I was never certain how wealthy my father was, at least on paper, much of which lost all value but for pulp when the stock market crashed and the Cotton Exchange collapsed. But that disaster was years away, and with the wedding of the young Stevenson fortune to the older Randall one, Franksville had a family that threatened to eclipse the Pritchards in prestige. The outward signs of my father's greater importance were comprised mostly of raidings from his dead mentor's home. The odd pieces of pseudo-Greek statuary were now scattered about our property, including a daringly draped Diana who arrived to grace the hall below the stained glass window, drawing great attention from my friends. A Persian rug from Mr. Randall's study, a grandfather clock, a candelabra for the piano in the parlor, law books, an oil portrait of Mr. Randall, which received a place of honor in the guest room refurnished with the bed, chest, and armoire of his late sister — all these traveled the distance from the crest of the hill to our front door. Bea and Lottie laid claim to an eccentric assortment of odds and ends: a brass hat rack, a Tiffany lamp, the dining room curtains, and several pair of oversize galoshes, which they felt would be useful in the garden during the April rains. I rescued the butterfly collection, a kerosene lamp, a *Collier's Encyclopedia* and several other books, and, after much pleading, the bearskin rug, which thereafter graced my bedroom floor.

Mrs. Randall salvaged some quilts, a few knickknacks to which she had become attached, and a chaise longue. She brought closets of clothes her late husband had bought her, jewelry, trunks, and bureaus. Amid all the sumptuousness came a plain wooden box like a miniature hope chest, which sat on the nightstand in the room called hers, which adjoined my father's and where she often napped. The box, secured with a small brass lock, was remarkable only for its homeliness. I asked her in the midst of moving what was in it.

"A few keepsakes," was all she offered. "I've had it since I was a little girl."

And for the moment that sufficed, as my eyes were drawn to grander stuff she had brought for her new life with us.

After the pillage, the remaining furnishings of Mr. Randall's home were draped, the walls scrubbed and the floors waxed, his clothes folded and settled into cedar chests, as if he had left on a trip and could be expected back in a year or two. Then the house was sealed. The bolts were slid across the shutters, and the front door was shackled with a chain to a great iron ring set in a block of cement on the veranda. From my window

49

or from the walk on the tower, Mr. Randall's house brooded through the twilight across the lawn, and after dark on those nights with no moon, it vanished altogether.

So it remained for many years — opened, aired, and cleaned every spring, then closed up again — till my father was dead. Then the contents were auctioned and the house and property sold to help settle his debts. I once thought the house remained intact so long as a kind of monument, my father's memorial to that man who had helped him so: encouraged his venture to Princeton and his practice of law; provided the counsel to make him a fortune, the drive to build a mansion; and, finally, left him a woman unlike any for miles and miles around. I concluded much later I was wrong. My father had let that house stand all those years, kept but empty, not out of respect but out of rage and vanity: rage at the old man who had given that child of clerks so much; vanity for having ended as master of it all. The spring of the wedding, if he had not done so before, my father surely took Mrs. Randall to the tower, looming there over the dead house lurking unseen, to seal in the same instant his love and his triumph.

Now, as I was going on thirteen, Franksville began to grow before my eyes. Not physically: places that had once seemed vast — the train station's waiting room, the lobby of the Mac-Kenzie Palace Hotel — now seemed almost cozy. Looking down from the hill in winter when the trees were bare, it was possible to see nearly the whole town: the courthouse, with offices and stores hard by; the spires of the churches, St. Peter and St. James, First Methodist, First and Second Baptist, Franksville, Central and West Franksville Presbyterian. The streets, especially in the newer districts to the south and east, spread in a neat grid, sign of the boom in the eighties when the cotton mills first flourished. Each was lined with trees: elms on Elm, maples on Maple, oaks on Oak. Only Chestnut Street ran anomalously naked because of the blight that had struck with the new century. In the hollow made by Brewster Creek sat the stadium, while to the west was Pallister Slough with its winding dirt streets and the houses near the banks raised three or even six feet on brick or wooden pilings against the spring floods. Finally, visible over faraway trees — the woods that ringed the town — were the steamy plumes of the mills, little cities unto themselves, the engines of Franksville's prosperity.

But what Franksville lost for me in size, it gained in nuance. With Bobby Brownrich, Tommy Allan, and Jimbo Cash, I bicycled endlessly, summer and winter, traversing that little world my father saw as his fiefdom: out of downtown, up Depot Street to Railroad Street with its warehouses, on to the woods, paralleling the tracks to Pritchard I, which rose humming and puffing out of a colony of cookie-cutter cabins, all identical, small and white.

And within we could see people, also identical, small and white — the mill folk: vaguely rickety children; silent, hard-eyed women given to sudden brays; fragile, pale men who sat unmoving on porches, breathing quick and shallow as fish, sometimes too with an ominous rattle.

Occasionally, we saw boys our own age, when words and then gumballs off the sweetgum trees and finally dirt clods and an occasional rock where exchanged. We would see more of some of them in high school, for a few would move beyond the tiny school the mill provided — always knotted together, underfed, badly clothed, teased by the students from town and often slackjawed with exhaustion from having worked the second shift.

Also within bicycling distance were Pritchard II and the True Harmony Towel mill, of which my father was part owner, as well as the new mill, which would later take on such sinister importance. The four of us visited them all, along with making summer excursions to the reservoir and autumn raids on the apple orchards far down the highway in the deep country toward the spa at Iron Springs.

In those two years, we saw the inside of every public building in Franksville — every fire station, courthouse, hotel, restaurant, theater, and church, including the A.M.E. chapel on the edge of Pallister Slough, where Jimbo said the congregation wailed and jumped like Holy Rollers. We laughed and called the old man who had unlocked the door to let us in "boy," as he watched us with an easy grin of furious patience. For a Southern town, Franksville had few black faces. There had been hardly any slaves there before the war, and with the boom and the construction of the mills, the managers, with consummate brilliance, had puffed up the white men, women, and children fresh off the land with the certainty that no nigger had the privilege of losing fingers to the loom or lining his lungs with lint. Downtown, only one business, Claude's Tailoring, was run by a black man; most of his fellows worked as Franksville's fetchers and carriers, the women scrubbing, cooking, and cleaning, all of them vanishing with the setting sun into the damp, secret precincts of Pallister Slough.

It was there, so Bobby told us around that thirteenth summer, that Franksville's men would slake their lust, now that the Moral Mothers League had closed Miss Wanda's bordello. It had been across from the King Cotton Hotel on Depot Street. Miss Wanda, as I recall, cut a fine painted figure in elaborate hats and dresses as she did her shopping on Saturdays. After state prohibition was passed, however, and Franksville's taverns were closed, Mrs. Pritchard — that is, Lemuel Pritchard's wife, the WCTU's local light and co-founder of the Moral Mothers League — turned her attention to white slavery. As a Baptist, she browbeat her preacher, Mr. Burnside, into a raging sermon on the matter at First Baptist's annual revival, and a campaign began to drive Miss Wanda and her girls out of town. Legal wrangles and harrassment — the Mothers massed in front of the house every Saturday night from eight to ten thirty, singing hymns — finally convinced Franksville's only madam to pack up her charges and belongings. She departed with the closing shot (so Bobby related) that she was off to a town where "men wore the pants and knew what to do once they had them off."

So, what prostitution occurred now took place in Pallister Slough: a casual, unorganized buying and selling, which, at least for the Moral Mothers, was not white slavery in that the women involved were black.

We all taught ourselves to masturbate that summer, again at Bobby's urging. He claimed to have learned all by himself at the age of seven and, having been a dedicated practitioner ever since, scoffed at our objections of hair, warts, and madness. As the youngest of five boys, he possessed a worldliness Jimbo, Tommy, and I lacked, as well as jaded distance from everything, peculiar in a child. Short, bespectacled, all his life the butt of his older brothers' pranks and recipient of their broader knowledge, he had developed a cynicism, a quick tongue, and the dirty mind he never lost.

Late in August, his second brother, Henry, brought him a reproduction of *September Morn* from Richmond, which Bobby soon began to rent out overnight at a nickle for fifteen hours. ("One-third cent an hour," he insisted. "Six P.M. to nine A.M. Plenty of time to do what you have to do.") Tommy returned it at ten that first week, for which Bobby fined him an extra three cents.

My chance for it came on a Tuesday evening the first week of school, when Bobby delivered it to me with the assurance that, though Yvette might have had hard use over the last few days, the session he had had not an hour before proved she could still more than satisfy a man. The brown envelope in which the French girl lay hidden looked sufficiently incriminating that, however I accommodated it amid my schoolwork, it seemed to betray me. On the way home, I shifted it four or five times among my papers, each new location more glaringly obvious to my eyes than the last. Finally, I unbuttoned my shirt and shoved one end down below the waistband of my trousers, so Yvette nestled against the incipient growth in my crotch and stroked seductively against my bare stomach.

As I started across the lawn, I saw Lottie and Bea taking in the dusk from their rockers, waving at me from the porch. I grasped my books tight and pitched forward slightly, my head down, barreling over the yard with my face set.

"Did you have a good day, dear?"

"A good day?"

"Fine," I said too loud, bounding up the steps, "just fine."

I caught a curious look on Bea's face as I shot past, certain my French companion was winking at my maiden aunts from that place no girl had any business being.

"Are you feeling all right, Gams?" I heard Lottie say as I slammed through the front door.

I bolted down the hall and into the sanctuary of my room, stumbled on the bearskin, and spilled my papers across the bed. I still kept one hand clamped over my middle, which heaved up and down with the effort of my charge through the house. I unbuttoned my shirt and pulled out the envelope.

It was slightly dog-eared, and the brown paper was dark with sweat. As I drew forth the reproduction, however, it was apparent Yvette was none the worse for wear, insouciant as ever in her innocence, her arms folded demurely over her breasts.

"Gams?"

It was Mrs. Randall's voice on the other side of the door. "Gams? Are you all right?"

Even in my panic, I was glad it was not my father, who after one rap would have simply barged in. With no time to think, I jammed the picture and envelope deep beneath my pillow, trying to catch my breath and decide on a reasonable excuse for my behavior.

"Gams?"

"Just a minute."

I counted deliberately to ten, listening as my heart quieted, then got up and went to the door.

She was dressed for dinner, her hair up, her white dress trimmed with lace at the neck and cuffs. She was wearing pearls, and I remembered then that Father Finch was due for dinner that night, a further obstacle to my orgiastic plans.

"Are you all right?" she said again, a trace of concern on her face.

"Oh, yes, yes," I said. "Fine."

"You gave your aunts a fright. Are you sick?" Her hand went to my forehead. "Do you have a fever?"

"Oh, no. No."

"Lottie said she thought you had a stomachache." She glanced at my open shirt.

"Ah, . . ." I stammered, "ah . . . I pulled a muscle, I think, today when we were running."

"Where?" Her hand moved toward my belly. "Are you sure? It's not appendicitis, is it?"

The feel of her palm where so recently Yvette had rested sent shivers of both shame and I was not sure what all through me, and I backed hurriedly away, clutching my side.

"No, no. I just have to work it out, that's all."

"Is it a cramp, then?"

"Maybe. I just need to relax a little."

"You're certain you're all right?"

"Fine," I assured her, smiling bravely. "I'll just stretch out a little bit and then change for dinner. What time is Father Finch due?"

"He should be here any minute now," Mrs. Randall said.

"Well, I'll get dressed," I said emphatically, cueing her to leave.

"All right." She moved toward the door. "But if you're not well, I can have Althea bring your supper up."

"No, no." I was horrified at the idea of anyone else coming to my room. "No, I'll be right down."

After Mrs. Randall left, I sank onto the bed, my knees weak. It was a minute or two before I snaked my hand under the pillow to pull Yvette into the half light. I slipped her back in the envelope and stacked my schoolbooks over her in hope that the weight of knowledge might straighten her out. That done, I pulled my blue suit from the closet to prepare for supper.

At nine o'clock, I took my leave, knowing it would be another hour at least before Father Finch took his. The evening had been pleasant enough, with Mrs. Randall playing "Anitra's Dance" and "In the Sweet Bye-and-Bye," and my father at his expansive best, speaking well of everyone in town and warm to the suggestion of financing new Whitsuntide vestments.

From my threshold, I could feel Yvette, seductive in the dark, as the rumble of ministerial conversation of good works and doctrinal disagreements was dulled to the vaguest hum by distance and the heavy door. Shaking with anticipation, I undressed, fumbling with the hangers in the dark, and padded naked through the gloom to where Yvette lay in silent expectation. I did not dare turn on a light, though I knew that meant I would be unable to make out the object of my affection. Unsure what to do, I finally grabbed the rug, my whole body shivering and my crotch already aching, and pulled it into the pool of starlight pouring through the window. Taking myself in hand, I stretched out on the coarse, thick bear's fur, Yvette propped beside me, and gave myself over to the French seductress.

It did not take long. Yvette, true to her nationality's reputation, was a mistress of all the arts of love, and thirteen-year-olds are not a hard lot to please.

Next day, I returned *September Morn* to Bobby, paying an extra nickel for the slightly creased envelope. He was annoyed at the damage, though at least, he noted acidly, I had not stained the print, which was his greatest fear. It was many years before I saw another reproduction of the painting. In little more than a week, Jimbo was caught *in delicto* and, encouraged by a barrel stave, revealed Bobby as Yvette's procurer. This led to her consignment to the incinerator and his own appointment in the basement. I was just as glad the temptation of the French girl had been removed, and within a short time all details of *September Morn* were gone from my memory. That left me, in the dark of my room late at night, to the faceless ladies of my imagination, their cool hands soft across my belly.

3

FROM THE FIRST, I was promised a brother. Peculiarly, everyone seemed to assume I would be delighted at the prospect. Even on the morning of the wedding, when I had solemnly taken part in the ceremony as ring bearer and later tasted my first champagne, I was assured by several doubtless well-meaning but obtuse guests that I might expect the companionship of a sibling, in almost all prognostications, a male one.

Initially, I had little interest in the actual appearance of a baby brother or sister. Bobby's and other friends' experiences convinced me there were few apparent advantages in being one child among many, and a number of obvious drawbacks. Indeed, old as I was, a new arrival would not even provide the solace of a playmate when none more acceptable was available. Whatever child my father and Mrs. Randall might produce would be more a curiosity than a companion for me, as far removed in generation as I was from Mrs. Randall, or she from my father.

What intrigued me most after the wedding was not babies but the mere presence of Mrs. Randall. Having a woman in the house — a young woman, one who had not surrendered herself to early spinsterhood and shut her body away in shapeless shrouds of brown and gray — was quite as thrilling as having an African gazelle in the garden or an Argentinian panther on the basement stairs. In the summer, I now sat with her in the parlor, reading and re-reading the same page as I spied on her placid face to my heart's content, watching her breast slowly rise and fall while she consumed novel after novel those humid afternoons. I watched her walk with that peculiar lightness in her step that men do not have, that my aunts had lost, that I had never taken the time to note in other women, though afterward — on my way to school, at the drugstore, simply out for a stroll — I would realize that women as a species (all of the young and even some of the old) possess that special buoyancy. I compared her shoulders to those of Diana, particularly the night she wore for some party a rather daring dress that bared them, and I wondered too how her breasts might compare to the one that peeked from beneath the tunic of the statue in the hall. Mrs. Randall seemed, I thought after perusing Bullfinch's (one of my acquisitions from Mr. Randall's estate), more of Diana's party among women than of any other. From the illustrations, Venus appeared too voluptuous, Minerva too mannish, Juno too mature and shrewish, to compare to Mrs. Randall. She was willowy, supple, and I could imagine her armed with arc and arrow, though I forgot that Diana's barbs were meant not to enamor but kill.

Further, of course, Diana was the moon, and Mrs. Randall was indeed changeable. She could be suddenly short with me, my aunts, my father — not often, but unpredictably. In the midst of some apparently innocent conversation, she might stiffen, as if a current of ice had passed through her. This happened most often, I came to realize, when some question arose about the past, or the subject of a child came up. She was not impolite but unexpectedly firm in diverting the conversation toward a topic less disturbing. Should that fail, she would simply leave, victim of a headache or a chill, taking to her room for an hour or the evening.

About that room, the one adjoining my father's, she was very jealous. It contained her wardrobe, which expanded constantly, thanks to my father's delight in seeing her in ever newer and more elaborate clothes. Scattered about on its tables and bureau were the miniatures she had brought from Mr. Randall's house, a photograph of her cousins and one of my father, and that tiny box she kept securely locked. There too was her dressing table, and I, on occasion, was allowed to talk to her while she prepared her face, particularly for a party, with painstaking care. Her hands would move expertly over the bottles, vials, and boxes as she spoke to my reflection in the mirror, advising, chastising, sympathizing, while I observed, half transfixed, her transformation into a woman of yet brighter eyes, redder lips, more translucent skin. She must have realized why I sat there, improvising problems to relate so I might remain party to such a private rite, but she rarely sent me away, as if she somehow understood how mysterious her cosmetizing seemed to me, and perhaps too because she enjoyed revealing to a man, even so young a one as I, her mastery of those women's sciences whose only purpose is to make what is perfect more perfect still.

It was almost a year and a half after the wedding that word spread through the house and then the town that my long anticipated brother was now en route. Mrs. Randall appeared no different than before, though in her confirming the news to inquirers, I noted a certain defiant pride I had not seen before: an angle of the head, a sharpness in her voice, as if someone, somewhere, once had challenged her to remake herself. Pregnancy did not impress me. Her body did not change in those first weeks, though I would occasionally wake to hear her retching in the bathroom. She tired easily and suffered occasional lightheadedness. Still, she seemed almost preternaturally pleased, holding court in the parlor with a parade of well-wishers from town, keeping my aunts busy fetching and carrying while Althea labored endlessly to concoct always more distinctive pastries and sandwiches to accompany tea.

My father turned absolutely cocky at the prospect of paternity. One would have thought I was conceived immaculately, that Gambetta Stevenson's namesake had arrived by means distinct from those which had now planted a child in Mrs. Randall's womb. He grew embarrassingly solicitous of his wife, but Franksville found such uxoriousness charming. His stock had risen higher in the town only on the occasions of my mother's death, Mr. Randall's funeral, and his second wedding. I realized now, more than at any time before, how the town endowed my father and Mrs. Randall with a specialness I did not fully understand. The sort of affection Mr. Randall had claimed now devolved upon my father for no other reason than his not having bothered much of anyone, his having been Mr. Randall's favorite, his having married the woman most people thought, deep in their hearts, had been too young and hence too taxing for a bachelor of a certain age. And, of course, Gambetta Stevenson was still a dashing figure and had a fine house and had been as able in grief as in joy. He was also very rich, and his wife, demure and beautiful, was the kind of thing of which fantasies are made.

Mrs. Randall lost the child at the beginning of the fourth

month. There seemed no real explanation. She had one difficult night. I left for school in the morning, and when I returned the house was abuzz and neighbors were already arriving to express their regrets. My father, in a new black suit signaling his mourning, manfully bore the condolences in the parlor. I started toward him, confused, but Lottie intercepted me and hustled me into the kitchen to explain the situation.

"Too many silly little sandwiches," Althea mumbled to herself as she checked the chicken pies. "Sandwiches and not enough greens."

"So she won't have the baby?" I said. Lottie's explanation had been more than a little oblique.

"Not for now."

"All them biddies comin' by. Not a minute's rest, poor Missus."

"But what happened?"

"The baby —"

". . . and tea. Enough tea to float away on . . ."

". . . just didn't want to grow anymore."

"Why not?"

Lottie sighed deeply. "The Lord just didn't intend it, Gams."

There was a murmur by the sink. "The Good Lord couldn't get a word in no-ways with all them biddies cluckin' away."

"Althea!"

Althea cast Lottie a murderous glance, fell silent, and scrubbed twice as hard at the skillet she was washing.

I went back to the parlor, joining the stream of the honestly sorry and the merely curious. It was an oddly ugly event, I later thought, in view of the intimacy of what had occurred. One would have thought a prince had died, or at least someone for whom there could be a coffin and a funeral. I shook my father's hand, noting, shaken, that he had been crying.

"I guess the Lord must not have intended it, Papa," I said, quoting Aunt Lottie for lack of any better source.

Father Finch, who stood at my father's right hand, tousled my hair and pronounced, "Yes, my boy. But there will be a new child. The good Lord will see you get a brother yet."

The minister had apparently misread the Lord's intentions. Twice in the next two years, Mrs. Randall conceived, and in both cases, around the third month, miscarried. Each loss threw her a bit deeper into despair, and she recovered a bit more slowly. More than that, however, I noticed that even when she was not pregnant, her distraction seemed greater, her spells of temper more frequent. Growing older myself, I found it easier to sympathize with her, excuse her; in my blooming adolescence, I attempted to adopt the wisdom and compassion of someone older, though her coldness could sting me as it had when I was a boy. She still, of course, enthralled me, though I did not invade her making up now and read with her less frequently in the parlor. I had new interests with high school to mold my life. But I continued to feel a thrill when she praised me, much more than when my father did, and noted happily that she could still ask after my friends by name.

That circle of friends changed a bit. Bicycle excursions were passé, or better, in hiatus till a year or so down the road, when girls would suddenly develop an attraction to springtime picnics in the outskirts of town or one of the city's three parks. I saw less of Tommy Allan after our taste for exploration faded, though our estrangement resulted too from his somewhat humbler station in Franksville's hierarchical little world. Before, his hand-me-down bicycle or patched summer clothes had made me, if anything, wish my own father's position a little less exalted, for Tommy's shabbier possessions could be scuffed or dirtied without fear of parental reprisals, or so I thought. I was amazed one day when he could not come with us for having torn his shirt the previous afternoon. I was too obtuse at the time to realize his shirts were endlessly mended not for comfort's sake but because his father's postal clerk's salary was stretched to the limits by the responsibility of four children, a wife, and a grandmother with a bad heart. In the years after, however, during which I obtained my first white linens for tennis, two new winter suits, a pair of British dress shoes, and a tie tack set with mother-of-pearl and three small diamonds, I came to know the thoughtless privilege money can afford even in a place like Franksville. It appeared most nakedly my sixteenth Christmas, when I ran into Tommy on the street and he showed me his family's gift, a Silverine watch I had seen in the Sears-Roebuck catalogue. I examined it, and then, with that smug cruelty of a teenager, showed him my Christmas watch — Swiss made, its silver casing detailed in gold — a ponderous and flamboyant thing, the overt sign of all that had come between us.

Of Jimbo Cash, I saw rather more, his car-selling father having been admitted into the Rotary Club and the family fortunes on the rise simultaneous with the boom in auto sales. My father was eager to augment his stable, which included a Pierce Arrow, a Packard, and a Scripps-Booth, with something more exotic, and Mr. Cash dropped by from time to time to share his thoughts on the matter. In any case, Jimbo himself had gotten the growth that would make him a natural football hero, one sure way to circumvent (at least temporarily) any obstacles social codes might put in his path.

Mostly, though, I palled around with Bobby, whose mind and tongue were more corrupt than ever. He was a dedicated Bull Durham smoker, with a murderous French inhale he had learned from his brother Henry, who in turn claimed to have perfected it watching a famous European gambler who smoked that way while winning five thousand dollars at a private black-jack party in a New York hotel. Given that Henry represented a shoe company and traveled only infrequently out of his territory in the upper South, his story should have rung suspicious.

But Henry, who was twenty-three and quite a dandy, sufficiently impressed us so that even if we had doubts, we kept them to ourselves. Ever since *September Morn*, he and Bobby had developed a special relationship, which meant any aspersions cast on Henry would be met immediately by an assault of words no one at fifteen in Franksville could withstand. Bobby's mouth often got him into trouble, but he could usually talk adults into surrender, while with the other boys, he could make any bully a laughingstock in front of the inevitable crowd. Still, as added insurance, he worked at being fast on his feet, tried out for wrestling, and always carried a pencil box full of marbles in his breast pocket, looking toward the day he would cast them behind him to send a pursuer slipping and crashing to a halt.

I took a liking as well to Bobby's niece Melissa, only a year his junior. She was apple-cheeked and a little plump, the picture, so they said, of her mother at that age. While the years and childbirth had transformed Bobby's sister-in-law, his eldest brother's wife, into a heavy-bodied and somewhat hypochondriacal mother of five, Melissa was in her prime. Long after, when I saw her on my first return to Franksville, it seemed astounding she had ever seemed attractive. But she was of that band who bloom early, are in their glory those first, uncertain years of womanhood, and who, by the time their slower-maturing sisters flower, are already pitied by those who once envied them.

Melissa and I spent many afternoons at The Arbor, a new ice cream parlor just down from the courthouse, quaffing phosphates and sundaes in summer, hot chocolate and Spiced Coffee Supremes (an Arbor innovation) in winter. I treated Melissa as often as I was able and was rewarded from time to time with a furtive kiss and on my birthday with a pen engraved with my name. It was not that I was more than usually fond of her, nor she of me. We simply shared enough — Bobby and other friends and an incipient interest in the high school Drama

Society — that each of us would do as well for the other as anybody else.

These too were the times I discovered the picture show. There had, of course, been a nickelodeon in town before I was born, and during my childhood Franksville had boasted three movie houses, one of which, when we were ten, Bobby and I had paid our five cents to enter on a dare. It was small and stank of summer sweat and a vague rancidness of old grease, in that the building had formerly been a diner. Movies, in those first years, were thought apt only for mill hands, many of whom could hardly read and often brought their children along to mutter the titles to them. In 1914, however, the Carillon Theater — besides the opera house, Franksville's only venue for traveling stock companies, vaudeville, and amateur theatricals — had been converted to a cinema, and the picture show rapidly became a respectable pastime not only for the poor and unlettered but for the town's better classes as well.

Of course, the dark auditorium proved a boon to surreptitious hand-holding and the occasional stolen kiss, particularly in those frequent moments the first year or so when the film broke or the projector malfunctioned. The crew at the Carillon took several months to master their new responsibilities. Still, the theater featured an eight-piece orchestra and sometimes included oleo acts in its presentations, which made ten to fifty cents an acceptable, if loudly resented, admission price.

With Melissa, with Bobby and Jimbo, but often alone, I came to know the Vitagraph and Biograph features and serials: *Suspense*, the locally unpopular *Sheridan's Ride*; the much more favorably received *Birth of a Nation*. There were a few ancient epics, remarkable primarily for scantily clad slave girls and boys cast about every scene like so much furniture, though the most titillating picture was *Traffic in Souls*. Based on the Rockefeller White Slavery Report, it purported to dramatize the smashing of the Vice Trust. More attention seemed lavished, however,

65

upon vice itself than its undoing. Bobby and I saw it three times during its two-day run, the last time seated four rows behind the delegation from the Moral Mothers League, who stalked out about a third of the way through, missing not only several even more educational scenes but those final five minutes or so when Virtue, so listless as to be nearly invisible throughout the rest of the drama, finally rises to unexpected triumph.

Traffic in Souls closed that night.

Bobby's disappointment was somewhat assuaged by the comedy mustered up to finish out the run. He liked slapstick, which had, after all, found practical application in his box of marbles. He claimed as well he could read dirty words on the lips of the silent players, which would send him into whoops of laughter at apparently inappropriate moments. I, meanwhile, had simply fallen in love with the movies. Settled in the silvered and music-laden darkness, I let epic or comedy or melodrama wash over me. Later, I would imitate Chaplin's walk or Theda Bara's stare for my friends and secretly practice the soulful mooning of romantic leads or the nonchalant toss of the head of the past week's swashbuckler in front of my bedroom mirror, assuring myself that, if such an exercise did not help me get a major role in the Drama Society's productions, it might at least give me a sort of sophistication lacking among my Franksville peers.

Certain old pastimes endured. In summer, Jimbo and Bobby and I often lolled at the reservoir, clothes heaped on tufts of swamp grass, avoiding the August sun and plunging from time to time beneath that cool, still surface to drive off bugs. We talked of girls and school and, more than once, the sinking of the *Lusitania* the previous year. There were movies to discuss, and baseball, and the plans for the future that began to assume shape.

"So," Jimbo said, spread-eagle on the bank, rippling with

66

summer muscles he was working up for football season, "what do you think you want to do?"

"Me?" I said. "I guess be a lawyer. That's what I always thought. Bobby?"

He had his arm thrown across his eyes, as if he were asleep. "A preacher," he mumbled. Then he laughed, sitting up and reaching for a stone to throw. "Hell, I'll sell stuff. My old man sells stuff. All my brothers sell stuff. I'll sell stuff, too."

"You going to college?"

"College!" Bobby sneered, sending the rock skiing over the water. "Who in God's name ever heard of somebody going to college so he could sell stuff?"

"Are you?" Jimbo asked.

"Sure. You can't be a lawyer if you don't go to college."

"Where to? To State?"

"No," I said, "to Princeton."

"Where's that?"

"New Jersey."

"New Jersey! A Yankee school!" Jimbo's grandfather had been the only one of six sons to come back after the war. "You'd run off and go to a Yankee school?"

"My father went there," I said defensively. "Mr. Randall went there. Lots of Southern boys do."

"What kind of Southern boy goes off up there? Hell, ain't it good enough at State? How can you talk about going someplace with all those Yankees around?"

"Aw, Jesus, Jimbo," Bobby grumbled, lurching up and walking to the edge of the water. "Let him be."

"But . . . but, god . . . goddamn it, Bobby." Jimbo rarely swore and only stuttered when excited. "Goddamn, a . . . a Yankee school!"

As Bobby reached the bank, he bent forward as if to dive, but instead reached around and pulled his cheeks apart. "Oh, lick my ripe Reb ass, General Lee."

Jimbo lunged up, but Bobby was already safe in the water, spouting several yards out, yipping like a playful hound. "What'sa matter, Stonewall, somebody stomp on the Stars and Bars?"

If he had wanted, Jimbo could have caught him, for if Bobby was a faster swimmer, Jimbo's endurance was better. But after a moment there on the bank, shouting — "Get in here, you yellow sucker. Get your yellow ass in here and I'll whi . . . whi . . . whip it for you! Yellow!" — to which the only reply was the impudent chitter of Bobby's laughter, Jimbo chucked a stone vaguely toward the retreating figure, then slumped down again beside me in the silt and coarse grass.

"Don't respect nothing, he don't."

I shrugged. "He's just got his ways, I guess." I plucked a seed-heavy stem and chewed the succulent end reflectively. "What about you? What are you going to do?"

"Me? I don't know. Sell cars?" Knees drawn up, sitting, he began to make patterns in the earth with his finger. Suddenly, for all that brawn he had acquired lately, he looked very much a child.

"You know?" he said. "You know the only thing I really like to do? Football. I wish I could just play football. Forever. I want to go to State and play football. You like it?"

Bobby paddled nearer the bank.

"I'm not big enough, Jimbo."

"Yeah, I guess. But you know what I mean? That thing you'd like to do really. Like you and track. You liked track when you ran last spring."

I snorted. "What am I going to do, earn a living running away?"

"I don't know. Like acting. You could be an actor, maybe."

I grunted a laugh.

"No, I mean it. You'd like that, wouldn't you?"

"Sure, I guess. But three parts in *A Midsummer Night's Dream* at Franksville High isn't going to make me a Barrymore."

"But if it's what you want . . ."

Bobby dragged himself up through the shallows, whipping water off his head like a dog.

"Oh, hell, Jimbo, he's gonna be a lawyer. And you're gonna sell cars. Everybody in the whole damn country's gonna want a car."

"You sound just like my old man."

"Damn right. That's 'cause we're all gonna end up just like the old man — selling cars, drawing wills, drumming up and down the whole damn state and a couple more, too, if I'm lucky."

There was a momentary silence, as if there were something too painful in that judgment to be dealt with.

"Hell of a world, huh?" I muttered finally.

Bobby sighed a laugh. "Bet your sweet ass, Gambetta. Bet your sweet ass."

After Christmas, 1916, it was announced quietly to me and to a few family friends that Mrs. Randall was again with child. It was considered best that the news remain private, though the doctor's decision to begin her lying in immediately gave rise to rumors in town. Officially, she had suffered an attack of "exhaustion" as a result of the holidays, and it was not till around the first of March, after her third month had come and gone, that my father informed me after dinner it would be all right now to confirm the gossip, that indeed it seemed my promised brother was on the way.

That was the spring of the war. Relations with Germany had been broken in February, though the declaration of hostilities would not occur till April. In Franksville, however, the decisions from Washington were mere formalities, the town's loyalties having been decided long before. If they had voted massively for Wilson because he kept them out of war and, more important, was a Democrat born in Virginia to boot, the citizens were pro-Allied almost to a man. There had been an explosion of outrage, intense if brief, when the *Lusitania* went down, and the following autumn the high school debating team had argued the topic "Preparedness." Henderson Pritchard, the youngest of the weak-chinned brood waiting to inherit Franksville's oldest great house, gave enraptured lectures at local civic organizations about his beloved Paris, where he had once spent a summer and where, the gossip ran, he had contracted a variety of esoteric social diseases. Meanwhile, the editor of the Franksville *Star and Informer*, Mr. McCready, maintained an ever more furious pro-British barrage in his newspaper, "Hunnish" having become, since 1914, his preferred adjective of horror. All those things that before might have been merely "awful," "dreadful," or "detestable" were now described in terms of the murderous kaiser and his spike-headed legions. In reading the history of the Great War, I have since discovered that McCready, after the initial German advances, found fit to repress nearly all news he felt might be injurious to the Allied cause. Hence, the disaster at Gallipoli, the true magnitude of the carnage on the Western Front, remained a bit unclear to the readers of the *Star and Informer*. It did seem from the newspaper's columns that the Central Powers had an almost masochistic hunger for destruction. The war news always carried gory reports of the barbarians indulging in some unthinkable outrage (boiling babies for machine oil seemed a preferred pastime, though sexual violation and crucifixion — particularly of Canadians — also ranked high on their list), till they were inevitably thrown back by right-thinking, clean-living Tommies.

News magazines arrived, of course — *Collier's*, the *Saturday*

Evening Post — along with more responsible newspapers from elsewhere in the state and nation. But Franksville rather liked McCready's war. Southerners preferred to hear about victorious Anglo-Saxons, having known firsthand the bitterness of loss. Boys slightly older than I talked about going to Canada to join the RAC, or perhaps the Lafayette Esquadrille itself. Though the Europeans had learned about their illusions too well in the trenches, we retained dreams of glorious battles; of sudden painless ends at the head of advancing troops; of flag-draped funerals we might observe from some comfortably homelike Valhalla surrounded by our comrades-in-arms, while down below our parents and all the girls we wished to impress mourned our untimely passing with profound but dignified grief.

In retrospect, of course, I realize Mr. McCready and the fast-dwindling Confederate Veterans, the DAR and the UDC, the teachers at the high school, and even the pastors in the churches were preparing us as fodder, and we, knowing even less of war than they did, were perversely eager to live up to their most sanguine expectations. But that is an old and oft-repeated story in this century, and certainly not unique to Franksville. But the bloody-mindedness consequent to the war helps explain, perhaps, some of what happened that spring, for our town, unlike many nearby, had over its hundred-or-so years of life been spared the kind of gruesome rites that had afflicted the South decade after decade. Perhaps, without those gory dispatches piled one on the other, without the sermons on the threat to civilization as we knew it; perhaps if, instead of the rotogravures of the fallen in stiffly creased uniforms striding across the clouds, we had seen the mangled limbs, the trench mouth, the terrified boys screaming as they bled to death, the supernatural green of the gas, then Franksville would not have given itself over to all the worst it held within it.

But it did not happen that way.

4

HUNNISH MURDER SHOCKS COUNTY!

AROUND THE TURN OF THE CENTURY, about five miles from the center of town, a drifter of indeterminate middle age had taken up residence in an abandoned cabin, with a woman presumably his wife, hardly more than a girl, and a baby. The drifter, red-headed and green-eyed, Granger Ellison by name, claimed to have moved north from Georgia as a result of a highly protean catastrophe — sometimes natural, sometimes manmade, depending on how deeply he had fallen in his cups when he delivered the tale. A devastating fire was, to most people's best recollection, the original cause of his wanderings, though they were also sometimes attributed to a flood of biblical proportions, a murderous tornado, a bastard brother who had cheated him out of an inheritance, and the son of an unrepentant carpetbagger who continued to leech the lifeblood out of good and innocent Southern people.

Who exactly owned the land where the Ellisons squatted was never clear, though it probably, one way or another, belonged to the Pritchards, who seemed the ultimate masters of most everything that lacked title in the county. The cabin was so dilapidated, however, and the ground around it so poor that no one bothered to find out. Ellison farmed with very marginal luck and probably pulled his family through the winter only with the profits from the still he began constructing almost as soon as he arrived. The whiskey was not very good, even of its kind, but it was cheap and hence popular with the sharecroppers, black and white, and mill hands, a number of whom were likely struck blind by the lead in Mr. Ellison's moonshine.

The family, or at least its enlargement, seemed Granger Ellison's other notable success. If he could make very little grow in the ground, he seemed hard-pressed not to make something grow in Larrissa, his incongruously named wife. She was a strangely pretty woman: small, intense, silent, copper-haired like Granger himself, less than half his age. Nearly every spring she was pregnant again, bringing into the world an apparently endless legion of Ellisons. They might well have taken over the county had she survived. The eldest child, Hoppy, the boy sucking when the family arrived, grew robust and was almost immediately followed by two brothers, who regardless of their given names were known in Franksville as Skippy and Jumpy. Then came another brother, then a pair of twin girls, severely retarded. There were other children interspersed, most of whom died of various childhood ailments, a couple more spectacularly in accidents. None of them was notably graced intellectually, though popular wisdom would certainly not expect that of drifters' children. They did, however, suffer a certain sinister kinship. Hoppy, with flaming red hair and a long, gangly body even as a child, seemed normal, respectful, and up to no more devilment than anyone else. Skippy, too, was friendly enough, but his left arm ended not in a hand but in a grotesque gnarl of flesh possessed of a single finger. Jumpy, all the more sadly in view of his nickname, suffered a multitude of nervous tics, while the next son, Wheeze, grew stunted, victim of some unnamed respiratory malady, which kept him spindle thin and flat on his back most of the time. Then came the twins, slightly pinheaded — affectionately dubbed "the idjets" by their father — who gabbled back and forth as if they possessed a special language all their own.

For the most part, the family kept to itself, and aside from an occasional run-in with the truant officer, who only halfheartedly attempted to enforce school attendance rules outside the town limits, they had little trouble with the authorities. The gossip ran that Granger Ellison drank too much, beat his wife, beat his children, beat his dog (a ratty hound named Major, who one day apparently had had enough and simply vanished), but that description would have fit any number of men in the county. As the family grew and Hoppy and Skippy fleshed into adolescence, the boys moved out of the cabin into a sort of lean-to on the edge of the clearing. About the time Mrs. Randall's pregnancy was officially announced, Skippy disappeared, presumably taking to the open road like his father before him. Granger, so the story ran, was furious, for Skippy had an inborn touch with the mash and was his father's favorite, as Hoppy was Larrissa's. Hoppy had sworn silence about his brother's plan, but Granger whipped the truth out of him. His howling alerted the neighbors to something amiss and made Skippy's flight public knowledge. Most people were not surprised at the boy's departure, and it was generally assumed Hoppy would follow in that course before the end of summer. That proved true, though a great deal transpired in between.

It was March, crisp but promising spring: buds on the trees, the jonquils, determined, thrusting leaves through the brown grass. Bobby, Melissa, and I were dawdling on our way to school, full of track teams, the spring talent show, and history quizzes, when we saw Hoppy Ellison — just before the sheriff caught him — running, screaming, down Depot Street. His face and clothes stiff with blood, half his hair singed away and his arm badly burned, he looked like hell itself, whirling around in the middle of the road, panting hoarsely, terribly: "No! Pa! Help me! Help!" Staggering past us, not even seeing Melissa burst into tears and Bobby holding up his books, as if they were a cross to ward off the Devil.

"Help me! Ma! Mama!"

That long body, like a scarecrow unhinged, reeled uncontrolled, and the air was suddenly thick with an ungodly and unforgettable smell: vomit and shit and old gore; the reek of burnt hair, cloth, and skin. I gagged and Melissa started to scream, her wails mingling with Hoppy Ellison's, he slowing, wobbling like a spent top, thinking perhaps in that mind past all thinking that those noises shattering out of Melissa meant he had found someone who understood his pain, who knew what had happened, so he need no longer try to form words but only shriek incoherently louder and louder.

None of us saw the sheriff or his deputy coming. They blundered into Hoppy, knocking the wind out of him so his cries were strangled wheezing, like the sounds his youngest brother made when he breathed.

"My God," the deputy murmured, "my God," as they cuffed Hoppy and led him away. They noticed us not at all, Melissa sobbing on my shoulder, Bobby staring at me, his eyes starting from his face as ghostly white as mine doubtless was. We remained there for I do not know how long, till others who had seen Hoppy Ellison that morning began to pass, mouths agape with curiosity or perplexity or horror, hurrying down Depot Street toward Main and on to the county courthouse.

What facts there were were simple enough. The Ellisons — every last one but Hoppy — were dead, murdered, butchered. The stories in the *Star and Informer* painted it graphically; the gossip even more so. The idjets had been decapitated, each with a single, smooth stroke, while Wheeze had had his skull split with a blow which parted his forehead and shattered the bridge of his nose. Jumpy had been hacked multiple times, his arms folded around him as if he had tried to stop the flow of blood from all those wounds by holding himself very tight.

Larrissa and Granger were found dead in their bed. She had been killed with one powerful thrust to the heart. Granger's throat was cut, though that was not what most impressed the sheriff and Walter Everhardt, who found, scattered throughout the room, various of his members: a hand, his nose, three toes, and (though the *Star* did not mention it) his genitals. It was not certain he had bled to death before he was mutilated.

Both his and Larrissa's bodies were badly charred. The bed had been set afire. That, Hoppy claimed when he finally regained himself, was how he got burned. For two days, he lay in the new county hospital, hardly alive at all, his head and arm heavily bandaged, his legs and chest bruised and torn by scrapes and scratches from the falls on his breakneck run to town. He looked, according to the few who saw him, like a body already enshrouded. Within three days, however, he gradually gained a hold on reality, and McCready could inform his readers of the tale Hoppy Ellison had to tell.

Asleep in the lean-to, Hoppy had awakened not long before dawn, vaguely aware he had heard something: a cry, perhaps only in a dream. He was almost asleep again when he heard another sound: a scream. He jumped off his cot, grabbed his squirrel rifle, and ran toward the cabin, firing a shot as he went. As he approached, a man darted through the front door, leapt from the porch, and nearly ran into him. As the figure staggered past, he lunged with what must have been a knife, for Hoppy said whatever it was rang like metal as it struck the rifle barrel. It was not yet dawn, so Hoppy could not see the intruder's face, though he did hear him grunt something unintelligible — "way back in his throat," Hoppy recalled — as he vanished in the darkness. The boy did not follow but dashed up the steps to find Jumpy in a pool of blood and then the rest of the mayhem. In the bedroom the flames were blazing on the mattress. Hoppy apparently smothered the fire with the dirt-encrusted rug that covered the floor, but by that time he was so deep in shock he could not recall it.

Hoppy could offer little more and was of no help in determining the identity of the murderer. A number of people, including the sheriff, suspected Hoppy himself, but the idea did not play well. First of all, the boy had been so dreadfully injured himself. Why, the reasoning ran, if he had set the fire to disguise the crime, would he then have risked life and limb to put it out? Beyond that, as far as anybody knew, Hoppy had no call to slaughter his entire family. Had it been Jumpy with his tics, or Wheeze, who always sounded like the promise of death, it might have been different. But to believe that Hoppy — the Ellisons' most normal offspring, the one with friends in town, a hard worker, according to the neighbors — had systematically butchered parents, brothers, and sisters would mean no one was safe, that any father might awaken one night to find his son leering over the bed, eyes glinting in the moonlight, the smiler with the knife.

The instruments that had wrought such violence were not found, but they were soon enough identified. In the rickety shed he referred to as the barn, high on the building's one truly solid wall, Granger hung the knives he used to butcher hogs. He had six of them, which he lined up in order of size, ranging from a heavy bladed monster that, with its handle, approached two feet in length, to a fine double-edged stiletto handy for cleaning close to the bone or the interstices of the joints. It was these two — the first and the last — that were missing from the set.

After the first seventy-two hours, then, McCready could set down most of what seemed the relevant details under the banner:

HUN FIEND, MURDERER?

But to what end? The Ellisons were absurd targets for robbery, and aside from the knives there was nothing missing from among their miserable possessions. Ellison's dealings in whiskey might have raised someone's hackles — but enough to dispatch the entire family? Of course, he could have been involved in some business no one was aware of, but that too seemed unlikely. Perhaps his bastard brother or the itinerant carpetbagger had arrived to extract some obscure vengeance. Most people in Franksville, however, did not believe in the existence of either man. Granger never mentioned them except when extraordinarily drunk and certainly did not indicate that, if they were real, they would have any idea where he was.

That left only one possibility: a maniac. Somewhere in Franksville, counting out change, drumming a table impatiently, cradling a chin, affectionately squeezing a shoulder, was the hand that had wielded the knives. It might be the one that put your cup before you at the MacKenzie Palace Tea Room, the one pointing the way to your package that had arrived Railway Express, the one clasping yours in greeting after a few days in which particular paths had not crossed. Franksville plunged into abject terror. Families who never locked their doors bought out the latches and bolts at the Ever-True Hardware and Feed Store, while others flooded Sears-Roebuck with orders. Men arrived late to work for having walked their children to school, and, in certain neighborhoods, women collectively cleaned one house a day. No one wanted to be alone, particularly at night, when whole families in some cases retired in one room.

McCready, in his own fashion, did his best to calm the hysteria. Hoppy had not recognized the killer, who must then have been a stranger, though that provided little comfort as visions danced in the public mind of a rabid psychopath lurking in the woods around town. Besides, the assertions of a boy rousted from a sound sleep, blundering around in the pitch dark to discover his entire family vivisected and suffer serious burns, were not, a number of people pointed out, entirely to be trusted. The killer might have been dirty or have blacked his face or been covered with blood — a likely circumstance, if Hoppy himself were anything to go by.

McCready, however, was resolute, and managed as well to find in the murder the conjunction of his various prejudices. America was ceasing to be too proud to fight, and in his head, surely, "Scotland the Brave," "The Bonnie Blue Flag," and "The Battle Hymn of the Republic" had melded into a single cacophonous anthem. Just as the Zimmermann telegram had revealed the kaiser's hopes of encouraging a revolt of Mexicans in the Southwest, so the massacre of the Ellison family signaled a reprehensible German plot to recruit "discontented Negroes" to their cause, to foment a dark-faced rebellion across the South all the way to California that would keep the United States out of the European war. Had not Hoppy Ellison himself identified the man as speaking some guttural tongue? "Like German," McCready suggested.

Here, the *Star and Informer*'s speculations approached a fateful fork in the path. If the killer were indeed part of a dastardly Hunnish plot, then he certainly could not be a local, black or white, since no one in town spoke German. It had been added to the curriculum at Franksville High only two years before and had never been considered a proper study for the colored. Further, McCready was convinced that a Negro would be incapable of learning a foreign language from anyone, while an American white man would be incapable of such a savage crime. The murderer, then, must have been a German agent, passing through Franksville on his way to provoke an uprising farther South. His own barbaric instincts having overwhelmed him, or simply wishing to refresh himself on the peculiar skills of slaughter, he had picked the unfortunate Ellisons as his victims. The plot went awry only because of Hoppy's unexpected intervention. Otherwise, McCready concluded triumphantly, the Ellisons would have been consumed in the fire, and no one would have been the wiser.

Such an explanation, even at the time, struck many as fantastic. But in those moments when the world seems to have gone a bit mad, people are loathe to express such reservations, and things that seem beyond all conceiving suddenly acquire an absurd plausibility. Unrestricted submarine warfare had been resumed by the Germans, the *Housatonic* had been torpedoed, relations with Berlin had been severed. Barely six months had passed since the Black Tom explosion, hardly two since the Canadian Car and Foundry blast. Now, with the Zimmermann note, people everywhere were swept into a fury against Germany and all things German. One morning in Franksville, the town awoke to find the display window of the Dresmann Bakery shattered, and the next day, the familiar sign above the door read "Dresman's." So, the extravagant fears of a bitter, limited, small-town journalist like John McCready — born of a white Southerner's understandable dread of ex-slaves still treated like chattle and of a Scot's undying devotion to the kilted legions at Culloden now battered by artillery shells and machine guns as they wormed beneath barbed wire — acquired a currency they would otherwise have lacked. People discussed in hushed tones the likelihood and implications of the German conspiracy, which with each edition of the *Star and Informer* grew more complex, more widespread, transforming itself from an editor's private fiction to a hungry reality awaiting propitiation:

HUN AGENTS COVER SOUTH!

For no more than a few hours, there was an attempt to keep the news from Mrs. Randall. As soon as I arrived home from the courthouse, too excited to go to school and assured of an excuse for my absence, I was cut off on the stairs and ferried to the kitchen by Aunt Lottie, who there interrogated me with Aunt Bea, Althea providing Greek chorus as my firsthand account was pieced together with the gossip that had already begun to circulate over back fences, across sales counters, and via the lips of deliverymen. The slaughter of the Ellisons had by then been discovered, so my description of Hoppy's capture did not have quite the impact it had enjoyed a bare couple hours before on the courthouse steps. Still, what I had to tell was grisly enough and much more detailed than the sketchy news available from the scene of the crime.

"His whole shirt was red, there was so much blood . . ."

"Lord, Lord . . ."

". . . like he was crazy. Just kept screaming . . ."

"Well he might. Lord, poor boy . . ."

Lottie and Bea remained silent, a parody of horror, Bea twisting the knot of her shawl, appalled but eager in that small-town way for every detail that might be repeated or, if heard again, consumed with the smug indulgence reserved for old news.

"There was no hair on one side of his head . . ."

"Little baby Jesus . . ."

"Screaming and screaming . . ."

"What he had to see. Poor boy."

"He just —"

My voice cracked. I did not expect it, retelling for the tenth time — the twelfth? — what I had seen. And suddenly my eyes were wet. Perhaps it was what Althea said. Perhaps across some other, inner eye the vision of a bloody, violated house flickered past, and a terror not even conscious rose to choke me. I blinked furiously, embarrassed, but they all had noticed, and the spell was broken.

"Well, it's terrible."

"Terrible."

"But you, Gams. You ought to lie down now."

"Yes, lie down."

"Lord, Lord . . ." Althea was back to her chores, which she had never really left, having years before developed the infinitely divisible attention of those who work in other people's houses.

"I guess . . ." I said, not wanting to, but confused by that unexpected rush of nerves which had silenced me. I felt too warm, and somewhere in the back of my throat was the taste of Hoppy Ellison's stink. "I think I will."

Lottie put her hand on my shoulder. "You're pale."

"Pale." Bea agreed.

"You just go upstairs," she said, leading me toward the door. "And" — she turned to face me, her finger raised, admonishing — "not a word of this to Mrs. Randall."

"She doesn't know?" The idea struck me as ludicrous.

"It would upset her terribly," Bea said.

"Terribly."

"And in her condition . . ." In the house, Mrs. Randall's miscarriages were never mentioned outright.

"Of course," I said. "Of course. I won't say anything."

When I walked through her door, Mrs. Randall was reading in the overstuffed chair by the window, the late winter sun falling brightly across her lap, her legs propped on the ottoman and covered with a pink and white throw. Her face, pale in the shadow, was as beatific as it always was when she read, her hair wound loosely back on her head. She did not look well. She had not looked well for the last five months. Perhaps it was indeed the pregnancy, perhaps she was too fragile of constitution, too delicate of body, to endure the labor of making a child. But I thought at the time, and still think it right in part, that it was the enforced idleness of the lying-in that drained her. That, and the awful charge pregnancy itself had become. She never spoke of it; but surely, the burden of carrying a child to term, the necessity of bearing the child alive, must have become almost unendurable. The premature loss of one baby was no shame — a common enough occurrence in those days — and even the loss of the second could be viewed with sympathy, a mean twist of luck. But the third miscarriage had the smack of judgment to it, and even if a word was never spoken, some would begin to think

there was something "wrong," not solely in a physical sense —
a canal too narrow, some wall too weak — but in a more profound way. A couple's failure to reproduce was a sign, in Franksville as surely as in a primitive tribe half naked in some jungle
yet unknown, and Mrs. Randall must have felt her joy at a new
conception give way to dread, as if she were again to be tested,
to see if she could fulfill her obligation as consort. If my father
and Mrs. Randall enjoyed the roles of native prince and his
foreign love, the town expected too that their lives be the fairy
tale promised in that absurd tower with its conical roof piercing
the sky. There was an heir apparent, of course, but I was a secondary figure in the myth, part of a different story, eternalized
in the town canon at the graveside of Gambetta Stevenson's
first, now vaguely recollected wife when I was six. The en-
chanted couple must bring into the world a child; that was the
burden of magic. It was simple as that.

"Gams?" Mrs. Randall said suddenly. "What are you doing
home so early?"

I hoped I looked as wan as I had in the kitchen. "I got sick at
school. They sent me home."

"What is it? Do you have a fever?"

She lurched clumsily to her feet, her belly now distended
beneath her dressing gown, her limbs heavy with the weight of
the baby and too little movement for months. She pulled the
throw around her as she came toward me, truly like a princess
then, like a lady in Van Eyck, but with a face whose beauty only
an Italian — Leonardo himself, perhaps — could have captured.

"Sit still," I said. "Please." I felt her arm around me and her
warm hand on my cheek and forehead. I wanted to tell her
everything then: about the day, about Hoppy, about the lie I
had agreed to. But differently this time, for the full horror of
what had happened at last was dawning on me, and I felt the
need to be comforted, rest my head, cry. But I steeled myself,
despising myself:

83

"No. It might be catching. Sit down. I'll be all right."

She let go, unwillingly, I thought, and backed away with a sad smile. "I suppose you're right. I mustn't get sick." She sighed smoothly into a laugh. "Poor Gams. You feel bad and I can't even take care of you."

"I'll be all right."

She slipped into the chair. "When this is over, you'll have to get sick again so I can nurse you."

I did not know what to say. "I'll go to bed, I guess," I blurted, but made no move to leave.

"Is there something else?" she said finally.

"No, nothing. Nothing." I backed toward the door. "I'm going to sleep. I'll see you at supper."

Safe in the hall, I felt lightheaded, and the lie lay sour in my mouth. Once in bed, I pitched and tossed and finally slipped off the mattress onto the bearskin rug. Images real and imagined elbowed one another behind my closed eyes: Hoppy and Melissa screaming and Althea scrubbing and the dead Ellisons and Mrs. Randall, her grace robbed now by that swelling under her dress, but more seraphic than ever, her hand held softly to my cheek.

My father told her. As soon as he arrived home. It was reasonable, I suppose. She surely, by late afternoon, had intuited something was wrong, for my own scene with her had been anything but professionally played, and during those couple of hours when I could not sleep, there had been an inordinate number of comings and goings downstairs as Bea and Lottie shunted neighbors back to the kitchen, there to gasp at the latest details.

She had been informed, then, by supper, but the topic was avoided over the meal — the good-mannered option, I realized in retrospect. The table talk, rarely scintillating, was unusually desultory that night, with Lottie and Bea echoing one another a good deal. For the most part, I watched Mrs. Randall. She had changed to a different dressing gown and picked at her food during dinner, both of which she did most nights, the former in celebration of the break in routine that coming downstairs signified; the latter because her appetite when she was pregnant came at the most unexpected times — three in the afternoon, one in the morning — so that Althea took to leaving cold plates prepared. She chose to have her tea in her room and went up while I stayed at the table to give my father an audience for the finale of his latest tale of financial derring-do. And to find out what news he had, of course.

"I saw Hoppy Ellison today," I said casually.

"I know," he said. "Ugly business." He got up and took the sherry from the sideboard. "Would you like some?"

I was never offered sherry except on special occasions, birthdays and holidays. "I think so, yes," I said, trying not to sound surprised. "Has there been any more news?"

"About the murder?" He handed me the glass. "I don't know what you've heard. The whole family dead. Stabbed. I spoke to McCready. He'd been out to the house."

In the years since he had married again, as his profits increased and his children failed to be born, as I grew older, my father and I talked less and less, and when we did, he affected that peculiar telegraphic speech so distinct from his usual loquaciousness. I stopped him up, as if I were somehow not to be trusted.

"Do they think Hoppy did it?"

"Yes and no, yes and no." He tossed back most of his sherry in a gulp. "McCready says no. A good boy. You know Hoppy, don't you?"

"Yes and no."

"Not crazy. He'd have to be crazy. McCready says only a lunatic could have killed them."

I tasted my drink. "Hoppy seemed pretty crazy today."

My father shrugged. "McCready said he didn't think it was Hoppy. He just had an intuition. And he's working on a theory."

"What kind of theory?"

"Didn't say. We'll read it in the paper, I suppose." He set down his glass. "I have a few things to do. You have homework?"

"Yes," I said. I didn't, of course, not having been to school.

"Well, get to it."

He walked away. He was not yet forty and still a handsome man, though he was becoming portly in the way men of his age and status are supposed to be at forty. A couple of his suits had had to be recut, and it had been years since he had taken me to swim at the reservoir. I went with friends, instead; he had ceded a father's place at the proper time to his son's companions. But I wondered if he were jealous.

I stayed at the table, relishing my sherry, wondering when a cigar might be tendered. Next year probably, when I was accepted at Princeton, as everyone predicted I would be, where I could go and learn French properly, and the law, and meet the sort of people it was essential to meet to play the stock market and wear fine clothes and live in a house with a turret.

"Hell of a world," I muttered.

I finished the drink, then crept upstairs, for above it was dark and I thought Mrs. Randall must have gone to sleep. But her door was open, and as I passed she called to me out of the gloom. "Gams?"

I crossed the threshold, reaching for the light.

"Don't turn it on," she said. Her voice was rough.

"All right."

There in the silence, my eyes adjusted slowly. I could make her out, just a silhouette of deeper darkness in the chair.

"You might have told me," she said.

"Told you what?" Knowing, of course, what she meant.

She laughed. "You're a worse liar now than you were this afternoon."

Though she could not see it, I flushed. "The aunts thought it would be better not —"

"Don't apologize." She had something in her lap, something I could not make out. "They mean well. Everyone thinks he means well." She sighed. "Every one of them dead?"

"Except for Hoppy."

"You saw him today."

"Yes."

"Tell me."

I hesitated.

"It cannot be any worse than my imagining it."

I told her, as I had not and had regretted that afternoon. Here and there my voice thinned, but I told her everything, not only what I saw but what I had heard. We did not touch. I leaned on the bureau, speaking softly to the darkness, her shape there slowly more distinct in the chair, with that unknowable object in her lap.

She said nothing for a moment. Perhaps she was crying. I liked to imagine she was, but even if it were only her silence, that was tribute enough amidst all the gossip, both to her and to the Ellisons.

"Poor Larrissa," she said finally.

It was not until the next day that the rumor would spread of that single thrust to the heart, and not until the day after that it would be confirmed in McCready's most graphic description. But it was as if Mrs. Randall already knew, just as somehow she already knew that Larrissa was pregnant when she died.

"It's hard to imagine sometimes what some people will do," I said, thinking that would sound very wise.

It was the first time I had heard her laugh bitter. "No, Gams. People can do things you would never believe anybody capable of in the flicker of an eye."

I could not reply, bobbled by that grimness from someone I

87

had thought so particularly innocent. And I wondered again what it was that set Mrs. Randall apart, what was that thing ineffable — unspeakable — there before she came to Franksville. I looked at her hands and still could not identify that shape, though later I realized it was the hope chest, locked as it would always be. Perhaps she never had the key at all.

"You should rest," I said mindlessly.

"I should always do that these days." I could see her turn toward me in the dark. "Were you really sick today?"

"No." I shook my head. "But yes, in a way. Can you imagine seeing what I saw?"

"No."

I turned to leave.

"Gams."

"Yes."

"It was right not to tell me, you know."

I snorted. "It's nice to think so."

5

IT IS IMPOSSIBLE to capture what Franksville was then. The hysteria, the terror mixed with impending war, whipped by McCready's fervor, the printed equivalent of the bloodlust that seemed to enrapture everyone, even Lottie and Bea. The Hun. The Hun! And mixed with reports of the atrocities of those Hellish legions (boys like our own — frightened, trench-mouthed — but from Bremen, Dresden, the godforsaken farming towns of Silesia) was the slaughter of Granger Ellison and all his kin but one. There in Franksville itself was the essence of barbarism, what the Central Powers represented, and — if you read McCready, as everybody did — the similarity was more than casual.

The Ellisons received a funeral none of them had any reason to expect. It was attended by everyone in town, including dignitaries who would have crossed the street before they exchanged the time of day with Granger. Hoppy was not there, of course. He was still swaddled in bandages in the county hospital. Everhardt, so the story ran, went to the trouble of cosmetizing the bodies, though the coffins were closed and, after both mayhem and autopsies, it must have stretched his skills to the limit. The County Council itself paid for monuments for the graves, including on Larrissa's the inscription "And Unnamed Ellison Child" for that baby which never saw light. The whole affair reminded me of Mr. Randall's rites five years before, a kind of parody of that civic funeral, for the dead Ellisons, thanks to the *Star and Informer*, had achieved a patriotic glamour in McCready's world as Franksville's first victims in the war against the Hun.

McCready's version of the events had been picked up by editors all across the state. Before, when he railed against the Germans, his fellows had treated him as a bit of a crank, interested themselves in issues closer to home. With the declaration of war almost assured, however, McCready achieved the status of a voice in the wilderness, a prophet without honor, and so on. I later thought it strange that it took so long to invent a suspect. Southern justice was usually swift if not especially sure, trotting might-be murderers off to the gallows with great alacrity and the assurance that, even if it were the wrong man, at least his fate might serve as an example to any who might be contemplating crime.

But more than a week passed before news arrived from down east of a drifter arrested, apparently for no other reason than drifting. A dark man, young, with no identification. Most intriguing of all, however, was his lack of speech. According to the report the sheriff received, the man made signs frantically but could make no sound except a low growl. Had he passed a month before through the swamps and across the sounds of that lazy world miles beyond Franksville, he might have moved on unnoticed, or spent a night in jail before being deposited next morning at the county line. As it was, news of his capture, news that would not even have been communicated before, must have fallen on our sheriff's ears like the music of heaven itself. All those days since the killings, McCready had fulminated not just against Germans and Negroes and devilish plots but against law officers who could not bring murderers to justice and conspiracy to heel. That sheriff, Oliver Benton, needed no harpy on his back, married as he was to one. He was an ineffective man who had little strenuous to do in Franksville aside from play poker, chase the boys who got rowdy on Saturday night, and occasionally venture into Pallister Slough on journeys of desultory intimidation. His wife, Evelyn, baited him unmercifully, publicly, treatment to which he submitted with quizzical, slothful stoicism. McCready's attacks stung him, however, though perhaps he had the wherewithall to fear more the pitch of terror the town had reached. In those weeks, there had been three more near-murders: an overdue boy mistaken for the maniac, nearly blown into eternity by his mother; a farmer cutting across his neighbor's field wounded in the leg by a trigger-happy sharecropper; and Elmore Lindley, one of the town drunks, crowned with a fry pan in the alley behind the Depot Diner. It was time to lay madness to rest, and an anonymous deaf-mute picked up half a state away would do as well as anyone else.

The day he arrived was electric — literally so, with a thunderstorm building in the south. An unseasonable muggy stillness over the town put everyone on edge. He was to be brought at two, and a crowd gathered, mostly men, with a few boys like me who had cut the final hour of classes, determined to see a psycho-path at close range. McCready had already painted a grim verbal picture and printed as well a sketch made by a Tidewater associate, showing a sullen, unkempt man with a vague expression. Perhaps, we speculated there outside the courthouse, that vacant look was the sign of a killer, though if so, Granger Ellison's younger children had certainly been marked also.

Two o'clock came and went. Bobby suggested they would not bring him till nightfall, especially if the deputy had notified Sheriff Benton about the crowd. Several of the men agreed, or at least took the idea seriously, as Bobby and I still held a certain prestige for having witnessed the capture of Hoppy Ellison.

"I hope if they're coming they get here soon." I was thinking ahead to track practice, which I could not miss. For the first time, we had been invited to the statewide meet in the capital, and Mr. Sink had scheduled daily practices for the next six weeks, even during Easter holidays.

"Do you want to go?"

"Let's wait half an hour." That would give me a good twenty minutes to get back and get suited.

The storm broke about a quarter past. There was only the most preliminary roll of thunder before a streak of lightning shattered above us and droplets thick as glycerine slapped the pavement. There was no cover nearby. I shifted to run.

"Be still!" Bobby grabbed my shoulder.

We stood there in the flood as the rest of the crowd dashed away, across the street into the bakery or the bank, up the block to the awning in front of the pharmacy. Instantly soaked, I started to laugh. Bobby took me by the arm and led me up the stairs through the heavy oak and glass door to the marbled court-house lobby, where we sat on the bench across from the brass clock Mr. Randall had presented to the county as a gift. No one, of course, could really ask us to leave — two drenched boys escaping the shower. Outside, the rain still slashed down the street in wind-driven silver blades.

Ten minutes later, at twenty-seven past two by Mr. Randall's clock, they brought the prisoner.

The car pulled up suddenly, and four men were hustling up the steps before we really realized it. They burst through the door — Sheriff Benton and two others in shiny rubber slickers, like huge black ducks. Once inside, they stopped. There amid them, shivering with fear or wet, was the killer.

He was no bigger than I was and looked not much older. He had a shock of curly black hair, which glistened with rain, and on his lip and cheeks was the stubbly shadow of a man who would never in his life grow a real beard. His skin was the color of oiled wood, and his dark eyes wide and bewildered. He did not look much like he did in the drawings. He looked even less German.

The sheriff exploded. "What in hell are you boys doin' here!"

"It was raining, sir," Bobby said.

"Lord help us," he muttered, turning to the others. "Let's get this one upstairs."

He pushed him, and I heard the clatter of the chains that dragged around his feet and clanked down from his wrists. But over that was his protest: a sad, animal sigh, as if his confusion were complete, as if he hoped his own keening groan might wake him from the dream in which he found himself. McCready had reported in the morning edition that the suspect seemed — or pretended to be — illiterate. I realized long after that if that were true, he would have had no notion of what they thought he had done, of why these men had put him in chains and taken him from one jail cell to drive him hours only to put him back in another one in a town he had never seen.

This would occur to me on a train racketing west, carrying me away from Franksville, as far away, it seemed then, as it was possible to go, though I learned as I grew older there were still more distant points where I might flee. As I lay alone in the clacking darkness, beneath the starch-stiff sheets of the Pullman Company, that face of external perplexity rose before me, and I wondered how many times men had thrown him roughly between them, speechless as a child or deer; how many times he had felt the bite of shackles on his wrists and ankles. He must have all his life inspired a foolish terror with his whinnies and groans and growls, his hopeless utterances of fright or love or wonder. Perhaps even as a boy he was mistreated. Or perhaps, at six or twelve or twenty, something had happened: some awful blow to the head, which had left him speechless, nameless; or some blow to the mind, something so awful as to strike him dumb and send him drifting through the world.

But he could not know, as neither Bobby nor I nor the sheriff nor likely anybody else in town could know, that his bonds that day were his penultimate chains, the jail in Franksville his final home. But for a murder and a war and a small-town paper, he might have wandered free for years and years. Perhaps I and the others would have recognized in those eyes his innocence, as I did that night, heading westward to escape that face — which followed me even there — and all it had come to mean.

"Hanging's no good. What good does it do to hang him? His neck's broke before he knows what hit him. You call that fair?"

"Dead's dead, far as I see it. Anything you do to a man, you can't make him deader than dead."

"Well, you can sure make it a lot meaner getting there."

"Ow! Watch my ear there, Sandy."

"Sorry, Gams. But the way the law reads, you gotta hang him or nothin'."

Perhaps the conversation was not exactly that. Memory is not like film. Images superimpose themselves; you can never be sure the words you hear inside your head are those that really go with a particular scene. Instead of in the barbershop, with Sandy cutting my hair as he had since I was three, clipping distractedly at my ear as he joined in the chatter around the next chair, the exchange might have been one I overheard at lunch in school, in a booth at The Arbor, in the locker room, on some street corner, passing by. In Franksville then, you could hear the voice of the beast — Mr. McCready's dream become real — wherever you turned. There was an object now, a human form: no caricature of the kaiser in the *Star and Informer*, no uniformed rags and a spiked helmet improvised with a saucepan and a scrap of broomstick, but flesh and blood behind bars awaiting judgment. And we were ready to judge, even I, who from that moment in the courthouse when I first saw his face perhaps was never quite convinced the man was guilty.

There were many suggestions as to what ought to be done. An example had to be made, for how many other agents had the Germans sent to stir up trouble across the South? A simple hanging would not do, down in the capital in a prison yard with nothing but jailbirds and a few newspapermen to watch. The *Star and Informer* ran letter after letter extolling public execution, executions of the grimmest sort. Readers recalled every atrocity McCready had fed them since 1914, committed by German or Austrian or Turk, which now might be avenged five thousand miles away by the citizens of a town it is doubtful anyone in Europe had ever heard of.

But the proof? There was no proof. The murder weapons had disappeared. No evidence had been collected at the scene of the crime to link the prisoner to the slaughter of the Ellisons. A confession of mayhem and espionage and sedition would be the easiest thing, the quickest and least troublesome for all. Surely they beat him. Surely Oliver Benton discovered within himself that peculiar sadism of Southern sheriffs. Likely, he was inept, that at first there was too much blood and too many bruises, and the burns from the cigar tip went too deep. Henry Brownrich claimed to have heard an awful howling one night late as he cut through downtown on his way home from the depot, but that was the only report.

They were not asking much. Only that he speak, that he form those guttural sounds he made into German, or better, German-accented English, which they could understand with no need to send out of town for a translator. But he did not speak, though he must have wanted to more desperately than at any other moment in his life, as they became more refined in their forcings, doing things we would have then, in the century's innocence still, have considered unthinkable.

McCready kept us informed of the killer's intransigence. Along with the headlines and statements from the sheriff and the news from Europe and Washington (now as far back as page three), he offered personal impressions of the prisoner he was often allowed to see. A "surly," "wily," "treacherous," "brutal" man, McCready reported. Bavarians, he informed us, were often dark. Further, in Germany and particularly the Hapsburg empire, there were endless mongrel races, half Asiatic, who would, for promises from Berlin and Vienna, enroll themselves in a dangerous and devilish cause. Poles, Bohemians, especially Jews, taken from the village or the ghetto and trained by sword-scarred Junkers — these were the perfect candidates for stirring up rebellion, more brutish themselves than the worst buck Negro.

"Buck nigger," of course, was what he said if not printed. Graying, bespectacled, not much thought of or particularly respected through the years he had labored for all purposes alone to bring the news to Franksville — writing the copy, managing the layout, helping to set the type — McCready was now a sage, a celebrity, and often held forth (often but briefly) as he hustled between courthouse and newsroom, newsroom and the Western

Union window at the depot. Requests for information poured in now, not just from elsewhere in the state but from places of moment: Atlanta and Baltimore and Cincinnati and Washington, D.C. The Department of Justice and the Department of War, McCready crowed, were prepared to take an interest in the case, were anxious for details, were keeping abreast. The *Star and Informer* printed extra copies, which went out on the mail trains to keep readers in surrounding counties up to date on Franksville's own experience with the looming war.

So it went, along with ever more frequent exhortations to duty and sacrifice, the sudden surging of patriotic songs at what public spectacles Franksville could boast. In spite of doubts, I drank it in, with Jimbo and Melissa, Lottie and Bea, Leonard and Father Finch, intoxicated with the united American voice, which blew away almost overnight sixty years of loyalty to the Stars and Bars. The Battle of Armageddon was about to be joined, and the time had come to take up positions among the ranks of the blest. And everyone fell gladly into line.

Everyone but Mrs. Randall.

Mrs. Randall did not believe. There was something that did not convince her. Perhaps it was being a Yankee; perhaps she had some sight beyond our own for being a stranger in Franksville, like the stranger in the jail. That first night over dinner, she insisted it was not just, that the deaf-mute was not the marauder who had killed the Ellisons one by one.

"Someone would have noticed. A man who can't talk? Probably wandering around half lost. Why hasn't anyone ever claimed to have recognized him? Has anyone?"

"Don't excite yourself, dear."

"Excite myself!"

She was well along in her fifth month. The point at which all the other babies had died had passed, but still the family worried. She kept — or was kept — to her room more and more and grew more and more frail, as if the tiny body in her womb consumed her. Her appetite was back, but however much she ate seemed too little to sustain her.

Day to day, from the time of the arrest, she quizzed me on developments, her face a cloud, her objections sharper and more frequent. There in her room, after school and practice: "What news?" What rumors, unspoken suspicions, half-truths? She wanted details, and her interest seemed finally more than in the innocence of that boy-faced man she had never seen. It was the man himself. Again and again, she asked me what he looked like, visualized those frightened eyes, that waving bramble of hair, the patchy beard. She somehow felt for him, sympathized. Did more than that? I thought it vaguely even then: wanted him? Why ought Mrs. Randall take an interest in this anonymous sacrifice to McCready and the public good?

"Then they know nothing about him?" Her feet on the hassock, she sank into the pillows of her chair, lost behind her belly.

"Nothing," I said, leaning on the bureau. "What could they find out? He doesn't talk. He can't read . . ."

By then I was casual. The room where she had made herself up — where now she lived, rarely venturing into that place she had conceived a child with my father — held no mystery now. My brother assured that. Brother? Sister? Sibling. Half-sibling unborn. But she herself, Mrs. Randall, she was still inscrutable, fondling that wooden box she toyed with more and more.

"What's in there?" I said suddenly.

"In where?"

"That chest."

She looked at it in her hands, as if she were surprised to find it there. "Oh, I just use it like worry beads. To do something."

"But what's in it?"

She folded her fingers over the old polished wood, nestled between her breasts and womb. A smile I had not seen before crept across her face as she raised her gaze to meet mine. It was not wicked, not malicious, but definitive, deceptive. And I knew suddenly that the box and whatever keepsakes it contained, whatever rattled when she turned it in her hands, was the most special, most dear, most secret thing she possessed.

"Well . . . what?"

"Hope," she said.

For the deaf-mute, hope began to dawn. It came in the form of a telegram from the State School for the Deaf and Dumb. Benton did not announce it. McCready did not publish it. But its threat could not remain a secret for long. The boys at the Western Union ate at the Depot Diner, where Maggie and Phil soon enough knew the text by heart and told first this friend and then that one, who themselves repeated the message, so the day after its arrival, I could recite it word for word to Mrs. Randall and her hope chest and the unborn child:

DEEP CONCERN RE: MURDER SUSPECT. WILL ABIDE NO MIS-TREATMENT. INFORM RE: CONDITION. RESPECTFULLY, MRS. WILMA EVERS/ASSISTANT DIRECTOR/STATE SCHOOL FOR THE DEAF AND DUMB

The unacknowledged telegram caused great unofficial consternation in Franksville. McCready spent long hours at the courthouse, presumably in conference with Benton. The *Star and Informer* continued to print daily revelations regarding the suspect, each more definite in its portrait of a mad German killer, though the source of such information remained obscure. More interesting were the rumors that did not see print: Mrs. Wilma Evers had gone to the governor; she had cast aspersions on McCready and on Franksville. Those who had connections in the capital or who found occasion to travel there bore news of new conspiracies, headed up by the assistant director of the School for the Deaf and Dumb, whose maiden name was Brauer, and who was divorced!

McCready finally could remain silent no longer, and the *Star and Informer* bannered: GERMAN-AMERICAN THREATENS IN-VESTIGATION. Mrs. Evers née Brauer did not fare well on the front page. She had brought panic to Franksville's authorities. The evening of the headline, as we sat at dinner, praising Althea's cooking for lack of a better topic, my father said suddenly:

"Well, this whole affair about the Ellisons should be over soon."

The aunts continued eating. Mrs. Randall raised her head slowly.

"Why so?"

"They're making preparations for the trial, apparently. They asked me to defend the killer."

Lottie dropped her biscuit. My fork floated in midair, and Mrs. Randall sat straighter than she was usually able.

My father cut another piece of his chop, relishing the suspense; or perhaps he simply did not understand how significant his reply would be. The topic of the murders rarely arose at the table — "for Mrs. Randall's sake" — and I do not know what was said in private, her to him or him to her.

"I refused, of course."

Some peculiar mix of relief and fury moiled around the table. Lottie and Bea assumed that beatific nullity associated with Murillo virgins, while Mrs. Randall's mouth plunged and I remained precipitous, uncertain, elated for reasons I did not fully comprehend and appalled in spite of myself.

"Why not?" I said before I had a chance to think.

My father looked at me with honest surprise. "What do you mean, Gams? I have a reputation."

The voice was a smooth purr; a mean, low sound. Mrs.

99

Randall's face was seraphic suddenly, her expression calm but brittle as glass, and through that transparency I could see the rage, the contempt.

"Good night."

She climbed the stairs alone.

The news from Washington was worse. The departments of Justice and War concluded there was little merit in the *Star*'s assumptions. McCready's monster was wounded, flailing, its very soul assaulted. And so was the public faith. It showed in "maybe"s, in a "perhaps" on the public street, those questions voiced when two or three were gathered together: Who really was the killer? Just suppose it weren't the deaf mute . . . And those questions threw into doubt that special and spectacular way Franksville agitated for war. If there were no German conspiracy . . . ?

Tongues moved. Even in the high school, among those for whom war was to be the grandest lark, a spectacular leap into manhood, the questions emerged, if only to be ridiculed, vituperated. In those last days, an odd quiet descended on Franksville, especially odd for the shrillness of the month preceding. Events in the larger world seemed inevitably locked. The president, they said, was at work on his war message. March, which had arrived with the shriek of coming battles and the Ellisons' slaughter, was going out like a lamb, just as the primers always promised. But this was no docile frolicker drawn by some spinster illustrator in Philadelphia. It was, instead, a beast escaped from Revelation: seven-eyed, protean, not of peace but of the sword. Perhaps only in memory was that lull so sinister. Franksville was a town of sane and sober folk. Even the kaiser and the dead Ellisons should not have driven us to apocalyptic dreams. But after all the deeds were done, it was hard to stand recollecting it in any other way.

6

THE SPUR to the Pritchards' new mill branched off the rail-road main just south of the town limit, where Franksville tattered into fewer and fewer widely spaced shacks and then into a patch of piney woods, the very same that the Ellisons' cabin abutted. The "new mill" had become, by 1917, a bit of a misnomer, as it had been abuilding off and on for the previous seven years, its construction halted variously by weather, cotton prices, and the vagaries of Pritchard fortunes. If, on the one hand, they repre-sented the region's sole remnant of antebellum aristocracy, they found themselves unable, for lack of will or incipient mental enfeeblement or bad luck, to maintain their standing in a chang-ing world, even one as slow getting about it as Franksville. Exhausted lands yielded less cotton; their real estate in town declined in value; the Pritchards made bad investments. And gradually, though no one mentioned it aloud, their florid, Con-federate past — service in the army of Northern Virginia; hero-ism in the Shenandoah campaigns — meant less and less.

So the mill, of dubious necessity anyway, rose by fits and starts, time lost in each new burst of shoring up or replacing what had weathered and worn or simply tumbled down since work last stopped. By that spring, no one had labored on the building for a good eighteen months, and down the middle of the rail line, pushing through the ballast, were the usual grasses and weeds, the wildflowers, and probably even the beginnings of a sapling or two, taking back the co-opted earth for the woods again.

I do not know exactly who went out in the darkness of that Thursday night to tear up the rails just beyond where the spur broke into the clearing. It could not have been a man alone, or two or three, and it took no ten or fifteen minutes to wrench the steel bands from their moorings, then pry up a dozen ties — fragrant with earth, creosote, old wet and steam — from their beds of stone and dirt, chop them in half to expose their drier hearts, then stack them in a neat, flat pyre with plenty of kindling: branches gathered from the forest floor, pine needles, stray scraps from around the mill itself. It must have taken a crew of men all night to craft so elegantly that pile of lumber, at the last hour before dawn, perhaps, driving in the iron bars looped at the ends — like the one set in cement on Mr. Randall's porch — which would receive the chains. What did they say to each other as they went about their noisy work? Were they silent, or did they jest obscenely, appalled or delighted by what they did, the preparations they made?

Perhaps if I had stayed in Franksville or returned there finally to live my life, I might have known. After one too many bourbons, one of them, or the son or brother of one, might have told me, revealing whether Benton himself was there that night, or McCready. I would have discovered how many slipped away (or did they leave their homes boldly, so assured of their righteousness there was no need to disguise their acts?) to congregate in someone's parlor or in the clearing itself, passing the whiskey bottle, talking trivialities while building courage for the act to which they were committed.

I do not know; I did not stay. Looking back, I am wonderstruck by that perverse miracle to which I was witness, in which something purely imaginary assumed form and walked among the living. John McCready, out of his dreams and demons, demons many in Franksville shared, confronted events he could not understand and forged a monster. And then, the fantasy of this hard-working, fortyish, white Southern bachelor, in the hysteria born of war and murder, grew strong and sired a reality.

I have asked myself in the years since why certain things were not done. Why couldn't they simply let him go? Why couldn't they have tried him? They could not prove he was guilty, of course, though a simple identification would have been enough. In the county hospital lay the witness to the crime, and one word from Hoppy Ellison would have condemned the deaf-mute without doubt. But then the suspect would have to be delivered over to the state, and in the capital questions might be asked, and Wilma Evers would badger the governor. There might be an appeal. Hoppy's testimony might be challenged. The deaf-mute might go free. And Franksville would look foolish. Its great patriotic façade would crack, and fear would seep back, along with the need to look to its own house for the source of mayhem. And that would be painful and frightening and might be avoided at so little cost.

Finally, too, there is that last explanation: simple evil. I do not know precisely who planned and executed the plot. McCready and Benton must have been among them, with the deputy; likely the mayor. Who else? Mr. Brownrich? My father? Overtly or tacitly: the butcher, the baker; field hands and mill foremen. As the idea emerged, as more details were planned, how many were seduced by the sheer horror of it? How many felt, somewhere perhaps where they were not fully aware, a thrill before the unthinkable act; recognized in their hearts the chance to take vengeance — on Germany, on war, on strangers, on fear, on life itself — by countenancing or assisting in the destruction of a man who could not protest?

The rumors began that morning. The Declaration of War had passed the House at 3:00 A.M. and had been sent on to Wilson. Before church services, we gathered on the street in front of Western Union, expecting news of the signature to arrive at any moment. Word passed too through the crowd that the murderer was to be set free, ferried out to the county line and sent on his way sometime during the afternoon.

"Let the goddamn Hun just light out," Lumpy Harris said.

"He sure as hell outfoxed us. What a bunch of bumpkins he must take us for."

Bobby glanced at him, bored. "Well, he never did talk," he said by way of disagreement.

"Training, that's all. The Huns just trained him good. He'd probably even fool that lady up at the capital, what's her name?"

"Evers," I said.

"Yeah, her." He wrinkled his nose in distaste. "He'd fool her, too."

Bobby shrugged, ironic. "Sure he could. She probably doesn't even own a rubber hose."

Torture was, by now, a widely held assumption. Not that it was called torture. Huns tortured Belgians, French virgins, newly democratic Russians. The deaf-mute was only being encouraged to confess.

"Well," Lumpy said, "we'll just see what happens. It seems to me there are a lot of people here that won't just sit by."

"Sit by what?" I said.

"Sometimes the law ain't right," Lumpy said piously.

"What does that mean?"

"Swell." Bobby glanced at the clock on the station platform. "Just what this place needs."

"What's he talking about?" I asked.

"We'll find out soon enough," Bobby said, bumping me away. "You can bet on it."

After services, rumors eddied through the knots scattered along the sidewalks: whispers of war, comments on the deaf-mute. With Bobby, I drifted toward the park, due at practice in half an hour. Ronnie Edmundson came with us, full of news from his paper route; a strange number of customers awake as he made his rounds.

"You'd've thought they was all comin' up from Pallister Slough." He laughed. "But they didn't have that beat-dog look, you know? Weren't slinkin' like they usually do. And there were too many."

"Who?"

"Mattheson. Elmore. Phil from the diner. Randy Keller's pa."

Mr. Keller, Prohibitionist, lay preacher, father of eight, was the yardstick against which most women in Franksville measured their husbands' respectability.

"Looks bad to me." Bobby sighed.

The mill boys, a few we knew who had moved on to high school, stayed tightly together as they always did. But today, bunched by the memorial in the park, they had a superior look, as if they knew what we had only guessed at. They came from houses where there were no secrets, where whispers breathed through walls like rice paper.

Bobby eyed the knot of them. "Let's see what we can find out." He strutted across the street, Ronnie and I in tow. "Hey! Lumpy!"

Lumpy was the one to choose: a foreman's son and so an outsider to the other mill boys. Fat and dull-witted, he was even less esteemed and often the butt of their jokes.

"What do you want?"

"Come here. I've gotta ask you something."

Lumpy shambled toward us, suspicious.

"Say, didn't you tell me and Gams this morning before church they're lettin' the killer go."

"Yeah."

"See, I told you, stupid." Bobby punched Ronnie's arm. "I told you I heard this morning. I told you they were gonna let him go. That's right, huh, Lumpy?"

"Ah, come on," Ronnie said.

"It's true." Lumpy stepped forward. "Just gonna let the Hun off."

"See! Tell him, Lumpy. About the law."

"It ain't right, lettin' him go." Lumpy was warming to it. "Gonna let him go and the poor old Ellisons, they just get forgotten and before you know it the niggers'll be up in arms and we'll rue the day we let that Jew get away. And if some folks are too stupid to see that, well, sometimes men have got to stand up —" He caught himself.

"And what, Lump?" Bobby said.

"Nothin'!"

"Come on!"

"Yeah," I said.

"Lay it out, Lumpy."

By that time, we were all around him, Ronnie sidling behind.

"Spit it out!"

"No! I told . . ."

"Told who you wouldn't say?" Bobby challenged, guessing. "Your Pa? Your brother? What'd your brother tell you?"

"You'll see. Today. You'll see!"

"See what? Huh, Lumpy? You liar. It's just a lie. You don't know nothin', huh, Lumpy." Bobby started to laugh. "He don't know nothin'. Not one goddamn —"

"You'll see," Lumpy shouted defiantly. "They'll get that Hun! You'll —"

"Shut up, Lumpy."

It was Eddie Nelson, one of the mill boys. He walked amid the three of us and gave Lumpy a shove. He was a senior, a pale, gangly six feet with discolored teeth and, already, a dark nicotine callous on his middle finger. He turned to Bobby. "Let him be, Brownrich," he said flatly. He led Lumpy back toward the Confederate soldier in marble beneath the trees.

Bobby smiled. "Son of a bitch. Got ourselves a little lynch mob right here in Franksville, do we?"

"What?"

"Don't be dense, Gams. That retard'll never get out of this

county." Bobby spat. "Sweet Jesus, what the hell's goin' on around here."

Lumpy was not the only one who knew; Bobby not alone in figuring it. I realized it was going to happen here like in the papers, like in the stories people told: the town was going to kill a man. Not just the hot-bloods; not just the mill hands. Mr. Keller was part of it, and Phil from the diner, Irish Phil, who was married to Maggie and laughed a lot and knew those soft arts of the kitchen, how to crimp pies and make soda bread. What had they done the night before? What had my father done?

Then I thought of the deaf-mute.

There in that cell. Innocent. Even if, by some unimaginable chance guilty of the slaughter of the Ellisons, innocent still, unaware of his destiny; unaware of why he had been ill-used, manacled, beaten, berated by a fat county sheriff, by his deputy — duller and so even more cruel — and by that other man: McCready. For him, McCready must have been Prince of Demons, which he was in his way, the demiurge who had reinvented the deaf-mute, transformed him from an anonymous wanderer into a homicidal celebrity, the Antichrist from Europe.

And he, the unspeaking, the hopeless; confused, more annihilated than ever before in a world of words, facing, though he could not know it, his own final annihilation, there in that cell, blind to the ruse that would free him only to take him again with more violent hands and bear him to destruction.

I walked to the stadium down serene holiday streets, my eyes registering one final time those trees, houses, yards, as peaceful places. Never again would they seem so in the same way. It was not just the war. Never again, I understood instinctively, would those sights touch me with like familiarity, though I did not yet know how bloody they would ultimately appear.

According to Tommy Allan, who swept up weekends and

holidays at the bakery across the street, they brought him down around one thirty. Benton and Horace, the deputy, hustled him through the courthouse doors as they had in the opposite direction nearly a month before, out to the car Horace had left running. There was no crowd. They drove off — all three — though the sheriff and the deputy would not normally both ferry a drifter to the county line: one would stay behind, alert for emergencies. But today there must be no one at the courthouse who might be called to intervene in the unexpected. They did not take the major county route, the well-traveled link north to south that carried farmer to market and drummer town to town. Tommy said they turned off it before they were out of sight, following backroads — macadam, gravel, dirt — anticipating trouble, Benton would later swear, trying to throw any pursuers off the scent.

So, through those fields awaiting crops of cotton and tobacco, the sheriff and Horace lazily chauffered the deaf-mute toward death. Meanwhile we, at Coach Sink's orders, exercised back in the stadium, the state meet barely two weeks away. On this holiday, we had been promised we would be home before three. Some were still warming up. I was already practicing dashes, my legs straining and throbbing with blood. Then suddenly, abrupt as the thunder of a summer storm, we knew. The war had come. And too, we knew what was to end that drama which had erupted in Franksville with Hoppy Ellison's crazed whirl down Depot Street. I never discovered the origin of the news. Perhaps Lumpy had talked; perhaps Eddie Mellors violated the silence he himself imposed; more likely the words that rolled into the stadium escaped from some other lips. But at the same instant, we knew.

"They're going to burn him."

There was no pause. We did not discuss what we ought to do. Coach Sink had no time to coax or bully us to concentrate on our running, our endurance, our speed, our duty to our young bodies. We simply flooded away as one, a few to the locker room but most, like me, striking out directly, leaving behind street clothes, each of us drawn like some insect clairvoyant to the promise of flame. Down through the arches of stone, feet slamming the cement with the echo and persistence of hooves, torn breathing erupting once, then twice, then constantly in a shout, squeal, barked curse as wild as the Rebels at Chicamauga, the Swamp Fox Francis Marion's boys, and on back across centuries and continents: Culloden, Bosworth Field, Hastings, to battles in Dacia, to the Rhine, to the tiny mounted men from the East driving all before them unto the doors of civilization itself.

We whooped onto the street, up out of the hollow where the stadium nestled, across the town, as the story was grunted one to another: "Burning." "The Pritchards' new mill." Certain runners fell behind; others scattered to gather brothers, friends; and I — alone, determined with the horrified triumph of the messenger of disaster — peeled away and up the hill, muscles crying, hearing only the wheeze of my own breath and the drumming of my heart, pounding up the incline, over the lawn, vaulting the steps and through the door to gasp the unspeakable:

"They're going to burn him."

As she slumped there on the landing, her mouth forming those hopeless words of denial, I stood below with not only the flush of exertion, not only the cruel pride of the bearer of bad tidings, not only the exhilarated horror before the fulfillment of the bloodlust sown these last weeks by patriotic exhortation and the Ellisons's slaughter and McCready's prosody of gore, but too and most profoundly the passion of the unsullied lover before the destruction of his rivals. This was Franksville's madness; this the consequence of frustration and unreason and my own father's inaction. And the deaf-mute was doomed. In that fevered adolescent wanting, had I remained a moment longer after she slumped against the bannister, I too might have fallen to my knees, to take her in my child's arms chaste and clumsy, dry her tears, and in that instant remake the world an innocent place free of hatred and fire and the fury of men.

But I did not stay. Even as that passion rose within me, something drove me away from her, from my father's house, back to the street in those ridiculous clothes barely hiding my nakedness, my hair flat with sweat. Down the hill, through the outskirts of town, out toward the mill. The sun sank lower toward a bank of clouds, some storm west of Franksville, and the air took on a chill as I found the rail line and bounded tie to tie, slipping sometimes, movements mechanical. The pine woods cast deeper and longer shadows, broken here and there by the dull light of afternoon. I did not think. Thinking would have stopped me, let me feel my exhaustion; would have opened my imagination to what waited where the forest bowed and the rails stopped, to the unfinished rawness of the unfinished mill, before it the mob of pandemonium.

I broke out of the trees. There was the clearing; there, the mill, the crowd of men and boys. I stumbled, panting, beside the rails, and rolled onto my back. My breath rattled in and out of my trembling chest, and weakness sent my thighs and calves jerking into cramps as my head floated dizzily toward the treetops.

"Gams? Gams!" It was Bobby above me, helping me stand, steadying me. "Come on, sonny," he said softly, sardonically. "You ain't missed the circus yet."

We wound through the crowd, my brain still starved for air, my legs numb. Around me, people were talking, but their voices seemed mere murmuring. Only occasionally did I capture a word: "Hun," "Ellison," "lesson." My eyes too were weak from the run, my vision aqueous as I moved beside Bobby like someone just roused from sleep. Amid the crowd there were business suits, overalls, cheap shirts forever salted with the lint from carders, spinners, looms at the mills. I saw as well three or four boys dressed as I was, shivering from exertion and the growing chill. Bobby threaded me past them all — their well-known faces unfamiliar to me in my exhaustion — up an earthen ramp beside the new mill, in amid the crowd till we were almost to the edge.

I saw the pyre.

He lay upon it already, chains snaking over him, looping around those iron rings, vanishing beneath timbers to re-emerge and bind him anew. He: strangling, writhing weakly against the steel, his face white in effortful confusion, in terror.

"Have a swallow, boys?"

The bottle floated into Bobby's hands. He tilted it to his lips for two long gulps.

"Here." He put the neck against my palm. "Drink some."

I started to shake my head.

"Don't be a jackass," Bobby growled. "You had to see and you're gonna see and this'll make it a damn sight easier."

The whiskey was hot against my tongue, raw in my throat, boiling down inside me with a shock that, for the moment, righted me, steadied my head and calmed the squalls in my legs. I took a second swallow, then a third, then handed the bottle back and passed my hands before my eyes.

Then I could see. And hear: the dull rumble of a hundred conversations; the jumbled snippets of those closest to me: ". . . but speeches and a band, by . . ." ". . . too good for . . ." ". . . so I say . . ." "I sold the damn thirty acres, and . . ." "Can't go too hard on a goddamn Hun."

And beyond, hooded men, a dozen or so, busily checking the chains, gesticulating broadly, their vision impaired by those rumpled masks, skittering back and forth with inexplicable and almost comic busyness, as if their attention to detail, to the construction and engineering of the act itself, somehow dispelled the reality of what they were about to do.

"Better get down to it," said the man with the bottle. "Might start to rain, then where would we be?" He laughed. "Why, that'd put everybody in a hell of a fix."

I did not know who he was. Some passer-through I never saw again. But his dark, too-handsome face — like a fallen angel's in some Byzantine mosaic — remained with me ever after.

As if they had heard him, one of the executioners motioned toward the sky. Another set off running, vanished behind the mill, only to reappear immediately with a large can. He danced around the pyre, the container juggling in his hands. The breeze wafting through the clearing blew sweet with kerosene.

These were the last moments, then, when instants grind suddenly slower and all that meets the senses is completely, simultaneously absorbed. One of the hooded men held up a pine branch, its end swathed in cotton, then lowered it ceremoniously as another soaked it with kerosene. There was no sound but wind and breathing. A third masked man took the firebrand; a fourth (McCready, inky fingers obvious even in the dying light); then a fifth, till the whole dozen had touched it. The last of them passed slowly around the human circle pressed close to the pyre, as hands strained in the air to brush the deadly stick. One after another, pulling back fingers slick with fuel or sticky with sap: participants, collaborators, brother murderers.

A match was struck, touched to the limb, and a flame shot forth. In that fraction of a second there was a sound, a wild, keening groan rising into the storm-threatened afternoon, before the shout, the triumphant crow of a hundred throats together, drowned it out forever.

"Jesus Christ," Bobby breathed.

The firebrand fell. The pyre exploded.

Many years — decades — later, in a theater in Rome, I sat in an audience of dinner jackets and furs, ever more breathless as the last reel spun toward its finale, and Ingrid Bergman, radiant and virginal in white, was led to the scaffold, bound to a pole, and a Hollywood torch was laid against an elaborate bramble of branches surrounding her. I lowered my eyes, faint and sick, till I heard the soundtrack swell, then looked up to find her in angelic ecstacy, a heavenly chorus of sopranos piping her into sainthood as she fluttered with holy passion at the stake.

It was not like that.

The second the fire raked the sky, the crowd's bellow ceased as if all breath were sucked from us by the column of flame. The heat blew us back into one another, and one executioner suddenly dove to the earth, half his hood ignited. Out of the heart of the pyre, distinct from the roar, came no ecstatic breath as the ghost was given up, but a hellish gibbering, screaming beyond human comprehension, the sound of the sound torn unwilling from the body.

Next, the smell as the kerosene was instantaneously consumed: the pungence of wood and a new sweetness of seared meat.

"Holy God," Bobby whispered, "holy God."

He stood transfixed, his glasses reflecting the fiery pillar that shot toward nothing, the smoke swirling to meld with clouds now scutting low from the west. I caught a breath and the air singed deep. Inside me, the whiskey rebelled, spewed with its own force up and out, burning my lips and nose as I staggered, gagging again, my ears full of screaming, whether remembered or that of men who suddenly recognize what they have wrought, I do not know.

I fell into Bobby, legs buckling, dizzy with smoke and vomit. He pulled me straight, though his eyes did not leave the pyre. My head rolled back, then forward again, and I saw the crowd melting, fleeing into darkness, away from that fire's absolute light. But for one: there, his shadow almost comic against the horrible brightness, his arms flailing in fury or desperation, a lone man pleaded, coaxed, demanded, his voice forged hot, whipped to us by the flames:

"Speak German! Speak German!"

THE CHILD was born dead.

It would have been a boy, my promised brother. Perhaps, without a crime compounded by another, he might have lived, and my life, Mrs. Randall's, my father's, would have been quite different. Mrs. Randall's last pregnancy would have gone to term and all that blue — blankets and bonnets and baby clothes — packed away from my own infancy might have known new light, if only I had not smashed through the door that afternoon to announce the deaf-mute's fate.

After I left the house, so I later heard, Lottie and Bea found Mrs. Randall, incoherent, hands rattling the stair posts like bars in unnatural, dry-eyed hysteria. They comforted her as they were able, afraid and unsure, determined only to somehow get her to bed.

"They cannot! They cannot!" she insisted over and over, and the aunts, with Althea there to back them, agreed, though not at all certain who "they" were nor what they intended. "Gambetta! Where's Gambetta? He has to stop them!"

And Althea was sent to retrieve Mr. Stevenson while Lottie and Bea wheedled Mrs. Randall toward bed.

"He'll be here in just a minute."

"A minute. Come now, dear. Rest . . ."

"Rest is what you need. Come now . . ."

"Come to rest."

They took her arms, and after long minutes brought her gently to her feet. Half-carried to her room, she suddenly found strength — "Let go!" — and pushed by them down the hall to the tower stairs, ascending high above the town, out to the widow's walk commanding a view not only of her one-time home but of the neighborhoods and shops and courthouse, the woods and farm-land rolling gently away on either side, the Piedmont swelling and falling like the sea. She stood gazing south, unmoved, not even answering Bea and Lottie's well-meant pleas for rest and quiet and the health of the unborn child. As the storm grew in the west, she must have looked terribly lovely in her tower there, like the woman of some ship's master awaiting a sail sign-ing not deliverance but catastrophe.

At last, inevitably, there was a flash in the midst of the piney woods, and a black plume rose toward the falling sun. And then, before the naked evidence that it was finished, done, she began to cry. Not sobs, Lottie later averred, but a soft, almost breath-less weeping, which continued as the smoke swirled toward the advancing clouds, as the aunts took her arms and guided her gently downstairs, as they settled her beneath blankets and propped her shoulders and promised to bring her dinner up that night — anything she liked — if only now she would rest, for-get, sleep. But the tears came still, through the arrival of my father, whom Althea located only after an hour's search (per-haps he had been with me at the mill, perhaps his lips had touched the bottle's mouth which momentarily gave me strength), came even into that dreaded and fatal labor, in which the boy she and my father had made together was cast out dead by a womb that would no longer abide him.

It was my fault, of course. The charge was never spoken; no one voiced the accusation to my face. But it was in the eyes of my aunts and the turn of their lips; the stiffness of my father's back. It was I who had brought disaster, son of another mother who would cede no space, who would pull down the temple of my own and my family's peace to remain the single son, the inheritor of my father's name and house and all he possessed.

After I arrived, sweaty, chilled, and sick, to the news of loss and the mist of unspoken blame, I kept to my room. I felt ill-used, surely: it was not I who had killed the child. It was what McCready had done, what Franksville had done, and those things that others — chief among them my father — had left undone. I had only borne news of the consequences. And yet, I could not forget entirely, much as I tried, that surging joy as I cast those words up the staircase, that unambiguous purity which only the powerless enjoy. I knew, though I resisted the knowledge, that a part of me had wanted the baby dead, and I flayed my conscience with the dark pleasure that my wish had come true.

On the third night of my self-imposed isolation, there was a knock. There had been others before: Althea bringing a cold tray; Lottie and Bea, in tandem even in judgment and concern, to make sure I was getting along; even twice my father, anxious to talk. But the food left by the door lay largely untouched; I remained for visitors dully "all right," successfully avoiding conversations, pleading the need for solitude even before my father's threats ("See here, young man . . .") and then before the sad phantom of the caring he and I had once possessed and somehow over the years misplaced and never encountered again.

"Gams?" he said. "Son." The word falling, caressed. "Gams . . ."

It was the quiet, confidential voice of the walks to the reservoir; the one soothing a six-year-old boy at the incontrovertible but inexplicable fact of death. It was different from the diction that, with the years, had become our mode, the two of us vaguely but surely mistrustful of each other, sign of the process that had transformed us from father and son into strangers — proud with that peculiar male pride — who shared the same house. There had been no drama: no wild, filial revolution nor brutal paternal repression. Simply, somewhere in those years of his construction of that fairy tale realm of his dreams, in my growing up, we had ceased to love each other.

But it was not his knock. I knew it was her even before her knuckles touched wood. Sprawled on the bearskin, my ear to the floor, I heard that special tread in the hall and the pause before her fingers called me. She rapped only lightly.

"Gams." It was barely a whisper. "Gams? I want to come in."

In all my confused silence, I had waited for her; absolution hers alone. I got up off the floor, passed before the mirror observing but unmoved by three days of adolescent stubble, the sunken eyes, my hair in disarray, clothes dirty and rumpled from my turnings on the mattress and the rug. I stepped across the room slowly, sluggish, my head light from inactivity. I threw back the bolt without yet having opened my mouth.

Framed in the jamb, the light of my bedside lamp weak against the dark of the hall, she was the specter of herself: disheveled too, eyes red, unsteady as she braced herself against the wall, pale from loss not only of body but spirit.

"Come in," I said.

She smiled, a wan curl of her lips, effortful as if she had forgotten in those last days what smiling was. She stepped inside, hopelessly fragile, tottering like someone very old. I caught her in my arms, to steady her, I thought, but did not cease after the first touch of her hand as I pulled closer, closer, thrust my head against her shoulder and my body against hers.

"I'm sorry. I'm so sorry. I'm sorry . . ."

Her fingers rustled through my hair to the nape where they kneaded me quiet, her other arm circling my shoulder, over my ribs.

"Shhhhh. Shh."

Her cheek rested on my temple, and I think now I could have stayed there forever, that if the death of my unborn brother boded no good for anyone, it at least once delivered me to arms that never held me quite the same way again.

"Of course you're sorry," she said softly. "We're all sorry."

I felt her breath on my ear, and as if that air itself blew into my brain an unexpected serenity, I felt my body soften, held her even closer as we rocked slowly back and forth. Tears coursed down my cheeks to blot on her gown. In my sadness, in her touch, there was some new and sweet release.

I regained myself, pride — and was it custom? — pulling me away. I held to her still, though, guiding her to the bed. We sat down, knees touching, my head bent miserably forward.

"But it's . . . if I hadn't . . ."

She took my hand. "Hadn't what?"

I breathed deep. "If I hadn't told you . . ."

"They blame you, don't they."

I looked up into her face momentarily frosty with rage.

"But if I . . ."

The fury vanished, sudden as steam. She smiled again. "But shouldn't you have told me?"

I shook my head.

"You knew I wanted to know."

"Yes, but . . ."

"I would have to have known. It was best I hear it from you. Better you than someone else."

That might be true, of course. But only partially. That, even then, I had the sense to understand. But such a half lie was easy, and I — anxious for exculpation, foolish enough to think she might believe it, and finally too young to even begin to confront my own desirings — let the words pass over me like the delivering hand of a priest.

I looked up. "I guess." I forced a silly, cockeyed excuse for a grin across my lips, determinedly optimistic. "And you're young. There'll be others."

"No."

The word lingered, gray in the lamplight. Absolute.

My face fell. I pulled away from her, certain I had misheard.

"No?"

She stood up, rustling toward the bureau. I followed.

"Why?" I tried to turn her to face me. "Why not?"

Her hand went suddenly, brutally to her face, her thumb and fingers white at her temples. Her mouth trembled, as if words broke against her lips like furious waves, as if the dike of all those years of control might in that moment crumble and the secret I had always sensed pour forth.

She drew a breath deeper than breath ought to be drawn, as if she were filling herself with the world, taking it in to roll back whatever threatened to flood out of her. She remained for an instant at the brink of revelation. Then her palm fell from her face, and she was once again mistress of herself — or better, whatever was within her was her master once again.

"There are things . . ." she said, her voice at first atremble, then smoother, "there are things not meant. Things not meant to be. I am not meant to have any more children. Your father and I are not meant to have any." She drew herself very straight, the simple rigidity of her spine the sign of some preternatural act of will. "There are things that cannot be changed."

"But why?"

Regained now, she relaxed, the battle inside her done. She shrugged, her face resigned. "We can only do what is given us. No more and no less. There is no escaping it. I have learned that, Gams. That is what I have learned."

That was all she told me. A cliché. Some homily learned in Sunday school. I looked at her with an awful emptiness, only imperfectly aware of how such pieties are meant to save us, to protect us from words impossible to utter.

"Take me back now —" She caught her breath sharply, then smiled. "Take me back to my room."

From those days on, it became forever her room. The last of

her things — knickknacks and hand mirrors and a patchwork quilt — were moved through the door that, closed and bolted, separated her from my father's bed. For the first time in my life, I found it in me to pity him, as he confronted, disoriented, his wife's rejection. I do not know what explanation Mrs. Randall offered him, how she repelled his advances, though I suspect she gave no reason at all, or only those transparent in their untruth. But my father was a small-town lawyer, a son of clerks, a player of stock exchanges in faraway cities he had visited long ago and had no yen to see again. His strength had never been insight into the human heart. Her threat to his vision of a charmed and happy Franksville life must have been unbearable, and his confusion and rage before her sudden frigidity tumbled him — particularly in those years after I was gone — toward liquor and floozies and greater self-indulgence in cars each more powerful and demonic than the one before. The throb of steel machines instead of his own would prove his undoing. But the resolve of Mrs. Randall to share no more her bed with him on account of some unexplained decision would be enough to drive any man to excess. More than once I heard him arrive late, brave with drink, pounding on her door to demand his husband's rights. Sometime he may have caught her, perhaps once she failed in her drowsiness to throw the bolt, but still I suspect she fought his passion or took him with an iciness that, for all his wanting, froze the lust in his veins, so that afterward it melted to a gloomy slush of dissatisfaction.

Through April, May, and into June, Mrs. Randall kept largely to herself, there in her bed with her books and mementos and her little hope chest. I would pass by on my way in from school for a few moments of conversation, and though she was often listless, she tried to show some kind of welcome, to make me feel that I, above all others, was somehow a joy to her. We talked mostly of my life, of my friends, of everything, after my short spell of darkness after the miscarriage, I thought I had regained. Like the child I still was, I could put all that had happened aside — or so I assumed — and live again in the present tense. My junior year was ending, and many of us, though we were still shy of enlistment age, talked of joining the army. I had few illusions, however, that my father would sign to send me off to France. Princeton was in my future, and the law, and, barring an extended war, it was all too likely I would miss the action, a probability that met with my father's approval. He, in any case, would not stand for my setting off to defend Paris till I had received a high school degree in Franksville.

Later that spring, two months and more after his appearance on Depot Street, Hoppy Ellison walked out of the hospital. It should not have taken so long to cure him, but a bout with pneumonia nearly killed him, and even on the day of his release he retained the ragged, ravaged look of a man tasted and spat back by death. His thinness was now emaciation, and his red hair, despite the nurses' best efforts at combing, whorled only unconvincingly over the bare place in his scalp where the fire had singed too deep and melted the skin in a patch like thick cream, which flowed in a one-inch-wide arc down his forehead, over his eye, to end at his cheekbone. Elsewhere the burns had healed well so there was hardly any scarring, but this one (which made him grotesque and half blind in that eye, squeezed into a permanent squint) would be with him forever. I glimpsed him only a few times; never spoke with him at all. The rumors, though, were many. He claimed, according to the few he would talk to, that he had no recollection now of what had happened that morning in March; that the murderer might well have been the deaf-mute, but he had no way of knowing, and photos of the man the town had killed did nothing to jar his memory. He spent most of May alone, back in that ruined cabin amongst his family's jetsome, their only monument but for those the county paid

121

for in the graveyard. He was never seen at the cemetery, and Franksville spoke of him in low voices, charged with sympathy. So, when after two weeks no one had seen him and a neighboring sharecropper passed by the cabin to find it empty, Hoppy's flight from Franksville was accepted as sad but inevitable.

"You couldn't expect the boy to stay," I heard Lottie say to the iceman. "I don't know how anyone could have thought he would."

"Yes'm. I expect he signed up for the war, don't you. That's a real opportunity for a boy like him."

The assumption became the town's myth, that Hoppy had vanished into French battlefields, so noble a fantasy that not even the doctor who treated him bothered to suggest his drooping eye would likely dissuade the army from taking him. It somehow soothed us all that the boy whose family's dying had driven us to murder was now himself face to face with the Hun. McCready's vision of the spring's events retained currency in those months. For most, the burning itself was quickly put aside. Even that evening, as the cinders steamed in the rain that came with the darkness, the thrill and horror began to subside before the reality of declared war. The Hun had been put to rout in our midst, but there remained a larger mission overseas. Certain doubts continued to be voiced; even a sermon or two was preached on the dangers of mob action. In early May, two officials from the attorney general's office spent an afternoon in Franksville, the consequence apparently of Wilma Evers's agitation. Their conclusion, after discussion with the sheriff and Horace, was that though acts of vigilantism were reprehensible, it would be impossible now to fix blame for the event.

The *Star and Informer* kept us conscious of the bleeding in Europe. The first of Franksville's boys — Mickey Edmundson, Tom Keller, Eddie Mellors's brother Ray — had answered the call and found themselves in training, from whence they would go thousands of miles to places they had never heard of, much less expected to see. By the Fourth of July — the most elaborate and, in a frightening, childlike way, the most heartfelt in my memory — Mrs. Randall had re-emerged, to the public eye radiant, sweet, and unidentifiably vulnerable as ever. Her estrangement from my father was complete but subtle, and the damning fact of their unshared bed would long be a secret. To anyone but me, Lottie, Bea, and Althea (mum for that profound and inexplicable loyalty of servants), our world in the towered house was once again its normal self.

It was to that tower that Mrs. Randall now seemed attracted. On lazy summer afternoons and, sometimes, long into summer nights lazier still, she retreated to that solitary room to sit in a straight-back chair, or to the walk to pace slowly all around and take in the panorama of the town below. Her privacy at those times was respected absolutely, so it was nearly September before I ever dared join her there. It was late one evening of a waxing moon, with Althea gone, my aunts asleep, my father off to bid farewell to an old friend's bachelorhood. I climbed the stairs angled up three sides of the tower, emerging out of the house's August heat into the silvered air, which poured through French windows yawning wide. She leaned over the railing, her chin in her hand, Franksville twinkling below her like that fairy tale kingdom she was supposed to rule. I stood for a long moment, first filled with a sweet excitement, then suddenly embarrassed, as if I had come upon her praying. I shuffled my feet softly, afraid to startle her.

"Mrs. Randall?"

She turned unflustered, almost as if she expected me. "Gams." There was no inquiry in her voice.

"Are you all right?" The question was absurd. There in the shadows, I could feel myself blush.

"Of course. Come out. This is the only place cool in the whole town, I think."

I walked to her side, still uncomfortable. There was a breeze, a directionless eddy, which bore faintly, weightlessly, the heavy summer scents from below: magnolia, mown grass, wild onion. The town spread before us, its neat blocks with their corner streetlamps, the brighter precincts of downtown, the gradual flickering away into farmland and woodland and the hollows of the stadium and Pallister Slough.

"It is beautiful," I said, settling beside her.

"Yes." She nodded. "So beautiful." There was a long, thoughtful pause. "You could never imagine what it had done."

"Done?"

"What happened here." She glanced at me; smiled at my half-quizzical face apparent even in the moonlight. "What happened. Last spring."

"Oh."

I turned my gaze back over the town. I knew what I would say then; what I had long wanted to say. Even if I had fought them, the words would have come anyway.

"Why did you care so much about him? About the deaf-mute?"

She sighed, her hands clasped before her. There was a hesitation, brief but certain. Then she said: "Did I care so much? Was I the only one? I suppose . . . I suppose there were many reasons. He was a stranger. I've known strangers. I've been a stranger myself places. Sometimes I think I'm still a stranger here." The slight nod of her head implied everything below. "And he was a victim. He was lonely, and confused, and when the time came, there was nothing he could do and no one to help him." Her voice lingered then, as if she understood that helplessness, that despair. Then, she straightened up, her palms on the rails. "And there are other things. There is justice, of course."

Her words, which had come in a smooth, sad song, resolved suddenly in that hard cadence.

"You blame us, then."

124

"Not you. You're a boy still, Gams. There is nothing you could have done."

"But the others. McCready. Benton." I caught my breath. "Papa."

She looked out over Franksville, that peaceful, pleasant American town which had burned a man alive, her face suddenly hard in the placid wash of moon. "Grown-ups know better than to kill something."

I have since reflected on those words, on their peculiarity, though I did not till long after Mrs. Randall was dead. Perhaps, for all her secretiveness, she gave me some clue then. Some sign of trauma. Some childhood loss? Something destroyed. But, looking out over Franksville that night, I could only wonder at her moral fury, at this woman wreaking vengeance for all the dispossessed — for the silent nameless and for herself, somehow — on my hapless father who lacked the courage or simple understanding to try, though he might fail, to forbid murder.

"It's late," Mrs. Randall said. "You should sleep."

"You, too."

"I'll stay a little longer." She kissed my cheek. "Good night."

I stepped away, dismissed, shaken. I was almost to the door when Mrs. Randall spoke again.

"Don't you think, Gams, there should be dancing here?"

"Pardon?"

"Dancing. A party sometime." She laughed. "We could put up little lanterns, hire a band. Before you go to Princeton."

I smiled. "It would have to be a pretty small party, wouldn't it?"

"And a pretty small band," she said lightly. "And you and I will dance. Won't it be wonderful?" She shook her head, self-mocking. "Oh, this night air makes me giddy sometimes."

I was helpless, mind-cuffed in my confusion, tenderness welling all through me. "Don't fall, then."

"I won't." She turned suddenly back toward town, the silly instant gone, her girlishness plunging away from me like a fading star. "I won't. Not tonight."

I backed toward the stairs, the beat of my heart swollen in my chest, uncomprehending, almost afraid she might jump. But I knew she would not, that she never would, for having once leapt into a darkness I would never know; and from that, drawing a strength I would never understand.

8

SUMMER ACCELERATED toward October and my last year of school. Though Franksville High fielded a football team that autumn, and though we had been promised track in the spring, most all purely athletic training had been abandoned in favor of military drill for the duration. In gym, we lunged at tackling dummies with sticks, wrestled, ducked and covered, but mostly we marched. We marched from the locker room to the playing fields; we marched the length, breadth, and diagonal of the baseball diamond; we marched around the perimeter of the high school. The usefulness of this in combat seemed questionable, though, as Bobby remarked, we would make a fine spectacle in the victory parades.

Over the summer, the school had been transformed into an exhibition of histrionic patriotism. Flags, never in short supply, were everywhere: classrooms, corridors, gymnasium, auditorium, and playground. Walking down the halls, those who had recently affected the habit of saluting Old Glory on all occasions looked almost epileptic. French, British, and Russian banners decorated the Victory Shrine beside the principal's office, where the rather forlorn portraits of Washington and Robert E. Lee were now all but lost in a galaxy of tinted photos of Foch, Clemenceau, Wilson, Pershing, the kings of England and Italy, and an elaborate Palmer Method copy of the war message. In each classroom, framed posters and slogans crowded the walls — "Beat Back the Hun!" "Join the Gas Hounds!" — though Bobby noted his favorite — "A Soldier Who Gets a Dose Is a Traitor" — was nowhere to be seen.

In such a place, unsurprisingly, boys and girls alike had little interest in Latin declensions or algebraic axioms, though we enthusiastically imbibed Scott, Kipling, and various romances of the Crusades. At the Carillon we were treated to *The Hounds of Hunland*, together with the exhortations of one of Franksville's numerous Four-Minute Men, who competed with one another in whipping moviegoers into a meringue of outrage even before the serial started.

Conscription was proceeding apace, but actually very little happened. The training, equipping, and transporting of a vast army to battlefields across the Atlantic required months, and no significant number of Americans would see action until Belleau Wood the next spring. Still, girls knitted, women's auxiliaries rolled bandages, Boy Scouts scavenged tinfoil, peach pits, lard. Consuming more than the necessary minimum of sugar, flour, meat, and milk near branded one a Benedict Arnold, if you listened to the Council of Defense, locally directed, unsurprisingly, by John McCready.

With the relative paucity of American news from overseas and the autumn's Allied reverses, McCready and his paper focused their attention closer to home. He headed as well the local chapter of the American Protective League and made it his business to guard the community against any unpatriotic elements or utterances that might undermine the war effort. Exhorting from the *Star*, declaiming at the Chamber of Commerce, the Rotary Club, and the Carillon, he managed to enlist over fifty leading locals in his organization, including my father, who carried his badge — "American Protective League/Secret Service" — in his wallet, eschewing the more common custom of pinning it to the reverse of the lapel. He proved a less than effective member, satisfied with warning Althea about her complaints over the shortage of pork fat and condemning Bobby's and my cynicism about drills. I did, however, late one night, hear his voice in the hall.

"You must stop with all that. What's done is done."

"Murder is murder, Gambetta, that . . ." It was Mrs. Randall, her tone shrill, then hushed to a low, dangerous drone.

"Do not talk about it, do you hear? No one . . ."

I was up by then, padding to the door.

"McCready's spoken to me. He's had reports."

"Damn John McCready!"

I started. I had never heard her swear.

"Damn John McCready and his damned pack of spies."

"Darling . . ."

"Damn his whole damned lynch mob."

"Darling, please . . ."

"And you, too. Damn you who wouldn't stop them. Coward!"

The word echoed, sharp and unexpected, followed by the slam of her door and the snap of the bolt. I stood in the dark, breathless, as I imagined my father wounded, silent, in the hall. I listened for his retreating steps but there were none. The shadow of a familiar satisfaction stole through me as I envisioned him outside her room, another little part of his perfect world consumed.

The leaves turned and fell, and through the ever-earlier dusk, the smell of their burning soothed a bit April's recollected fire, a reminder that flame too might bring warmth and light in winter nights ahead. Gradually, each in turn, the trees revealed themselves naked and gnarled, but for the pines in defiant green. The flowers vanished; apples were cheap; lawns turned brittle and sear in the burning frost. I had a new winter coat to try those first chilled nights and began to pass the last half hour before sleep, after dinner and homework, reading about Princeton, trying to imagine that mysterious North now already braced for snow.

Late one afternoon as November slid toward Thanksgiving, I sat in The Arbor waiting for Melissa, sipping a Spiced Coffee Supreme while thumbing *As You Like It* in preparation for tryouts for the winter play. The place had nearly emptied when Bobby barreled through the door, out of breath, snapping "Gimme a dope" at Freddy as he thumped down across from me. His cheeks were red from the cold and exertion, and there was a peculiar grim excitement in his eyes as he pulled out a cigarette. Freddy brought the cola, from which Bobby took a long, satisfied swallow, followed by a deep drag on his Bull Durham. Then he folded his hands against his chin and smirked.

"Well?" I said.

His smile widened. He was enjoying his performance. He tipped the cigarette in the ashtray, blew a few smoke rings, then said flatly, "They found a body."

"What?"

"They found a body."

"Who?"

"Phil. Phil and Rex Peal. Hunting."

Phil and Rex, who toted at the hardware store, were old rifle buddies given to long autumn expeditions in search of anything from squirrel to deer. Neither ever bagged much — a possum on occasion, sometimes a couple rabbits — but they enjoyed the excursions and talked all through the winter of their exploits, till spring came and fishing sparked their interest.

"What body? Where?"

"In the piney woods, down near the marsh. This morning."

He took another sip fom his glass, relishing the suspense.

"So?" I said, hoping annoyance covered curiosity.

"Buried."

"Buried?"

"Yeah."

"Well, damn it, Bobby, tell me!"

"Not too far from the Ellison place."

In the small of my back, there was a tightness, a stirring of knowledge not yet conscious.

"Who was it?"

Bobby nodded, still grinning. His eyes narrowed behind his glasses. "Well, of course they can't be sure yet. There's no real positive way to tell until they get a good look at him at the funeral parlor. That body's pretty rotten, down there in all that damp, you know."

I reached over the table to catch his wrist as the cigarette moved to his lips. "Who was it, Bobby?"

He pulled away. "Hell if I can be sure, Gams." He shrugged. "But Rex and Phil both say that from the little bit you could tell when they dragged it up, there sure was something funny about that dead boy's hand."

Skippy Ellison's corpse — what there was of it — did not rest long where I saw it, on a marble slab at Everhardt's, nor did it merit the expensive casket and civic funeral lavished upon his family. It was buried within a day, and the stone set later was flat and bore nothing more than his name and dates. That it was him, there was no doubt. The cadaver was of an adolescent boy, and the remnants of clothing were identified by several people. Of course, most damning of all, there was the stump, the arm which below the elbow melted into a solitary finger. There was little else the body could tell, but for that single blow with a sharp-edged object that had shattered the skull from the back, parting the head to the nape of the neck.

When I came through the door, they were all at the table, Althea removing the roast, their cups ready for coffee. Bea and Lottie sat with their backs to me, while my accustomed place opposite stood empty, dishes shining. My father looked up sternly.

"And where have you been, young man?"

I hardly heard him. I was lightheaded and very hot, as if feverish. I floated toward the table. As I looked at Mrs. Randall, I felt my lips rise in a gentle smile. My father continued.

". . . has to leave, you know, so you can take care of your own supper."

"I won't be eating."

I could not be sure I was speaking. I heard the words; concluded logically they must be mine. I pulled my chair out and sat down.

Mrs. Randall was to my right, her dress a rich Irish green, on her face a cautious curiosity. "What's happened, Gams?"

"Skippy," I said.

There was a silence. I stared straight in front of me, past Lottie and Bea's perplexed faces into the gloom of the parlor.

"Skippy what?" my father snapped.

"They found Skippy." That seemed enough. Then a voice within me reminded me they did not know what I knew; had not yet thought what I had thought. "Dead."

Lottie and Bea gasped, and from behind the swinging door to the kitchen came Althea's muffled: "Lord, Lord!" My father jerked back as if pushed at the word, then caught a breath and muttered, "So that devil got him, too."

I could feel a laugh somewhere in my chest. Though the scene was unrehearsed in my head, those last words hit my ears as if foreordained. A terrible sadness coursed through me, a coolness that must be very close to the serenity of the certainty of death. Though I could not express it fully, I knew what I next spoke was as doomful, as violent to all that had seemed assured, as the thrust of a knife.

"No."

It did not feel lethal. It did not come charged with emotion. As if physical, that simple negative lay on the table. I turned toward Mrs. Randall.

Her eyelids fell for an instant, then rose, and her face was calm. It was as if she had dreamt this moment.

I heard myself speaking. "He'd been buried. Phil and Rex found him. Everhardt says it's been months he's been dead. Killed. His head was split open."

Lottie and Bea were shaking their heads. On the edge of my vision, I saw Mrs. Randall's jaw strain and her eyes fill suddenly as she stared down the length of the table.

"Remarkable," I heard my father say. His chair whispered over the carpet and there was a pop as he uncorked the sherry. The mouth of the bottle beat a tinkling alarm against the lip of the glass. "Remarkable he would have taken the time to bury him. Just him and not the others. You would have thought . . ."

"Hoppy did it."

I did not shout. There was no need. The words were enough.

I did not hear when Mrs. Randall began to cry, nor know exactly when I spoke again:

"Hoppy did it! He killed Skippy! He killed them all! It was Hoppy! Hoppy did it! Hoppy did!"

The accusation echoed louder and louder out of my lips, hurled into the dining room, out through the parlor and into the town. Suddenly my hands were before my eyes and the fever upon me again, the house wheeling around me.

Then cool fingers guided me into a calm, deep green as Mrs.

Randall pulled my head against her offered body and rocked me gently as that night after the deaf-mute's sacrifice. "Lord help us! Lord help us!" rang out from somewhere, and on my tongue somehow was the sweet taste of sherry.

I was all right. I was in bed in my pajamas. It was very late, and the only light came from the stars beyond my window. But even there, beneath the blankets in that familiar silence, there was no safety now. In the dark, before my sleepless eyes, the story played itself like an endless loop of film, though each time a little different, till as the sky began to pearl I saw it as it happened, as it must have happened.

Once, in the hills of Georgia, in a hollow or some other hidden place, there lived a man named Granger Ellison. He grew up, neither exalted nor demeaned, one more element of nature, not lost to measles or the croup or the rapids of the river, and perhaps as little more than a boy he took to wife another child of those cabins, filled her with child, and built his own house from the logs and stones that the earth and trees provided, as had his father and grandfather and so on back before him.

And so he pushed on past his thirtieth year, mastering the skills of survival and the secrets of that mash of corn or wheat or whatever grew to excess that particular year, which yielded the clear, hot brew which made life in the hills somehow bearable. Perhaps he was drunk when he first saw her, or took notice of her. Perhaps she was the aunt of his own children; his wife's best friend. Or his own first born. But the child-woman, breasts mere buds beneath cast-off gingham or tater sacks, seduced him unawares before he had a chance to catch his breath. And with the lust of a man who in that world had long since passed his years of stud, he desired her hopelessly, willfully, though it mean the loss not only of all he loved but all he had ever known.

This was the catastrophe then — not fire, brother, or carpet-bagger, but unbridled desire. When her monthly flow stopped and her belly grew, Granger and his child-love fled the Georgia hills for the highway that eventually led to Franksville. There had been no thought as to how she felt, as to what she wanted, that incongruously named Larrissa. And who knows but what, from the moment she was ripped untimely from the place that was her home, from the instant of her rape upon a forest floor, from the day she knew another soul grew there within her body, she had not dreamt of some vague vengeance on the man who had imposed his will upon her.

On the road, near Columbia or Waxhaw, Sumter or Darlington, her waters broke, and in a mill cabin or simply the gravel shoulder, she brought into the world the one perfect child she would ever know, that first-born boy more brother than son. And as she swaddled him warm with the afterbirth and first gave him suck, perhaps her own unexpressed and inexpressible wish for Granger's destruction flourished in the blood of that red-faced baby pressed against her teat.

So they came to Franksville: Granger and Larrissa and Hoppy. Perhaps the father from the first discerned his rival, so dubbing him with a ridiculous name which would make him and his later, equally malmonikered brothers the logical objects of ridicule by Eddies and Otises and Toms. But destiny favored the first-born boy, who grew tall and robust, flushed with health, with hair like the setting sun, even as siblings succumbed to tetanus and snakebite and scarlet fever, while the ones who perversely survived bore some mark of disfavor upon them: a withered arm, a shriveled brain. Was it Larrissa's doing? Some prayer so potent to God or the Devil that only that boy almost her contemporary might be blessed with wholeness? Or was it instead some intricate trick of blood: the skein of generation upon generation of intermarriage, which, in its exhaustion, could produce only one child complete before burdening all those who came after with some grim variance of nature.

There is no answer. There is only speculation, as there is only speculation as to what actually occurred out there in the woods in that shabby cabin and the shabby world around it. The years passed, children were born and died, Granger took his pleasure with Larrissa amidst blankets destined to be their winding sheets. He adopted as his favorite his second son, marked from birth perhaps with malleability, while his wife lavished her love upon the boy she had carried out of the Georgia forests. She would have made no move, attempted nothing untoward, till he touched fifteen or so and she herself saw thirty looming, as she felt her teeth, here and there, grow loose in her mouth and knew those years of bearing not just children but loathing had begun to wear her body into dust. Perhaps they were berry picking, while Skippy learned the intricacies of distilling, and Jumpy, shuddering with his badly soldered nerves, kept watch on Wheeze and corralled the idjets. Hoppy in nothing but badly patched knickers, and she — green-eyed, sandy-haired; mother, sister? — reaching down behind him and up through his legs to his delighted horror, pulling him to her to reverse her violation and make ready the weapon of her vengeance. Kisses there along the barbed wire and the promise of more, in exchange only for his silence. That for the moment; later there would be his desire and that blood-borne want of revenge and possession, which would make him his mother's natural ally.

Was he just sixteen when she delivered herself to him, after months of preparation, in the woods or the barn one afternoon or nightfall, as Granger delivered moonshine to some liquor-starved sharecropper or tippling preacher a county or two removed? Did Skippy find them then, entwined, and with that threat of exposure, was his destiny determined by the two-foot blade intended for the throats and bowels of pigs?

But what occurred demanded mutual desire, which Hoppy embraced with the headstrong certainty of the first-born boy and blind self-destruction of a feeble child. Confronted with the choice of Larrissa or his brother, faced with that potential Judas, it was he who would have grabbed the knife and dealt the blow, he who dragged the shattered corpse deep into the forest and opened the grave in the piney black. But surely, as he tumbled the dirt and rearranged the leaves over his brother's tomb, as he washed from his hands the blood of the boy with whom he had shared roof and bed and board over all those years, he himself pitched finally into a realm unknown to you or me from which there is no escape. As he took that beating from his father's strap — willingly, as the remorseful criminal takes the blows — only to howl the lie that would bring him respite and cauterize his father's love for the son he did not know was dead, Hoppy's fevered brain fell further into a paradox of wanting and denying. And finally, on that last day, perhaps he was told — or perhaps only intuited — that his mother was pregnant.

As the moon rose late that night, a waxing scimitar of spring promise, he held the knife in his hand, gross and thick on his palm, and then, nearly as an afterthought, took too the double-edged stiletto from the rack on the wall, pressing it down beneath his belt, the hilt cool against his belly as he glided across the yard and onto the porch.

He lifted the latch and slipped within, ghostlike. There it was quiet, but for the ominous rattle of Wheeze as he struggled for breath. First were the idjets, huddled together. He reached down, almost tenderly, forcing his forearm against their jaws to stifle them, drawing the blade smooth as a fiddler's bow over their throats. Wheeze's snores stopped; modulated into the birth of a cry as Hoppy pivoted and the bloodied steel flashed down to silence that breathing forever. Frenzied now, panicked at the deeds yet undone, he fell on Jumpy — still abed, asleep — who woke only for his own destruction, sent into eternity in narcissistic embrace, that body unquiet finally still in death.

There was no sound. Nothing but the racheting of his own breathing. He pressed against the bedroom door in the pale moonlight, aqueous, unjudging. His feet, long accustomed to the creaks and groans of those uneven planks, inched forward, possessed of a sight all their own, till they brought him, almost unwilling, to the head of the bed. There, his eyes now attuned to the darkness, he could see them: his father; his mother, sister?, wife. Granger snored, his life's breath echoing through the house of his dead children. Hoppy thrust his arm against his father's chin and pulled the knife across his throat.

Granger did not die like his daughters. There was a terrible gurgling noise, like the fountain of some unnamable curse bubbling forth, and his arms flailed suddenly as he sought to rise and his head flopped backward as his chest thrust up. But Hoppy was now beyond fear or alarm. Larrissa, struck by Granger's fluttering hand, started awake: "What?"

But Hoppy silenced her. Larrissa, his only love. Larrissa for whom he had killed them, every one. There beside her, behind her, that coldness gone from beside his belly, his voice soft as a lover's.

"It's just me, Ma."

After that, his mind stopped. Hoppy — utterly and forever alone: through the rage of mutilation; through the fire he started and the fire he quelled; through the birth of the lie that would save him from hanging and send a stranger to the flame.

Not until dawn broke, as day poured full bright into the room, did he recognize his family had been slaughtered. He rose, and on his way across the yard passed the outhouse and dropped the knives into its depths — depths which would not be plumbed for thirty years, till after another war and another boom, when Franksville devoured the piney woods all the way to the Pritchards' new mill and beyond.

He passed the clearing and found the road toward town.

For the first time, he screamed.

9

I DISCOVERED COLTON COLLEGE accidentally. It appeared on the map of Los Angeles I studied in the Carnegie Library, in November, after my sickness had passed. My attack of nervous exhaustion, as it was called, acutely embarrassed my father, who found it shameful, especially in a son who had never before displayed any signs of "sensitivity." Early on, there had been some talk of sending me away to one of those resorts in the mountains favored by neurasthenic women and tuberculars. But I was young and strong and recovered quickly — I missed only two weeks of school — so that plan, which I would have welcomed, was abandoned. When I first went back to class, I was treated with caution by both teachers and friends, as if I were a fine bottle of volatile liquid, which, joggled, might spew forth cataclysmically. Jimbo, riding the crest of his glory as Franksville's football darling, privately stuttered his regret to me that my collapse would likely mean the army would have no part of me. Bobby was different, ironic as might be expected, but abashed and more than a little disturbed for having been the one who brought me the news of Skippy's death and the one who stood with me by that marble slab at Everhardt's.

He was not alone in his perplexity. I myself had drawn a curtain around the source of terror and despair that found me,

the morning after, unable to rise from my bed, mute and given to sudden wellings of tears. Althea, efficient as ever before catastrophe, explained it simply as the malign influence of the corpse, Skippy's demons having chosen me as their victim, and she left talismans unobtrusively under my bed — a necklace of feathers, a bowl of brightly colored stones — which she bought from the Magic Lady. One evening around supper time, I awoke in my shuttered room to find two small candles sputtering on my nightstand, one white, one black, the waxy remnants of which Althea removed when she took away my untouched tray, presumably to be read that night by the shaman of Pallister Slough. Next day, she was loud in her proclamations of my imminent recovery, the prognostications having apparently been fortuitous.

For Althea, my collapse was explicable within the natural order of things, and so she treated me much the same as always. For Lottie and Bea, however, such weakness in a man was a frightening and foreign plague, accustomed as they were to my father's perpetual charm and to Southern Presbyterians and Baptists quite capable of fury but incapable of tears. In the first days they sat vigil, as if my condition were fatal, a crisis so deep recovery was obviously impossible. For the first time in my life, I saw them apart: one came in the mornings, the other, afternoons; gray- or brown-dressed, knitting with the concentration of the Fates themselves. In my vague consciousness their faces were interchangeable, the same mask of abstract mourning before a phenomenon neither could quite comprehend.

Mrs. Randall came at night. She would light the kerosene lamp I had saved from her old home, the glow so blurring the room in its softness that objects once familiar ceased to be either shadows or their natural selves. As I drifted in and out of fitful dreaming, she appeared bathed in that autumnal light, ineffably beautiful in ineffable grief, her eyes always

upon me and her hand at my cheek in those moments of un-anticipated tears. She knew: she knew everything that had happened and might have happened; knew those things I did not permit myself to know.

It was to her I first spoke, that third night, bolting upright out of bed from a sound sleep to cry, "I have to leave! I have to leave!"

"Of course, of course." Her warm breath brushed my ear. "Of course . . ." Her hand crossed my forehead. "Anywhere. Anywhere you want to go. I'll help, Gams, I'll help you."

I slipped away again, soothed, ignoring the other voices — two spinsters gabbling and a bewildered baritone. They might as well have spoken in tongues. Their concern should have touched me; it was surely sincere. But from that moment forward I was unmoved by them, as I would find myself in the weeks ahead unmoved by the entire town. The events of those extraordinary months — the birth of the war, the extermination of the Ellisons, the incineration of the deaf-mute, and the discovery of the truth — also marked the torching of my innocence, the annihilation of my past. Franksville ceased to be any place at all, and after my delirious assertion all that mattered to me was determining the place to which I would escape.

Even there amidst the pillows, as I recovered, I found myself searching remembered maps in the hope of encountering that river, town, or mountain which would set me rocketing out of the town that had cradled my childhood and coddled my youth. It would not be Princeton. Princeton was Franksville writ different: Franksville with snow; Franksville with connections throughout the continent and especially the South. New York was not far enough, nor was New Orleans, nor Havana. France would not have me; nor I, France, whose civilized language my father spoke so flowingly. Its battlefields would only recall for me the small patch of ash gradually vanishing in the year's

rains beside the half-built Pritchard III. Santiago, Melbourne, Batavia, Samarkand in Russia now consumed in revolution — these were the names that shimmered in my mind, places so many thousands of miles and imaginations from Franksville.

Which is what brought me, on that gloomy afternoon only days from the year's longest night, to the atlas in the library reading room, with its dark wood and green-shaded lamps and tables of whispers. And what more appropriate to draw me from the demonic place where I had witnessed in miniature all the horrors man could commit (or so I thought) than the angelic city, that factory of dreams by the ocean whose very name meant peace. Even repeating the circling towns — Pasadena, Pomona, Santa Ana, Ventura — seemed to calm me. Three thousand miles. Three thousand miles to the west, in the one state dubbed not with a garbled Indian word, not for a province or personage of the old continent, but for a magic land of no sorrow or pain; the state whose motto proclaimed: "I have found it." And there, in Monteclara, hard by the mountains, fifty miles from the sea, stood Colton College, my response to Princeton, the Pacific refuge of a pack of West Coast Yalies. There was my excuse to fly as far as I could go.

I wrote them, to Sumner Hall (called that not, to my relief, for the crippled radical senator from Massachusetts but for some obscure Congregationalist preacher), enclosing my own envelope, stamped and self-addressed. Even so, when Lottie distributed the mail one day, she said to me, "And what is this from California?" But I had already the well-rehearsed lie: "I had a question about a movie I saw." And that satisfied her. My attack had made me wily. Through Christmas, through steely January and February's dulling chill, to March — one year since Hoppy's reel down Depot Street — I maintained that correspondence: shipping the documents, finagling the letters, offhanded, serene. ("A whim. Just an alternative to Princeton.")

141

Going through the motions of a Southern Ivy Leaguer whose one goal was that tiny town just off the line from Philadelphia to New York, till the day the acceptance arrived: yes, of course; yes, they would, yes. And only then, after months of dissimulation I would have been incapable of before, did I stand before Mrs. Randall, documents in hand, to announce my decision.

In the interceding year, she and my father had cemented their arrangement. Upstairs they maintained a strict separation, he to his room, she to hers. But below, at dinner, at parties, as they walked down the street, no one might notice their union dissolved. There were the first rumors, of course, gossip here and there about my father's increasingly urgent appointments in neighboring towns, in the capital, in Richmond, and, once, in Washington itself; presumed assignations, but nothing concrete. About Mrs. Randall there was no whispering. A woman had no call for out-of-town visits, except for a trip to see cousins in Knoxville, an invitation never apparently proffered.

She studied the letter, dressed in Colton College's signature and seal, there on her chaise, and handed it back with hardly a gesture.

"And?" she said.

I smiled.

In those months since my illness, since Skippy's corpse was found, our relationship too had changed. I had been cooler toward her and she to me, polite but distant over meals, ungiving of visits between our rooms. We sensed, perhaps, though allied in our rejection of my father, that our courses must be different ones, for her tie of vows was in its way stronger than mine of blood. Also, I was growing older; and finally, though we might recognize it only unconsciously, there was the lesson of the Ellison's horror to keep us apart.

"That's where I'm going," I said flatly.

"To school?"

"Yes."

She glanced at the letterhead skeptically.

"Near Los Angeles."

A slow grin crossed her lips, and she shook her head. "He won't let you."

"He has to."

"He won't."

"I won't go to Princeton."

"He'll demand it," she said.

I walked to her vanity and pulled a cigarette from my coat. I had recently affected smoking, something encouraged in equal parts by the war and Bobby. I dragged on it dramatically. "Then you must convince him otherwise."

It was clumsily played. In later years, I would never have been quite so crass. But I was a child and had never called in promises, though I would do so — in fiction and in fact — many times later, till the moment came when even promises possessed no honor. I stood there self-assured, and that woman, not yet thirty and already too wise, who doubtless had suffered even crueler betrayals than I was to know, nodded and said, "You haven't forgotten, have you."

"No. 'Anywhere you want to go.' I heard you say it. 'I'll help you.' This is where I want to go. And you have to help me get there."

Her smile changed then, infused with sadness, and for an instant her eyes were far away with remembrance. "Do you think you can run away, then?"

I wanted more than ever in my life to convey that strength only a small-town scion possesses at birth, the utter certitude that his hair and eyes and bones and flesh endow him by right with a peculiar independence from place and history. But her words had shaken me, pricked my confidence and raised new fears.

She closed her eyes, blinking away whatever had clouded the moment. "Of course I'll help."

She reached to the nightstand, to the lower shelf where the chest sat, locked, like a sign of her heart.

I smiled. "Worry beads?"

"My rosary, perhaps. If you go to California, you'll need to get used to them." She fingered the smooth wood. "I'll talk to him this evening. Go to bed early, so he can't come for you."

"All right."

I heard them in my bright unsleep, my head restless on the pillow, from the study below and one wall over from my bedroom. I heard his footfalls on the stairs and her voice behind him, arresting him in midstep as he neared the landing. I could not make out the words. Then below there was more talking, low-voiced and so uncaptured.

I had drifted off in a sleep incomplete. It was much later. Suddenly light poured in from the hall and the silhouette of Mrs. Randall played across the bearskin rug.

"You will go to California," she said. That was all. I realized vaguely in my drowsiness she had been crying.

In June she and I walked out to Pritchard III. We had gone downtown to shop, to buy me yet another suit and a pair of shoes I might need when September came and I stepped on the local to Atlanta to catch the express to New Orleans, and after that a new and unimaginable limited to California. We found the suit — a gray ready-made, which needed only minor alteration — though not the shoes. On the sidewalk we glanced at the headlines about Belleau Wood and expressed our regrets to Mrs. Nelson, Franksville's third Gold Star mother. The town had not expected the war to hurt so much. The flag-bedecked extravaganzas continued, the Four Minute Men exhorted, the drives for foil, lard, and Liberty Bonds went on unabated, but the reality of the ghastly cost of mere yards slowly filtered into the mind of Franksville and perhaps, at night, shook forth in even the most vociferous patriot a shudder of dread.

We wandered out of downtown, into an afternoon still fresh with late spring, digesting sundaes from The Arbor, discussing the likelihood that the draft board would find me inappropriate for service; for the rumor now was that, by summer's end, the army would conscript down to the age of eighteen and up to forty-five.

"I wonder if it will come back on me," I said.

"What?"

"Not having served. It could, you know. They've been baiting Randy Keller about being a slacker, and everybody knows he couldn't find his way to the front door without his glasses."

"I don't think you have to worry," she said. "Besides, you'll be leaving before you're eligible."

"You're right, I guess." Seeing Mrs. Nelson had unnerved me. "I just don't want to be haunted by it."

She gave me an odd look and stopped. We were on Lytton Street, which soon enough faded into rough macadam and then forked, part dying away in a gravel lane that wound through the woods, the other branch dead-ending at Pritchard III.

"Will you take me to the mill?"

"The Pritchards' new mill?" I asked uncertainly.

She turned away. "It isn't Pritchards' mill anymore, or it won't be much longer. The True Harmony Corporation is buying it. Your father's been negotiating the sale for weeks now." She flashed a bitter smile. "So it's our mill now. Part ours. Your father's and mine and yours."

Had Bobby told me, I would have thought it a joke. The mean irony of it would have delighted him. But it was not a joke, of course. My stomach plunged for an instant toward my feet, and then I found myself laughing. "He must hate us very, very much."

Since March, my father and I had barely spoken. My betrayal of him and of Princeton had singed forever the little green left in our relations. Mrs. Randall's intercession for me simply made me twice-Judas in his eyes. Dinner conversation was now largely directed by Lottie and Bea, whose limited repertoire of topics tottered under the load. I had once, as a sort of conciliation, brought up my upcoming journey west, speculating on what might be the most interesting route: north to Washington, south to Atlanta, winding up the Clinchfield to Cincinnati. My father had dabbed his lips with his napkin and said tightly, "Please wait till I'm finished. Then you can discuss the matter more profitably with the ladies."

"Hatred has less to do with it," Mrs. Randall said, her voice tired, "than the price of cotton." She looked up the road. "Will you take me?"

"Do you really want to go?"

"No." She shook her head. "But if I don't now, with you here, I know I never will."

We walked silently through the pines I had last passed as I staggered away with Bobby half sustaining me through that spring day turned bleak with smoke and clouds, the taste of vomit still fresh in my mouth. Today, I could hear the birds, robins and jays, and the rustle of a slight western breeze through the boughs above. The road was half obscured with foliage. Work on the mill had been suspended again months before when the Pritchards, inept even in the midst of the war boom, found themselves without funds to continue. Mrs. Randall kept pace, though it must have been difficult in pumps appropriate for city sidewalks but not for the potholes and washouts of a half-abandoned country road. She wore a cream-colored dress that day and a hat with a partial veil which was out of fashion but which she had always liked.

The trees thinned, the road curved, and then we were in the clearing. The mill rose, foreboding, forlorn as that day seasons before, the detritus of construction renewed and broken off scattered here and there, half and sometimes wholly hidden by weeds green and tall from the spring wet. On the rail line, a boxcar sat, one door thrown open to its gaping emptiness, the darkness within so intense in the brilliant June day it seemed infinite. Mrs. Randall stopped, frozen; will-less. I took her arm, leading her farther, hearing in my own head the cacophony of that April afternoon, all the sounds together: the conversational murmur, the rage of the fire, that ungodly scream.

I took her onto the ramp where I had stood in gym-suited ridiculousness before the one moment in my life I was least able to forget, to the spot where that man with the face of an evil angel had given me drink as we watched those hooded figures go about their business.

"This is where I was," I said.

Her eyes followed as I pointed.

"And they did it there."

The boughs overhead singed, in the first rush of the explosion, were green again, unscarred, at least from a distance. Still, we could see a few charred thrusts of tie peeking through the grass and thistles. Mrs. Randall remained transfixed, somehow trans-figured, her creamy clothes fluttering in the late spring breeze; she, the one who would have stopped it all, her eyes liquid in wonder before the scene doubtless even more horrible in her imagination than it had been in fact.

"Why did you love him so?" I said suddenly, brutally.

She turned to me, uncomprehending, like an archangel in-explicably brought down to earth on a whim of God.

"What?"

Her voice trembled, and I might have pressed my advantage then; might have unlocked the secrets of her past, her heart, of that small wooden casket she kept at her bedside. But I could not, disarmed as any man in the presence of divinity.

"Love him."

The smile, the pained and generous smile, spread across her face, certain and obscuring as wings drawn across a countenance that, revealed, would incinerate with the brilliance of its truth. "I told you," she said softly, "last summer. In the tower. Don't you remember?"

"Yes, but there must be more. Did you know him?"

"No. I don't think so. Perhaps." That little veil seemed to have grown, swirled around her like her mourning weeds, hiding her completely from my questions. "That's all I can tell you."

And that I accepted, though I had yet to learn that what we might wish to speak and what may be spoken are often, especially in matters of the heart, two worlds discrete. We stepped down then, out through the green sea of June toward the site of the crime, the very place of sacrifice and loss. The noises now were louder in my ears in their confusion. I held her arm tighter, drawing her closer to me against my memories, grasping her free hand so we stood like two dancers amid the heavy-headed weeds.

"What did you threaten him with?" I said unexpectedly, absurdly, grasping some question related to the present to wrench myself from that place and its past.

"Who?"

"My father."

She turned to me as if the words came from another world. "With what?" she said. "I told him I'd divorce him."

"That's all?"

She raised her eyebrows, suddenly practical, worldly. "A divorce would mean a division of the fortune. A reckoning. There is too much peculiar in both men's schemes to allow for that. I knew that." She stepped away from me. "That's why you can go to California."

It was just a question of riches then, my escape contingent

on marginal frauds and the cigar smoke and laughter drifting beneath the study door. The tawdriness of it sickened me at the same time its very smallness represented what I meant to flee, still believing then that elsewhere such petty and earthly concerns would have no power over questions of love or the soul.

"That's all?" I said, incredulous.

"All," she repeated starkly, absolutely.

We remained a moment longer, almost up to our waists in implacable nature, which, regardless of Pritchard fortunes or perhaps even the True Harmony Corporation, went on building its kingdom and rebuilding ad infinitum despite pillage and fire and trampling feet. Finally her elbow disentwined from mine, and Mrs. Randall stepped away, diaphonous, bending down to pluck from the earth a cinder, one of those charred remnants of wood, iron, flesh, still scattered among the growth. She cradled it in her palm like some rare treasure, and I, who ought to have looked away, said boldly, ironic: "For your hope chest?"

It wounded her, but she willed away the hurt in her eyes with that awful gift of control — how earned? — and smiled. "No, there's quite enough in there already." She cast the long-dead ember into the brush. "We should get along now."

"All right."

I swooped low in an exaggerated bow and pointed to the passage through the weeds, watching her, laughing, sweep past me. But as my fingers stroked the ground, I gathered in my hand a piece of that seared memory, which that night I would leave on her nightstand, on top of that box. I shoved it deep in my pocket, down to where it might glow again with the heat of my own body, and then hurried to her side, above me the confused chatter of the mockingbird and the joereaper.

10

I DID NOT RETURN to Franksville for fifteen years. I did not stay away truculently. It was not a question of money. In those first years, Mrs. Randall would doubtless have paid my way, and subsequently, as I took trains from Los Angeles to New York, to San Francisco, to Chicago, and made the first of my European journeys, I could well have afforded it myself. A couple of times — in 1919, again in 1924 — plans were conceived, only to wither because of other obligations or opportunities. Somewhere within me, though, as I stepped into the vestibule of the 7:19 in the muggy August dusk, I must have decided, having made good my escape, only the most weighty of obligations would ever draw me back.

Still, I could not have known at five o'clock, after an early supper, the study curtains half drawn against the heat, that I would never see my father again. In his eyes I remained unshriven, a renegade of the worst sort, and our relations were as chilly as they had been in March. Still, he felt obliged to offer some kind of blessing, or at least some advice, to a son setting out into the world.

He paced as he talked, the Polonian lecture as narcotic as the heat. To give at least the appearance of attention, I let my eyes follow his measured tread across the carpet. Past forty now, he was going to fat, his neck swelling below his chin, his waist slowly vanishing, his face showing the first puffiness, though for a man his age he still cut an imposing figure. He had a boxer's grace in his walk, and the silver just brushing his temples made him look less old than experienced. Over the years his voice had grown more resonant, and his smile had become even more winning — though that afternoon, of course, I did not see it. Briefly, he touched the subjects that might be expected: money, drink, the choice of companions, even, obliquely, women both honest and otherwise.

He stopped suddenly, his fingertips resting lightly on the windowsill, and looked through the sheer silk panel of drapery, across the wide lawn to the shuttered mansion beside our own, dazzling even in the dying light.

"You have," he said, "disappointed me very much. I do not approve of this adventure . . . ." He drew a deep breath, arresting the complaint. "I trust on your own you will make better account of yourself."

Perhaps I ought to have defended myself; perhaps doing so might have brought us to shouting but then to understanding or at least a cordial truce. In that moment I felt a fluttering emptiness, and wished I could make some gesture, some sound. But I could not. The silence continued a few seconds longer.

"I should check my bags one last time."

I stood up. He made no move; remained by the window, stiff as the dead, his gaze fixed on the home of that man who had been good as a father to him. I went to the door.

"Good-bye," I said.

"Good-bye."

The parting with Lottie and Bea was hardly less strained. Gradually, as relations deteriorated between my father and me, as he and Mrs. Randall established their distance, blood had asserted itself and made them assuredly of their brother's party. They were not cruel to me, simply more phantasmal than ever in that house where they never felt they belonged. In the foyer, they kissed my cheek as they might some ritual object in which they had long ago lost faith, likely relieved that one source of their brother's pain would now be absent. Althea wept, took me to her bosom, making no judgments, speaking no re-proaches. She surely had opinions regarding what had happened in the house over the last months and years, but with the sly and silent wisdom of those beholden to others for their daily bread, she remained pointedly oblivious to the turmoil.

We took a cab to the station — Mrs. Randall and I — something I knew would raise eyebrows in the town. My father, who loved his automobiles, had never shown any interest in hiring a chauffeur, nor any in Mrs. Randall's learning to drive. Our ride, with my two trunks and three valises, was a crowded and quiet one. I watched the hill and then downtown slip by: The Arbor, the courthouse, St. Peter and St. James. Much as I detested it, Franksville was the only place I had really known, and on that ride the exhilaration I had felt all through the preparations for leaving was replaced by terror of the loss of the familiar. Mrs. Randall chatted at me from time to time, then finally fell silent, reaching over to slip her hand gently, weightlessly, over mine.

There were no friends to see me off. I had wanted it that way, and in any case there was the growing meanness about my certain disqualification from the draft. Some of my classmates had been taken; various more had enlisted. Even my defenders — those who had not concluded my collapse was only a rich boy's ruse to escape battle — were forced to admit it betokened a sissiness they previously had no inkling of.

The baggage was checked in good order; the ticket had already been purchased. At 7:15 we walked onto the platform, where so many years before Mrs. Randall had arrived, where her first husband's casket had been unloaded, where now, usually late at night, trains bulging with materiel, specials heavy with fresh recruits, pounded by in the darkness toward eastern ports.

We spoke hardly at all. This was the moment I most dreaded, as had she, I imagine. I was all in Franksville she loved, perhaps had ever loved, and my departure would drive her more solidly into herself, behind that mask of reserve, than she had ever been before. We knew each other well enough, cared deeply enough, that we made no attempt to fill the silence. Only when the whistle wailed in the distance and the first plume of smoke appeared down the tracks did she turn, enfolding me in her arms as my fingers locked behind her.

"Good luck. Think of me sometimes."

I choked back tears. "Of course, of course," was all I could muster, my hand reaching to touch her hair. "Thank you."

The train was there, groaning to a halt, and other people were around us, alighting, boarding. Mistily, I saw my trunks wrestled into the baggage car. I squeezed her very tightly one last time and then, crazily, kissed her hard, only for an instant, on the lips.

"Good-bye," I said, backing away. "Good-bye."

She raised a gloved hand, the other held to her mouth, and I leapt up the steps of the car, my resolutions of strength, of leaving at all, creaking under the strain of that parting. I shoved my way to the men's washroom, locked the door behind me, and slipped down onto the toilet as my eyes welled over and three deep sobs escaped my chest. Then I sat, there in my new gray suit, my lower lip gripped in my teeth, till I felt the train moving around me. I got up slowly, washed my face, lit a cigarette. When I stepped out, I turned onto the vestibule, where the top half of the dutch door was still open. Franksville was gone.

It was the colors that first impressed me. The colors of the earth itself: the mountain's ochres and rusts moving across a pastel spectrum as the day swelled and declined; the shimmering gold-white of the sand beside the gold-struck sea, beneath a sky blue beyond conception in a light so pure I had to squint. And onto that subtle earth — so different from the bloody clay of home — rising into the tropical glitter, men had planted fruit trees with leaves of impossible waxy green, heavy with lemons and oranges; palms, bougainvillea, and grasses eternally dewy from the sparkling jets of sprinklers. Beside the soft adobes with roofs like wine stains, they had thrown up buildings of turquoise, ocean green, pink, and lavender, bejeweled with neon — whole fanciful towns, joined by trolley cars of shimmering red, reaching out to Newport Beach, to Venice-by-the-Sea, San Berdoo. And Colton.

Colton attempted to restrain its fantasy, proper elms and oaks and pines as well as more exotic eucalyptus dotting its campus, which was vaguely Florentine in design. The founders were New Englanders after all, and the entire town tried very hard to suggest the ivy-draped sanctity of a place with colonial roots. California, of course, betrayed the masquerade, the naked peaks lofting behind us, jasmine filling the evening, the electric breath of the Santanas sweeping out of the desert to send temperatures soaring and leech every drop of moisture from the air. But they seemed not to notice, those determined Yankees, comfortable in their anomalousness in that world of anomalies, secure, in a land so insecure that even the earth itself might move, that no one would find their caprice too odd.

The sense of a peculiarly matched but pleasing jigsaw puzzle was borne out by those who shared my suite, two bedrooms and a study overlooking the tennis courts. Alex McGilvary was Jimbo Cash made over, but more perfectly: a gentle six feet of football prowess. Still shy of eighteen, he talked eagerly of signing up and doing his part when his birthday came, and he wept with naive loss the delirious day of the Armistice. Andy Bethune, across the study, felt no such regrets. He was short, dark-haired and dark-eyed; it was long into October before we knew his legal name was not Andrew but Andrés and his full family tag Bethune de Pico. Related vaguely to a Mexican governor of the state, his people had managed through guile and politic marriages to retain at least a fraction of their wealth and standing. Product of Jesuitical training, which left him with a loathing of Catholicism but the subtle wits and classical learning of such an education, he had a charming Latin cynicism and languor, which perhaps influenced my later fascination with things Mediterranean.

But it was the fourth resident of the suite who was, for me, the most intriguing. Harvey Feldman was the first Jew I had ever met, or at least whom I really knew. Wiry, fair-skinned, and black-haired, he talked faster and seemed altogether funnier and more intense than anybody Franksville had ever produced. It was he who, on the first night in the dining hall, tried to dub me "Grits" for the regional specialty I had rarely eaten and never liked, but which he assumed to be the major source of Southern sustenance. Over my time at Colton, Harvey seemed able to produce liquor at will despite school rules, and he had a flashy Ford roadster and a complicated romantic life. But most magically of all, his father was in the movies.

That is not quite accurate. Mr. Feldman did not appear in movies, nor did he film or direct them. He was among those who had come in the initial migration from New York to Hollywood, the Lower East Side children of parents who had felt the czar's pogroms. Mr. Feldman's fortes were raising money, wrangling with lawyers, and exercising a remarkable sense of what small-town, Gentile America would like to see on the screen. In the industry, he was indispensable.

I first entered the Feldman's house, and thus the world of the movies, on Thanksgiving Day, 1918. For all his fearsome reputation in his trade, Mr. Feldman seemed a benign figure, generous and self-effacing, while Mrs. Feldman — a handsome woman who had once, briefly, danced with the Ziegfeld Follies

— clucked and groaned over me in a motherly fashion: "So far from home, poor boy. Like my Allan . . ." Harvey's oldest brother was in New York, while a sister lived in Santa Barbara and another brother worked for Famous-Laskey. Before dinner we drank vermouth and smoked imported cigarettes, something I had never tried, and I worked very hard to impress Mr. Feldman with my knowledge of films, dazzled by the names that salted his conversation. There was wine with dinner, which — in a household that had long ago broken Kosher — was served by a butler and prepared by a woman to whom Mrs. Feldman spoke nothing but Spanish. The meal was not like the one described by Bobby's brother, after which plates were broken for having been touched by goyim. Over brandy, Mrs. Feldman asked after my Christmas plans, and I, straining to be polite, replied, "Over Hanukkah?" Harvey doubled up with laughter.

I had thought of a return to Franksville, since the college closed down for two weeks for the holidays, though somehow the South, after only three months, seemed far away as China, and the eight-day journey out and back seemed hardly worth the trouble and expense. I stammered something about my present indecision, when Mr. Feldman remarked that he would be happy to show me around the studios a bit during the break, and we could all go to some of the holiday parties, which were sure to be terrific, especially now that the war had ended.

"We'll even have a Hanukkah bush," Harvey inserted, and the decision was made. After a tour on Friday of Hollywood-land, still a suburb where the Feldmans and other movie folk were more than vaguely suspect, I returned to college to pen a letter announcing I would not be home for Christmas, though my reasons were spelled out only in a note to Mrs. Randall.

Even she expressed some reservations.

But that balmy December, as we tooled through the city from one production to another, to this party or that, the ruins of Griffith's Babylon looming through the darkness or noon, I knew I had found my place, that this was where I belonged. The Feldmans were my ticket, full of advice, encouragement, and the sort of connections those who poured in from Fresno and Iowa City only dreamed of. By chance and distances impractical to traverse in only a vacation, I stumbled into what at the Carillon or Franksville High's *Midsummer Night's Dream* had seemed beyond all imagining.

During that Christmas, I played my first part, as an extra in a Universal serial. Throughout the winter and into spring, I answered other casting calls: now a Union soldier, now a French revolutionary, an Egyptian slave boy, or simply a man on the street. My studies slumped as I borrowed Harvey's roadster more and more often to sweep down the highway in the day's first light to arrive in time for the selection. By May, I was ready to throw my lot with Hollywood. Colton had been a happy place for me: sniggering over Catullus; admiring the Shakespearean who insisted on reading aloud in class the bowdlerized passages of *Hamlet* and *Troilus and Cressida*; emoting on the auditorium stage. Still, my gentleman's C's were a bit disappointing to the college, and more so to my father, who, though he had been satisfied with the same at Princeton, saw them as a sign of the frivolity of my West Coast excursion. In June I left the dormitory overlooking those tennis courts, Andy and Alex and Harvey toasting my future stardom with cheap tequila, to move into an apartment in the Echo Park district, in a building shared by an almost constantly changing cast of transients from all over the United States. Mr. Feldman found it for me, paid the first three months' rent, and made sure I met the right people: not directors or Mabel Normand, but men who knew about make-up, who could show me how to be a pirate, an Arab, a Roman, a boche. In my building lived Melody and Oscar and Minnie and Frank and Tom and Su-Su, who were very modern and smoked marijuana and who, one dizzy July night, took all the virginities I had to offer in one delicious swoop. My recollection of that ecumenical initiation is sadly vague. The images that remain are of parts of two people who, before Christmas, had vanished into the anonymity of drug stores and service stations, which, in Los Angeles, absorbed those who lacked good teeth or fortune, who became bored or disenchanted or corrupted by pictures and ended grease monkeys, prostitutes, or both.

The news from the South was not good. Gambetta Stevenson was appalled. He wrote me furious letters, demanding my return, asserting his humiliation. I ignored his notes as I devoured those from Mrs. Randall, admonitory but thrilled, concerned for my health and moral well-being, but full too of what I took to be admiration for my audacity. I exaggerated to her my own importance and especially that of my neighbors — bit players at best, extras out of work much of the time. Still, I made sure to tell her often of the Feldmans (whose name, for local sensibilities, I transformed to Felton), so she might rest assured I had a patron looking out for me.

As the last of the brush fires of September burned in the hills, the smoke and sometimes even the flames visible from the roof of the boarding house, Su-Su, her hair cropped in that severe geometry later immortalized by Louise Brooks, brought me the telegram informing me of Lottie's death. I must have paled.

"Bad news?" she said.

When I didn't reply, she took out a cigarette and hung it between my lips. I handed her the telegram.

"Who's Lottie?"

"My aunt."

"Are you going back?"

I looked at her, my face blank.

She lit the cigarette for me. "They tell you when the funeral is."

"I know."

"You shouldn't do it," she said simply. "I bet it was the influenza that got her. Traveling's the worst thing you could do. You'll get it. You get tired; you're around all those people." She put her hand on my shoulder. "Don't go, Gams."

I remained mute. Here Lottie was gone, and the date and hour of her funeral marked, though even if I left that afternoon I would not arrive in Franksville in time for the services. But it was family, after all: Lottie, who had carried me squalling as a child and made the move to the big house by my side and watched my caromings on that red and gray bike; whose ghostly presence was hopelessly tied to all that my growing up in Franksville could ever mean. And here beside me was a woman only a year or two older than I, who with her husband — or boyfriend or paramour — had mere weeks before not only seen me naked (which Lottie had not done in years) but touched me naked and watched me touch her husband naked and led me along in things never even considered physically feasible in Franksville, telling me not to return, telling me it was dangerous, even deadly, to do so. And I knew without a moment's reflection she was right.

I took a drag on the cigarette. "No, no, of course. I couldn't get there in time anyway."

Bea followed her sister within three months. That was the influenza too, though surely it must really have been just Lottie's loss, for no Siamese twins were ever as surely joined as the two sisters. I had written after the first death my reasons for not coming back, at which point all letters from my father ceased. When Bea died there was no telegram, only a special delivery letter from Mrs. Randall, full of calm assurance that I had acted rightly before and that there was no reason now to return because of the second passing.

Soon after that, early in 1920, I began to be noticed. I was no star, surely, but with the Feldmans' help and, too, with my Southern and Protestant reliability, I gradually became desirable. Minor directors sent for me, and in comedies and dramas and epics my face came forward out of the background, never dominating the screen but appearing more and more often for one minute, two minutes, five, a cumulative twelve or fifteen throughout the film until finally, in a Western, I actually landed a part sufficient to include me in the cast list. Gambetta Stevenson, I was told, would not do: too long and foreign sounding. I was allowed to try to choose an acceptable name, and that entire weekend, drunk most of the time with my neighbors (these in a more respectable building near Westlake Park), I pondered the possibilities. On Monday, I caught the Red Car to the lot to announce I was now Steven Gambet, which was changed to Gambit for the move in chess, and it was as Steven Gambit that I made my Hollywood career.

The details of those years of the twenties have been well-enough chronicled in the studio biographies and the magazine profiles of later years. Unlike the official histories of many other actors, which are more fanciful than most of the scripts they played, the public record of my roles, of how I came to be contracted, of the foods I liked and where I took tea, were accurate. Except for the shabbier scandal sheets, I cannot quarrel with my treatment by press or publicity department. Illusions at large over my Hollywood life arise not from calculated misinformation but from omission. And, even so, my life in the era was likely no wilder (perhaps less so) than those of my contemporaries, the lot of us transplanted to California without roots or obligations except to the studios; required only to be punctual, tractable, and to maintain our looks. That, of course, and sate whatever peculiar appetites we might possess discreetly, for this was the era of the Arbuckle and Wallace Reid scandals, of the

Hays Commission and the William Desmond Taylor murder. And I, as a Southerner of a certain class, had imbibed discretion, if not in my mill-worker mother's milk, then in the air of that house on the hill, from the Episcopal church, from years in the presence of that most secret of women, Mrs. Randall.

So I got on well, establishing myself as a pleasant fellow, easy to direct, a loyal friend. I sharpened my childhood talent for mimicry but was careful to couch my imitations of Jack Pickford, Mr. Feldman, and Clara Bow in kindness. I was popular at parties, and with my runner's body, which, as happens in one's twenties, maintained itself without much effort on my part, popular afterward as well. Tom and Chi-Chi had endowed me with a sexual catholicity that served me well when I and my career were young, as did a calculated moderation in drink and drugs which left me viable long after many other young men had lapsed. I was uncommonly proud that I never had to resort to artificial means of satisfaction, such means as were presented at a very private affair to Ramon Navarro by Rudolf Valentino, the signed leaden toy that, decades later, would prove Ramon's undoing.

My good repute, then, both at work and more privately, gave me entrance to places that a solid but unimportant secondary player might not be expected to have, living as I did in an unpretentious bungalow off Western. Had it not been for *The Jazz Singer*, I could well have spent the rest of my life in those comfortable but unglamorous circumstances. But with talking pictures came the demand for voices, and mine — gift of my father, pitched slightly higher than his at the unthreateningly masculine range between baritone and tenor — was my ticket to Hollywood's more celestial spheres. That, and my ability to be now English, now Irish, now a boy from the slums, now a genteel Southern aristocrat, till my character was fixed in 1931 as the suave and worldly cad in *Betrayed!*

Throughout all this, I remained abreast of events in Franksville through biweekly letters from Mrs. Randall. Apparently abreast, in any case, for her communications were as void of allusions to the unhappier moments of her life as mine were of the more intimate ones of mine. On occasion, she would slip. Some past disagreement, an unknown woman's name I took to be that of a former mistress of my father's, a stray remark about loneliness (and how bleak that house now minus even the single presence of the collective Lottie and Bea must have been) — these would occasionally surface, and I would mine her past letters in search of further clues.

It was likely around 1925 that I first suggested divorce. It was obliquely put, as I remember, though I myself found the step unremarkable after five years in the movies. But I recalled Franksville with sufficient vividness to know that, even where Mrs. Randall was concerned, the suggestion might seem a bit scandalous. She had ignored my earlier innuendos. Now I grew bolder.

> You really might consider divorcing him. There's never any sign in your letters that there's much chance of a reconciliation, so each of you continues sharing a house with someone you don't really love anymore. It hardly seems just or fair for either one of you.

I was quite taken with the adultness of it all, how wise and even-handed it seemed. I even suggested, should she need a place to think things over, she might come to Los Angeles, where she could stay with me.

I mailed the letter next day, and returned home to find her latest. Then there was a pause. I imagined she was pondering the separation, quite struck with my finally voicing what had so long been in her heart. Perhaps in those days she was packing her bags, or already on the train to New Orleans and thence the Pacific.

The letter that finally arrived was exactly like those before, the tone indistinguishable, the news very much the same, as if my last missive had never reached her; or if it had, had not touched her. Then, coiled at the foot of the penultimate paragraph, it appeared:

> The idea mentioned in your last letter strikes me as both vulgar and inappropriate, a lapse perhaps occasioned by some of the company you keep in Hollywood. I long ago ceased to inquire after or meddle in your private affairs. I would ask you to extend me the same courtesy.

The letter puttered on through a few more domestic details, ending with the pregnant mention of a possible journey to White Sulphur Springs and her usual closing: "All love, my darling Gams."

The day, a typically sparkling, seasonless one, turned arctic for me. I went out to the garden, returned to the house, took a bath, left for an aimless walk. Only after many blocks — innumerable palms, uncountable oleanders — did I cast with sufficient skill the explanation: her past. Just as she knew the financial irregularities my father and Mr. Randall had committed made the threat of divorce a weapon of catastrophic force, perhaps she had let slip in the first years of their marriage sufficient clues that my father knew their revelation would ruin her. I was overwhelmed then by the selflessness of her threat in my name: willing to sacrifice both my father and his fortune and her own good name simply so I might go to college where I chose.

The idea raised my spirits and took my mind away from present matters by resurrecting older and more tantalizing mysteries. What of Mrs. Randall's past? Had she been some kind of show girl? Or worse? Perhaps a carnival dancer, lurching from town to town, dreaming of finer things. That was how she knew the deaf-mute, who worked as a clown or roustabout.

They had had a sweet, silent affair, and then were separated. In Knoxville — a chance encounter on the street, a petty kindness, or some more contractual arrangement — she had met Mr. Randall, and he, smitten, had taken her away; convinced some trusted friends to pose as her surviving family; concocted the story of her parents. And so she had arrived in Franksville, free but burdened with the reality of her former self, which could never be spoken of. That, and the memory of a lover who could not speak.

A dime novel, of course. The kind of thing featured in shoddier women's magazines or ground out at studios doomed to failure in the coming depression. That I ever invented such a pathetic little tale now strikes me as fantastic. But for a while, embellished here, pruned there, it soothed me, till returning from downtown one day I stopped at the produce stand two blocks from the house to buy tomatoes. I set them in front of Arturo, who said: "That's all?" "All," I said.

And then the exchange at Pritchard III returned, and the absoluteness of her voice. There on a Los Angeles street corner, I realized with queasy certainty she had lied. There had been more. She had slept with him surely, to seal their bargain of mutual silence. He would have demanded it: in the tower; his bed. And had she then slept with him again and again — the two nauseated with contempt for each other — although she was not meant to have his children? But she would know ways to assure that did not happen, those ways I had learned of these last years in Hollywood.

"Mr. Gambit?"

I turned away from the counter. "Never mind, Arturo. Nothing today. Nothing."

I received pictures of the trip to White Sulphur Springs. She had not gone alone but with a group of Franksville ladies. She smiled at me out of blurry Kodak snapshots, lovely as I remembered her, dressed in fashions she must have ordered from Atlanta or New York, more ethereal than ever for the years since I had seen her last and her traveling companion's photographic ineptitude. The trip awakened some wanderlust in her, for from then on, for a dozen years, she made such journeys often, in the first years Southern excursions to Virginia Beach, Asheville, Charleston, once to Florida. She apparently took great pleasure in them, while I, who by blind luck and the discreet manipulation of more powerful friends earned a passage to Rome for the ill-fated filming of *Ben Hur*, was filled with superior amusement. St. Petersburg and Miami Beach seemed silly little places when put beside Europe, beside Italy, which, even in its fascist incarnation, made me drunk with cheap wine, bread, and pasta; with monuments of every age, sunny *pensioni* and sin innocent for its very ancientness. It occurred to me occasionally that she and her respectable lady companions might, on their journeys, take lovers, but the possibility, which fascinated and repelled me, seemed unlikely.

My Italian opportunity aborted a long-postponed trip to Franksville (quite to my father's relief, I suspect), and by the time I returned, my finances were a disaster and I took on as much work as possible. Then sound arrived, my opportunities blossomed, and most fortuitously of all, I accepted the part nobody wanted in *Betrayed!*

Many film historians still consider that my finest performance, and more than a few have written that it remains the definitive portrayal of a cad on film, all the more remarkable for my being so young at the time. One critic, some twenty years after, found I combined "the insouciance of the neighborhood truant with the jaded charm of a decadent aristocrat," some grotesque cross, it seems, between Peck's Bad Boy and the not completely invented public persona of Erich von Stroheim.

I was, from that moment, hopelessly typed, though again, it was a faust event. The cad is a durable character and proved quite popular in films of the thirties of a vaguely social-democratic cast, as well as in more escapist comedies of manners. In the years after World War II, there was even a certain vogue of cads a bit long in the tooth, which, until the troubles, suited me admirably.

Most lucky of all, however, was that *Betrayed!*'s popularity coincided almost exactly with the renegotiation of my contract, and I found myself virtually overnight a much wealthier man than I ever could have imagined. My first act was to vacate the comfortable bungalow of a bachelor supporting player to take up residence in a wildly pretentious mansion in Brentwood, built by a star whom age, sound, and fortune had treated nearly as badly as they had treated me well.

I had photographs taken of the place by a professional, which I sent to Franksville, pointedly addressing the package to my father. I reveled in the impressed — awed, I thought at the time — tone in Mrs. Randall's letters, and though I heard nothing from Gambetta Stevenson, I imagined him livid and green both at once at my success, though my triumph was short-lived.

I worked rather less. The studio had no yen to squander my face in minor pictures. With more time free, I held elaborate dinners for twenty and intimate ones for two; frequented Muro and Frank's for lunch, the Garden of Allah in the evenings, with occasional literary evenings at Stanley Rose's bookstore. The summer of Roosevelt's nomination, flush with dollars as banks failed daily, I rushed from party to party. I made a memorable scene at Lili Damita's, throwing a punch at Charles Farrell in an argument about F. W. Murneau's funeral. I left my house for the weekend to Mary Astor and George Kaufman, while I attended a get-together of questionable repute on Catalina Island.

But too, I spent many evenings alone, reading, with records, glancing up occasionally with all the satisfaction of any man in his first moments of material well-being. I had made my place. I had a swimming pool, a glazed tile terrace overlooking a lawn perpetually green, which ended in a bougainvillea arbor and a tiny Grecian temple. There was a vast oak library, a sunken bath, Persian rugs, and a vaulted foyer with a marble floor and a brass-banistered staircase tumbling down one wall.

The stairs were not so grand, of course, as those Norma Desmond immortalized in the sweep toward her final close-up. But before their bastard Mediterranean splendor, with a nude Phoebus in a niche alongside, I felt like a true señor, established in the eternal spring of that angeline paradise, lord of a life gorgeous, outraged, refined.

It was down those stairs one late January afternoon, hungover still from a post New Year's revel, that I descended, dressed in silk pajamas and a smoking jacket sent me for Christmas by Ramon, to open the door to the uniformed boy. He smiled and I liked his face and reached to the silver bowl nearby for a tip.

He handed me the telegram.

11

HOW I HAD FORGOTTEN it, and how weary it had grown, that Southern earth in the full blast of the depression. Chuffing south from Washington, across Virginia ravaged, here and there Hoovervilled, worse than California, which at least was a land of bogus hope. These tents and cardboard shacks pitched along the tracks provided not even the simulacrum of optimism. There was the winter, the mean, Southern winter which hurts capriciously, inconsistently. Down through the naked trees and the evergreens and the raw, red clay, the abandoned fields already exhausted before and now left to fallow, past broken-windowed mills and the tobacco barns' gaping doors yawning forlorn over the desolation. Down to the capital; picking up the local; deeper into the lost world of my boyhood, the place I had never returned. The land grew familiar, the smokeless stacks like profiles of somebody's father, the curves of the rails known not only from within but from without the train. We plunged steadily into the early dusk, the engine's moaning like the half-remembered pleading of some other life.

It was a car that did it. A 1927 Stutz. He was drunk, I assumed, roiling back from some midnight assignation one county distant, his eyes and mind bleared with whiskey and sated desire as he drove that road, too many luckier times maneuvered sightlessly. And that night, was it a deer or rabbit, a displaced cropper, or simply the imagined specter of his own lost dreams that set his right foot too suddenly on the pedal, skiing him into and out of the curve and against the pine break, which shattered the Stutz and shattered his skull in that instant it takes to utter a single curse?

We steamed in slowly, the old, squat station, shingled and eternally in need of paint, looming beyond the glass. There was a single platform now, not two, and the arcing shed that had sheltered them was gone. As the train heaved to a stop, I saw a crowd of a couple dozen people stamping and moving against the chill, jabbering, the cloud from their breaths competing with that from the train's boiler, brakes, and heaters.

I left my compartment. (I was long past open Pullmans, much less those coaches I had once taken uncomplaining.) I squeezed down the aisle, emerging into the lounge intended to give the train a touch of elegance, out onto the observation platform and the December air undefinably, indisputably Franksville.

"There he is!" a girl squealed.

I looked down upon a single face. Then there was another, and another, mostly women, young women, though there was a boy or two among them; some children brought along. Out of the night a hand-lettered sign emerged: WELCOME HOME STEVEN GAMBIT. And as I held back, half a dozen arms stretched toward me with slips of paper, a book, a copy of *Fotoplay*. I realized that even here — more than ever here, ludicrously, hideously — I was a movie star, the only movie star who had ever visited Franksville, certainly the only one to come from there. But too, even here, I was no longer Gams, not Gambetta Stevenson, Jr., son of the recently and prematurely dead man who lived in the house on the hill, but Steven Gambit. In the more than a decade away, at least for that crowd of people before me (many of whom had barely drawn breath when I had last set foot in Franksville), I was an altogether different and much more valuable person than I had been when I left.

"Please, ladies. Please!" I heard the conductor say as two or three attempted to mount the stairs or clamber up the ironwork of the open vestibule. He turned his face up to me. "So you're Steven Gambit."

"Yes, yes." I handed him my attaché, adding absently, "I'm here for a funeral."

He had planted himself on the second step and pushed roughly at one girl who had gained a foothold on the grating. "Yeah?"

"Yes. My father's."

"Oh, Lord."

He was a young man, sharp in his stiff blue uniform and cap. Some other men appeared out of the station.

"Hey! Get over here!" he shouted to them. "Let the gentleman alone. Let Mr. Gambit be. Get over here!"

The men from the baggage room — was one of them Randy

Keller? His younger brother Elmore? — pushed through the crowd.

"Get back, ladies!" He turned to me. "Somebody waiting for you?"

I had wired from Albuquerque, from Chicago, from Washington, signalling my impending arrival in dashes and dots.

"I don't know. I think —"

There, at the back of the crowd, her arm raised, I saw her.

Her widow's weeds were different than before, her hem revealing much of her calf, her hat flat across her head, its veil barely covering her face. Two sharp, almost ridiculous black feathers stabbed above her, glistening in the frosty light. Her coat was seal, or sable. She glided unaccompanied to the edge of the crowd, and they let her pass, recalling incompletely perhaps that I was someone before I was Steven Gambit, that this woman in black possessed rights to that other, former self, which superceded even the hunt for an autograph. She reached a gloved hand toward mine as I descended.

I smelled her, the unmistakable mix of her self unchanged as we embraced. Her touch was the same, and the veil misted her face so her features were those of years before, when I, barely eighteen, and she, just touching thirty, had last held one another, body to body, on the same platform.

"Dear Gams. I've missed you so much."

Her voice, full of breath and secrets there close to my ear, struck me dumb, and I could not believe that nearly fifteen years had gone. I held her tighter and felt tears in my throat, which I swallowed, shuddering.

"You must be exhausted. Come on."

She led me through the crowd, which was silent, a bit surly at its loss, though just as we reached the door of the station there was a flash, the photographer from the *Star and Informer*, I found out the next morning from the newspaper's front page:

"Film Star Returns for Father's Rites." I wondered if Mc-Cready still wrote the headlines.

"Are you all right?" Mrs. Randall asked when we were securely in the car, a monstrous, somber Packard. She had gotten in behind the wheel.

"Yes, yes. I didn't think . . ."

"Ever since your father died. The idea you might be coming even got the stadium off the front page."

I barely heard her, my attention drawn outside to those still-familiar shadows; inside to her, incongruous behind the wheel.

"You're quite the favorite son, though everybody tells me they can't imagine how such a nice boy could play such a terrible man."

I laughed, then cut myself short. "But you. How are you?"

She turned to me, the streetlamps shimmering momentarily across her clothes as we made a turn. She signed. "All right, I suppose. It hasn't been easy, these last few days."

"Years," I said.

She shrugged. "Those haven't been that hard, Gams. We all make our adjustments."

We were silent up the hill. The big house loomed ever larger before us. Light poured from the French windows of the parlor, but otherwise it was dark. Getting out of the car, I stopped, the tower thrusting over me ghostlike in a three-quarter moon. Mrs. Randall came around and slammed my door, then took me by the arm and led me inside.

She had redecorated in the twenties, so that much of the massive and overstuffed furniture I had known, the bric-a-brac, the heavy drapes, the tassels and cords, were gone. Still, there were reminders: an Oriental rug, Diana on duty in the hall, the baby grand in one corner by the windows, surmounted by Mr. Randall's candelabra. There was a great silence over the place.

"Sherry?"

She brought me rather more than I should be expected to drink and rather more for herself as well. She sat in a wing chair, eased off her pumps, and stretched her feet across an ottoman. I remained standing, confused, lost in my own house. She gestured toward the other chair.

"Sit down."

She was different. Her hair was cropped short. As she removed her hat and set it casually on the floor beside her, I could see the wrinkles that cut across her temples, a deepening crescent that marked her chin. She was stouter, not yet matronly, but thicker of body, though her figure was still good and her neck proud as a swan's above all that black. Her gaze was the same, and the way her hands moved flawlessly, cautiously, as she spoke.

"And the trip?"

"Good enough, I suppose. I should have come through New Orleans." Absurdly, I began the litany of the journey: the accommodations, the scenery, the delays, the food, the difficulty in making the best connection. She produced some Chesterfields and an elegant gold lighter. I stopped in mid-sentence.

"Want one?" she said, puffing her cigarette to life and offering me the pack.

I sat speechless. She began to laugh.

"Oh, Gams, for heaven's sake. I'm not a fallen woman."

I had to laugh too, as if she, here, had not lived the past decade and a half, as if all those starlets lighting up on the screen would not have convinced even the most demure of ladies that tobacco was no sin.

There was an uncomfortable pause. I looked up to the ceiling; at the draperies.

"How did it happen?"

She told me about the accident.

"Killed instantly, no suffering."

"Was he drunk?"

"Perhaps. Probably. I asked them not to tell me," she said, then smiled. "We still have a certain influence." She swirled her sherry in the glass, a sad, soft gesture. "He often was. It's been worse since the Crash, of course."

"Did he lose quite a lot?"

I had asked in letters, watching the price of cotton plummet, and was always assured that while things were not rosy they were very much better than might be expected.

She barked a single, bitter laugh. "True Harmony has been nearly bankrupt for two years. And your father had done quite a lot of speculating. Then, when the stadium burned . . ."

"What?"

She took another sip of her drink. "I didn't think you heard me in the car. Ten days ago. They'd been using it to store surplus cotton, hoping the price would rise. The county couldn't maintain it. But then it caught fire. It was spectacular from the tower, the whole hollow in flames. The stands were destroyed, one entire side collapsed. We can go and look after the funeral, if you like."

I should have been shocked by her casualness. But I was more struck by my father's ruin, and so Mrs. Randall's.

"But how will you live? If his investments have gone bad, what will you do? Do you — "

"Don't worry, Gams." She snuffed out her Chesterfield. The smoke poured languidly from her nose and swirled around her face. "I'll manage. Just the rents are enough to get by on, and we hold the mortgage on the MacKenzie Palace, and I've wanted to sell the old house for years and now I'll have the chance."

The Randall place, embalmed season to season.

"Do you have a buyer?"

She nodded, smiling slyly. "The Cashes. They've wanted the property for years."

"Jimbo's people?" I said incredulously.

173

"Jim Junior, Gams. Cars sold very well in the twenties, and Mr. Cash went into auto parts, too. Everybody, your father included, told him he was crazy. But it's the mechanics who are on the soup lines now. They'll tear the house down." She gestured dramatically, draining the last of her sherry. "I've seen the plans for the neocolonial Mr. Cash has been dreaming of. Both my husbands would be appalled."

She was harder, colder than I had imagined for those fifteen years of joylessness, of assuming faithlessness from the man she once loved, and perhaps matching it herself there in Miami with a salesman, a bellboy. I felt sick.

"And Althea?"

"She comes twice a week now. It wasn't the cost. She makes nearly as much as she did before. But after your aunts died . . ." She pressed her fingers beneath her chin. "I always knew how to cook."

I could not hate what she had become. She was, in spite of the years and what they had brought, still beautiful, and if the bitterness of the last decade and more had steeled her, had stolen her youth more than a bit, it had given her strength a brilliance that made it even more potent, something I could only admire.

"I should sleep," I said.

"Althea came by today especially to make up your room," she said. "I'll sit up a bit."

I started for the stairs.

"We brought the bearskin down from the attic," she said to the empty parlor. "The moths had gotten to it some. But we both decided you wouldn't know how to sleep if it weren't there."

On the way back from the burial, on the way to the wake, we stopped at the stadium.

The instructions confused Clive Everhardt, who was driving,

and doubtless a couple of other people from out of town who had decided to follow the chief mourner's car. Althea had missed the interment to make sure everything in the kitchen was in order, while the vestrymen's wives would take care of serving. Our tardiness would cause no remark. It was expected we would use the backstairs, remain private with our grief a few moments in our bedrooms before descending to accept the condolences not only of Franksville but of those from the capital and elsewhere in the state, and even from a few of those Princeton classmates, one of whom came all the way from Norfolk. If we detoured on the way home, it would be put down to the eccentricities that mourning allows. Even if not, neither I nor Mrs. Randall was particularly concerned that Franksville thought us peculiar.

It was, inevitably, smaller than I remembered it. Accustomed to the freshly minted Colisseum in Los Angeles, and having seen the original in Rome, I thought the hometown hippodrome a paltry thing. And yet, when we finally stood beside it, our perplexed chauffeur left behind, Mrs. Randall on my arm, it seemed somehow grander in ruin, moreso even than the ancient one, not scrubbed up and fit for tourists. Here, Alaric had only recently passed by.

One side, as Mrs. Randall said, had collapsed, ill-plastered beams beneath the stands seared to nothing by the flames. Or perhaps it had been the explosive force of the cotton itself, dried by an unseasonably rainless fall, ignited bomblike in seconds beneath those benches intended for stamping, stammering crowds of autumn or the thin band of aficionados who followed track in the spring. As we walked onto the field, the smoke-blackened arches rose like the bones of an aqueduct or basilica, all that was left of the proud dreams of the town where I was born.

The destruction was less on the other side, though more sinister. There the bleachers had been saved. Indeed, in one corner they had not been touched at all, the wood gray, splintered, but whole. Elsewhere, however, the benches were charred black, as if at the final game of the year Franksville High had taken the field against hell itself, its legions in attendance scorching the bleachers with their fiery behinds. I smiled. There again, this was the home team's side.

"They suspect arson," Mrs. Randall remarked.

"Wouldn't be the first time," I said dryly.

When Clive turned onto our driveway, the street was already thick with cars. We pulled behind the house. I noticed the Cashes — Mr. and Mrs., Jimbo, his two brothers and three sisters, accompanied by who I assumed to be their spouses and children — at the far side of the lawn, sniffing the shuttered Randall house. Mrs. Randall saw them, too.

"Voltore or Corvino?" I said.

"Pardon?"

"Italian for Cash."

I offered her a cigarette. She brushed the pack away. The circumstances did not permit it, much as she must have wanted one.

In the kitchen, I hugged Althea, who wept unabashedly, sincerely. She was old now, her breasts, still firm when I left, now those wide, flat pillows which give no suck and do not harden with desire but instead offer succor in sorrow, some motherhood beyond blood.

"Lord Jesus," she said. "Too long. What they got out there in Hollywood? What boys you act! And your poor Daddy . . ."

It was an unselfconscious grief, which moved me even as it struck me cold. I did not understand how she could so unambiguously mourn him as she welcomed me. She knew it all. She knew more than I could: the snippets of conversations, the meaningful looks, the occasional sidelong confession, the veiled gossip out of Lottie and Bea; and more, from those other maids and cooks and gardeners from other houses who accumulated the stray remark, the snipe, the "Thank God we don'ts," all intermingled in Pallister Slough — so the mosaic of Franksville fit together in wondrous and revealing ways unknown on the hill or downtown, amidst the white congregations of First and Second and so on Baptist, Presbyterian, Methodist.

We went upstairs. I had been there less than twenty-four hours. The funeral had been delayed in the hopes I might come. I had a headache, and my mourning suit, bought hurriedly on Wilshire Boulevard, was too small. The images of St. Peter and St. James sat heavy in my mind, coursing through me like rum: a weighty, too-sweet vagueness. It was all too much like Mr. Randall's dying, like the wedding, like some silly film in which I'd been an extra or played a minor part. I still had no idea how I really felt, adopting manly grief for lack of a better solution, unsure if I should feel happy, sad, triumphant, furious, guilty, or vindicated. I longed for a script, or Tom and Su-Su, a delirious party with reefers and liquor to the point of forgetfulness, all in the soft, damp chill of the California winter.

"Are you ready?"

Mrs. Randall stood in the doorway. She had changed her dress, her new one black too, of course, but less encumbering, more flattering than the one she had worn at graveside, as if the widow's cloud had already begun to lift from her. I remembered those other times I had seen her framed like that: in pearls on the evening of my *September Morn* episode; three nights after the burning; during those fevered visions after my collapse; the moment when she told me, "You will go to California."

"Coming?"

"Of course." I sighed. "But I don't think I'm going to enjoy it."

"I don't know what the etiquette books say about giving autographs at times like these," she said lightly, offering her arm.

It was as awful as I had imagined. Half those in attendance treated me with the deference accorded before the war to reigning monarchs of significant powers. One young lady curtsied. Some women and girls huddled together, whispering and giggling, making judgments. Was I as handsome as I was on the screen? Was my suit too tight? A few men attempted old-time affability, which would have included guffaws and backslaps had this not been a wake. A large number of people seemed utterly at sea as to what to call me, a problem some avoided by addressing me as "sir." This, in view of the fact I was ten or twenty years younger than many of them, only increased my sense of royal isolation. I had a stab at conversation with the pregnant Melissa, who answered in monosyllables and seemed dumbstruck with wonder and fury, one for my being a film star, the other for not having held on to me when she at least assumed she had had the opportunity.

My brief interview with Jimbo was a disaster. Though Mrs. Randall had commented that a few months' work with an elocution teacher some years before had cured him of his stuttering, he stumbled over every third word, while his wife, a woman from the capital, surveyed us two old friends with a smile frozen with contempt for him and loathing for me. She had the unctuous manners of an accomplished poisoner and flinched every time I called him "Jimbo." "Jim Junior" had obviously been her idea. He, the bright young god of the backfield, had developed a paunch and grown a bit broad of breech. The five minutes or so were so excruciating I finally, rather abruptly, excused myself and slipped into the bathroom, where I slapped my face with icy water from the tap. Surreptitiously as I could, I stepped back into the hall and, just before reaching the foyer, ducked into the study.

There, ironically, I found respite, in his little redoubt. The books he had left were still scattered on the tables by the easy chairs, and figure-loaded foolscap littered the desk. A half-smoked cigar graced one of the ashtrays. Through the sheers, I could see the Randall house.

I gritted my teeth as I heard the door swing open.

"For a slacker you look pretty good, far as I can see."

I snuffed a laugh and turned around.

"Mind if I come in?"

Bobby's glasses looked a bit thicker, and the frames were different. Perhaps he had lost a little hair. But his face fell in that same expression of cynical estimation — a little wiser, a bit more tired, but undeniably his.

"No, as long as you close the door."

He clicked the latch behind him and walked across the room, surveying me critically up and down, nodding his head. He stuck out his hand.

"Nice to meet you, Mr. Gambit. Any man who did what you did to that girl ought to be horsewhipped."

"Thank God somebody here's got the guts to say it." I glanced over at the bookshelf. The glasses from which my father and Mr. Randall had drunk were there, the decanter alongside. "Sit down. Scotch?"

I splashed each of us two fingers neat.

"Whiskey's mine," Bobby said as he took a sip.

I laughed, sipped my own. I coughed, the taste unexpected. It was a blend, a cheap one.

Bobby shrugged. "Kentucky's a lot closer than Scotland." He took out his Luckys. "Talk to Jimbo?"

"Yes. It was a little . . ."

"Got him by the nards, doesn't she?"

"Yes, I guess . . ."

"Not that he had very big ones to begin with. Even with all that football. He always had a collar just waitin' for a leash."

I nodded. It was Bobby, surely. Bobby unadulterated. I settled into the other chair. "So, what —"

"Drummin'," he said. "Atlanta Lock and Safety Box. Four-state territory. Thirty percent of my time on the road. Thirty percent in hotels. Thirty percent at home."

"What about the other ten percent?"

He smirked. "Bars, cafés, and whorehouses. How 'bout you?"

I talked a bit about the studio; about the house.

"Done all right, then. That's good." He threw down half the whiskey in a swallow. "Hah! Well, I guess I was right a long time ago. We all did end up pretty much doing what our daddys did."

I cocked my head. "What do you mean?"

"Oh, me on the road; Jimbo with his cars; you acting."

"But my father wasn't an actor."

Bobby raised his eyebrows. "Oh, he did pretty good those first few years. You weren't around long enough to see it, I guess."

I shifted uncomfortably, knowing what he had to say would not be pleasant. But I knew too it would be the closest I would come to truth here. I gestured for him to go on.

"Oh, for a long time nobody knew there was anything wrong — between them, I mean. With you, well, everybody just figured you were about the biggest bastard this town ever saw, especially when you didn't come back when your aunts died. You know: you were a slacker, you had a swelled head, you'd got thick with all them 'actors' out there. You got dragged through the dirt good" — he French inhaled — "by all those same people who were just suckin' your toes out there."

I smiled, nodding.

"But nobody figured there was any problem particularly between him and Mrs. Randall. She's a hell of an actor, too. There was some gossip, of course. But, hell, what else do you do in a burg like this? Up till twenty-five or so, I don't think anybody took that kind of stuff seriously. I sure didn't, till I ran into your old man at that cathouse in Richmond."

I reached for his cigarettes.

"After that, we ran into each other time and again," he said, ignoring my discomfort. "Here the last couple years, he took to inviting me over when I was in town. And he was. It was about the same time he switched to blends." He shot his cuffs and put his hands behind his head. "If there's Scotch, it's in the left bottom drawer of the desk."

"Thanks," I said. The bottle was hidden in the back. I poured some into my empty glass.

"Whiskey's mine," he said. I brought over the decanter. "Yeah, me and your old man talked a lot in here, just like we're doing now. He talked to me a lot about you."

I closed my eyes. I could see what was coming: the recriminations, the sense of betrayal, the self-doubt, the assertion of a father's love and the awful perplexity he felt.

"He hated your guts. I think half the dirty stories about you here he started himself. Just two weeks ago, right where we're sitting, he told me that you and Valentino and that Cary Grant fellow were all fairies. He tried to hate her, too." Bobby nodded toward the parlor. "But he was never very good at that. Whenever he tried to — hate her, that is — he looked like such a hurt dog I never believed it. It's a sad thing to see a man with his tail between his legs like that."

Bobby was hard, the hard younger brother of four other boys who is allowed no illusions for the disillusions of those who came before. He cocked his glass back and tipped down some more whiskey.

"He wasn't a bad fellow, Gams. I don't know what you think. He sure as hell never knew what to make of you. Probably Randall was the worst thing that ever happened to him. He'd have been a good salesman. If your mother hadn't died, maybe he'd 've been okay. But there was too much money. And Randall wanted a boy too much. And then there was her." He gestured again. "I don't know whether she's the Virgin Mary or a hell-bitch, Gams, but there's something about her that'll rot a man out. Something happened to that lady once, and it did something to her. Your old man knew that, even though he never figured out what was wrong." He shook his head. "Or maybe he did, but he could just never bring himself to tell anybody."

He poured himself some more whiskey. He drank fast. Too fast.

"Hell, what do I know?" he said vaguely. "When do you leave?"

"A couple days. I'm due back next week." It was a lie, but I had practiced it since I arrived.

"Good," he said. He looked at his glass. "I talk too damn much."

"No, not —"

"Shut up. Yes, I do." He looked up suddenly. "Just get the hell out of here quick as you can, Gams." There was an urgency to it; a wild protectiveness. "There's not a goddamn thing for you here." He shook his head, whether in negation or to clear it I didn't know, and stood up. "You've got to get back in there. They're gonna come looking."

"I suppose." I clapped him on the shoulder. It was like some illustration off the cover of one of those Honest Dick books of our childhood. He shrugged my hand away, but kindly.

"Don't get all sticky, damn it. This is a funeral."

We walked back into the parlor together.

No one stayed much past four. My father had made many friends, not intimate ones. It was hard to tell how the town felt about him. He was not Mr. Randall. He had not been their legate to the halls of the capital, the man they trusted with such business of state as affected them, and who in turn curried them, respected them, listened to their problems and called them by name. My father, risen from the ranks, had assumed an air more imperial. He obtained the purple not by election but adoption; his obligations to one man, not many. The mourning, then, was more polite and perfunctory than that for the town's leading citizen two decades before. The towered house on the hill was like Capri, its impact on the lives of those below peculiarly indirect, mediated through the agents of empire: the True Harmony mills, the Fidelity Savings Bank, the Brotherhood Fund of St. Peter and St. James, the Chamber of Commerce, and the Rotary Club. Even with his reverses, when he died my father was the richest man in Franksville. The Pritchards were falling ever faster into the dissolution and idiocy that made Southern fiction of the era so popular, and the Cashes and others (the barbarian hordes, to follow the accelerated history of the metaphor) were only beginning to breach the walls.

I sat in my room, embarrassed by its immutability. Even the kerosene lamp, frivolous and nostalgic, was still in place, along with the bearskin rug. I might as well have had Yvette hidden under the pillow. All the Hollywood years were false as film, and I belonged to this place as much as ever, despite Bobby's remembered voice, urging me every moment to collect my bags and leave immediately for the station. That room, house, town, was a vortex of something unfinished, unfinished since my flight fifteen years before, and, having plunged into it by my simple returning, I now must have done with it.

Up to the end, though, I could not make my proposition. I waited, and in that waiting watched her, crafty and obsessive as some Jacobean villain-hero. Her loss of the youthfulness I had first loved at eleven and seen still at eighteen made no difference. Her ripe forties became as attractive to me as the diaphanous teens she had first shown me. Our daytimes were passed in reminiscences and short walks through the winter briskness.

Dinner, with wines from France and candlelight and Althea (not completely silent) serving, the two of us at opposite ends of the table, laughing over the past, took on a suggestiveness that encouraged me. Then there were drinks and the fire and the long, slow evenings. Even though her door was shut and bolted each night, I, alone in my adolescent lair, gave rein to my fantasies without question or regret. My desire, spiced by mourning, fed my bravery, made me ever more ready to declare myself.

Then I was out of time. Wednesday had come, and no more dreaming there amidst my childish things would do. We were in the parlor, sherry in hand, the embers fading slowly, me prattling story after story about Hollywood, Italy, fan magazine gossip, all to avoid the statement, all couched in indirection sure as seduction, sensitive always to a sign, searching her words, her laugh, for a trace of mutual wanting. But her ambiguities were finer honed than mine. Toward midnight, her eyes heavy, mine dry with liquor and the effort of wit, there was no further avoiding it.

"But seriously, what now?"

"What?"

"Will you really stay here?" It was the incredulous interrogative, demanding furious or amused denial.

"Of course," she replied with gray-eyed serenity, as if the thought of leaving had never crossed her mind.

"But why?" I said easily. It required every grain of my actor's training. I poured another splash of sherry for both of us coolly, unbetrayed. "There's nothing for you here now. Papa's dead. True Harmony is hopeless. The bank can manage your affairs. Why not get out of here once and for all? Come to Hollywood with me," I added lightly. "California's much cheerier this time of year anyway."

She shook her head with a knowing grin. "Don't be silly, Gams. This is my home now. I couldn't leave here."

"Why not?"

"Oh, briefly perhaps. Traveling. But . . ."

"Why not?"

She looked up, surprised at my insistence. Then she said deliberately, "This is my home."

"This? Home?"

She sighed. "As much as I've had one. Gams, Los Angeles may be fine for you —"

"And you! What has this place ever given you?" I injected sharply. "A lot of bad memories and Papa out —"

"That's enough."

". . . at play."

It struck home, but not in the way I would have hoped or quite anticipated. A slyness came across her face, a comprehension, a rising to the challenge.

"They've taught you well out there," she said, her finger on her goblet's rim. "It's a nasty world all over, I suppose."

"Not nasty," I said defensively. "Realer than here. You'd see. It would be better for you there. It's a freer, fuller place. People care more and less about each other. They've never liked you here, what with all the gossiping right from the first." Touch. "There you can do what you want, with no one judging, no one nattering behind your back. Or even if they do, no one listens." Most palpable. "With a bit of discretion, your life is your own. With no past and no relations." Coup de grace. "Just like you."

For an instant, it worked. The wound ought to have been mortal, deep enough to free her of her old self. Briefly in her eyes there was the gleam of the notion of flight. But she resisted; drew deep within herself to snuff it out. She would not die and rise transformed, unbound. She fondled the half-full glass of sherry, her face impassive now, certain in an old faith.

"I don't think I was ever as young as you, Gams," she said quietly. "If I ever was, I can't remember it now."

"Don't patronize me." My voice was harsh. I knew what I

wanted, what I had returned to Franksville to obtain. "Come with me tomorrow," I said briskly. "It's perverse to stay here."

"I have my reasons."

"What?" I snapped. "This fire-trap of a house. The MacKenzie Palace?" I changed tack. "Or who? A sharp old bachelor with an eye for the ladies? A shopkeeper's boy he took as his own?"

"That will do, Gams."

"Or some dumb bastard burnt to a crisp!"

"Enough!"

"Some bastard whose dying was enough to make you —"

"Enough! I am your mother!"

"You are not my mother! I love you! You are not my mother!"

"No. No. No. No. No, Gams." She shook her head in wide, slow arcs, back and forth. "That cannot be." Her hands rose to meet her face, and out of her came a noise, a breath like the last reverberation in the far distance of some terrible battle; the single, final sob not of buried love but of the burial of the soul's permission to itself to love.

Perhaps, had this been a film, I might have assaulted her, at the least grasped her fingers, tearful and obsessive, and pressed them to my lips. But suddenly histrionics made no sense, and my lust withered, collapsed terrified upon itself, there in my father's house. No resolve remained, only exhaustion; the knowledge of futility. I had no desire left, only memories of other men, while she survived, eluded, witnessed. Abhorred and absorbed it all. And Mrs. Randall would not deliver herself to dreams. To Hollywood.

"I'm sorry," I said weakly. The room wheeled around me, stuffy with some vague reek of violation. "I'm sorry. Do come if you'd like. I'd like that."

Slowly, she revealed her face, breathing deeply, her eyes on the fire as color slowly crept once more across her cheeks.

"I do love you, you know," I added quietly, hopelessly.

She turned her eyes toward me. "Gams." The word was sweet, Italian, not my name but some deeper knowledge of me. "Gams. Go back. Leave me here. I am your mother, after all."

And perhaps, as for all those others, old and young and lost, she was. I saw her, wedded to her pain for all of them: Mr. Randall and my father and my brother unborn and most especially that stranger mute and beloved. And what others unknown?

I could no more demand. I fondled my glass and, absurdly self-conscious, sent it shattering into the logs.

Mrs. Randall nodded. "Worthy of you, Gams," she said sweetly. "Your own best director."

"And you yours," I said. "And you yours."

12

MANY AFTERNOONS, toward sunset, I went down to San Vitale. There, beside the alabaster altar meant for the soft light of lanterns within, I gazed into the stern face of Justinian, believing, fleetingly, there was justice. But then I turned to Theodora, to that serene understanding of unreason in the world, potent in the countenance of the secret and beautiful courtesan, and knew the depths of my illusion. Later, reading Gibbon in bed, or Frenner, or Finlay, about the vagaries and intrigues of the Constantinopolitan court, of the wars and persecutions of the very man who presumed to cast up the world's most magnificent church and call it Holy Wisdom, I realized fully there could be no justice and very little reason. And then my only comfort came at the Arian Baptistry — below that naked Christ so frail beneath the hand of John the Baptist — kneeling there, lit by candles, for I knew the sexton.

This I did many nights.

I was never a communist. I think I might have liked to have been: the millenarian vision, the self-control, the triumphant quashing of private demons in the service of irresistible history. But Colton's Congregationalist liberalism or Anglicanism's easy tolerance, the inheritance of Southern provincialism or my being the jaded rube I was in my twenties, or something within I could not know or would not name, prevented me; that, and my own hopeless skepticism — or was it truly cynicism? — which made me finally such a perfect cad.

But I did try, after my fashion, after that cross-country journey upon my father's death through mile after mile of bewildered misery. It was not conscious. I was too deeply bound by my own private disappointments and frustrations to be converted by some ardent professor or labor lawyer in the club car over Scotch between Altoona and Pittsburgh. No Pall Mall legend appeared over the Santa Fe near Winslow, Arizona, beneath a hammer and sickle instead of a cross. But back in Hollywood, the visions of that trip converged with the words of screenwriters, actors, even directors, along with the tide of Europeans who, in ever greater numbers, swept over California, bearing news that rubbed old wounds and the echo of the word "coward."

So, in the thirties, I traveled with the fellows of the Party, made my pitches for Spain, and on occasion wrote a note for *The Nation*, *The New Republic*, even once *The Daily Worker*. I expanded damningly in the last on my visit to Germany in 1935; less brutally on less brutal Italy, perhaps because on that trip I first discovered Venice, and then Ravenna. But I was not altogether convincing, as an intense young extra who looked like Mayakovsky and died on the Ebro dramatically announced to me at a cocktail party at Dorothy Parker's that very year. My activism was confused by pressures brought to bear: contracts, a run of bad parts, and the studio's unmistakable suggestion that I marry. After the Harlow-Bern scandal, all bachelors fell under suspicion — public suspicion, which the studio dreaded — and so, I wed successively an Ohioan, a Belgian, a Lett. The Popular Front and my standing in Louella Parsons possessed an odd co-equality in my mind, though doubtless my inchoate ardor for socialism surpassed any I ever felt for my wives. My divorces were acceptable; reinforced my image, really, as a suave but heartless man. Where my politics were concerned, there was the ugly inconvenience of the Hitler-Stalin Pact, but with Pearl Harbor and the Lend-Lease, I appeared both patriotic and prescient. Even afterward, with our bright postwar hopes and Wallace and our loathing of Truman, the world of the ridiculous house in Brentwood was a kind one, and the challenges of what later were called *noir* films the sweetest an actor now face to face with fifty could imagine.

But there were signs. There were signs even before that burnt body in Berlin. I knew as early as 1944, when I was first referred to as a "premature antifascist," that I had played with a different fire, but the smell of smoke adhered. Happily, I had also exercised enough capitalist good sense to remain a very wealthy man and, as the clouds grew darker, made ready my escape. In 1948, at Christmas time, not long after a holiday celebration at which a guest unknown to me seemed far too interested in both my and certain friends' opinions past and present, I arranged my departure, sailing from New York on the *Queen Mary*, then making my way to Rome, to ruined Padova, to Bologna, and then Ravenna, assuming a committee that pronounced Brecht with two syllables would not attempt the name of a foreign town with three.

They didn't. I was, in the end, unimpressive game and absent

189

to boot, very occasionally traveling by train to London for a minor part in a Rank Organization production. This was before the renaissance of Cinecitta, where I played endless pro-consuls, sycophants, Frankish bishops in the not-so-spectaculars of the late fifties and early sixties.

For the most part, however, I lazed away my dividends in the late-nineteenth-century splendor of a tiny villa complete with valet and maid, not far from San Apollinaire at Classe. It was only eight rooms, a quite petite Petit Trianon, built by an aged count of one petty state or another that finally became Italy.

So I lived in the capital of exarchs, in that land where the trains, once again, had taken on their practiced freedom, and America was very far away. But I was never out of touch with it. There was Mrs. Randall, after all.

Two months after the earth pattered down upon my father's casket, after my declaration so ineptly stated, so definitively dismissed, she wrote me. When I was married, working, she passed through Hollywood; met stars. She got on well with my wives; they were pleased but a bit perplexed before the intense Southernness she had affected. In those first years, the five or so after my father's death, she traveled ever more widely, most often alone. I received a letter postmarked Havana; a souvenir from Montreal. But she journeyed not only to capitals. Postcards arrived from obscure fishing ports in Louisiana and mining towns in Pennsylvania and elsewhere; tinted scenes of cornfields in Illinois or Iowa, of the largest oaks and widest cave mouths and highest and lowest points in this or that region, state, or county. The last card was perhaps the most absurd of all: the statue of some Spanish queen, gracing the square of a hamlet set amid an obscure mountain chain in that part of the country where the Midwest tatters into the South.

Her cards never told me much, and somewhere in 1937 or 1938 they stopped altogether, as if her yen for new places and people, sparked by that visit to White Sulphur Springs, had been snuffed out as suddenly as it had struck. Afterward, she seemed perfectly content to remain in Franksville with an occasional West Coast jaunt, her letters assuming an accustomed rhythm, closed as ever with "All love, my darling Gams."

There was never any mention between us of that final evening in Franksville, buried deep and sure as her husbands, her past. The last time I saw her in California before my departure for Italy she seemed as effortlessly flawless to me as ever. Her legs were still shapely, her hair dramatically streaked with gray, and she was stylishly turned out. We spent an easy pair of weeks eating, shopping, driving up the coast to Santa Barbara. I suspect then — though there was no sign and she made no mention of it, and would not in the letters I later received irregularly by the Italian post — that she had already begun to die.

My mail came care of a trattoria near the cathedral where I lunched two or three times a week, letters arriving at my table with the menu, bread, and a bottle of the local wine, and along with my meal, I would imbibe news from home. Most of the correspondence was shunted through my agent in Los Angeles: Hollywood gossip, New York gossip, the continuing grotesqueries in Washington, together with Mrs. Randall's chronicles of Franksville's births, deaths, and scandals. On occasion, if business were slow, Fabrizio, the proprietor, round and always sweaty from the kitchen, would join me for a glass of wine; or it would be donna Constanza, his mother; or his son, his brother-in-law, or his raven-haired and ambiguous cousin Giancarlo. They would settle down for a chat with *il attore*, and in my wine-soothed brain the transgressions of America, of modern Ravenna, and two thousand years of lust, mayhem, and sacrifice all flowed together in comfortable synchrony, and it was hard to imagine a life more serene.

May passed with no word from Mrs. Randall, and though I

assumed the blame lay with the posts, I asked my agent to call her for my own reassurance. I read Arnie's response in a warm June haze:

> She insists everything's fine and that she's very busy. But I think there's something fishy. Why don't you visit? The committees will be in recess. Besides, a short trip would be no problem if you don't come to the Coast. No red-baiter will think to look for you in Franksville. They're all more interested in the State Department anyway. I'll stay in touch with her week to week, and it would be a terrific surprise if you showed up.

A return did not particularly appeal to me. But it all did seem a bit suspicious. Next day I traveled to Venice, and at Thomas Cooke arranged passage on the *Île de France* out of Le Havre two weeks later. I wired Los Angeles, then spent the next two days with friends on the Lido, returning to Ravenna on a brilliant Saturday morning. At the station, I had my bags sent ahead, anxious for lunch. When I arrived, Fabrizio seated me, brought my usual accompaniment, and then, in a nasty reprise of a scene played before, handed me a telegram. It was from Arnie, and consisted of a single word: "FLY."

Franksville Memorial Hospital rose on the far side of the Pallister Reservoir, its main entrance, not coincidentally, facing away from the center of town. Of the Slough, with its stilted houses, Magic Lady, A.M.E. Chapel, casual sex and families, there was nothing left, all lost beneath the still, dark waters of the flood control project the New Deal had brought. Downtown, the McKenzie Palace had grown more than a little shabby, its tearoom now a coffee shop with vinyl booths and a counter like Woolworths. My room was stuffy and smelled of summer damp. I sat down to wait by the phone.

When I had contacted the hospital earlier, they had told me that Dr. Murphey was unavailable. His answering service would have him call me.

"As soon as possible. This is urgent," I had said. "G-A-M-B-I-T. He'll know who it is."

Four days before I had been in Ravenna, though I had nearly lost my capacity to measure days, mangled by hours in airports, on planes, at banks of phones with my pockets bulging with change which felt so oddly foreign, by my drive through the darkness down the new state highway in a rented Chevrolet. Only one train a day made the stop in Franksville, and it would not get me there fast enough.

The town began several miles before I remembered it, a strip of businesses strewn along the road: billboarded and neon-lit. Franksville had fallen victim to the creeping ugliness devouring all of America, sending its tentacles out across the landscape, blighting field and forest and the quiet vistas that once were the reward of travel. I passed burger houses and drive-in picture shows, beer palaces, tire stores, and "CASH BUICK/CADILLAC," a sprawling lot of autos regimented beneath a glaring light cold and perfect as a photo of the South Pole. One part of my mind registered it all; another part replayed the scene like an old movie.

"It's cancer."

I fumbled in my pocket, another dime at ready, a dull pain coiling somewhere down below my stomach.

"God knows how long she's had it. The doctor wouldn't tell me. It was all I could do to get that out of him, even when I told him you were coming and wanted to know. It sounds to me like she's had it for years. Did you know? You there?"

"Yeah. Yes, Arnie. It's just taken me a little by surprise, that's all." I pawed for some response. "What kind?"

"What?"

"What kind of cancer?"

"Wouldn't say. A real tight-lipped son of a bitch. Murphey. Dr. Murphey. His number's . . . hold it . . . *Webster two, two, two, two, eight.*" Then it was Arnie who paused. "You okay, guy?"

"Yes, yes." I rubbed the back of my neck. "I've got to catch a flight now. I'll call from Franksville."

The phone rang.

"Mr. Gambit? Or Stevenson?" His tone was mean, rehearsed.

"Yes. Dr. Murphey?"

"Yes."

Nothing more. No sympathy for the relatives. No bedside manner.

"Yes, regarding Mrs. Randall. I wondered —"

"Mrs. Stevenson?" he said brusquely. "I can meet you at the hospital in half an hour. I have a patient to look in on."

"Very good. I —"

He hung up.

I shaved, put on a clean shirt, wondering absurdly where I might find flowers or candy at ten-thirty at night. The desk clerk glowered at me as I strode through the lobby.

"Door locks at eleven."

I whirled around, furious. "No one on at night?"

"Nope."

"There's no bell?"

"Yeah, but —"

"I'll be sure to ring."

I swept out, teeth gritted. Slamming my rented car into gear, I streaked down Broad Street.

Dr. Murphey had not yet arrived. I sat down on one of the sofas by a sickly rubber tree near the door. It was a few minutes after eleven. Five minutes passed. Ten. A tall brush-cut man

194

appeared at the desk. The nurse there leaned forward, speaking low, glancing in my direction. He turned. I walked toward him.

"Dr. Murphey?"

"Yes. Gambit?" I had begun to extend my hand. He turned back to the desk to exchange charts. "Or do you prefer Stevenson?"

I pulled up short; willed away my anxiousness, imagining the sound stage, my cues. But the cold now in my breast was real.

"Either will do." I paused. "Consistency is what's important."

It flustered him a bit, and for an instant I felt a silly pride about it. He was facing me again: a young man, muscular, a veteran, with his American Legion pin prominent on his lapel like a clove of garlic to ward off pinkish actors with unpredictable tastes. His hair was close-cropped, his mouth set, shoulders squared, bristling order. In my head, I heard the word *Wehrmacht*.

"About Mrs. Randall."

He looked me up and down, appraising, taking stock like a rival in an audition.

"Yes, yes. Mrs. Stevenson. Come along. You should see her."

We walked to the elevator, waiting in silence. The doors opened. The young black woman who handled the joystick smiled at me. It was the first smile I had seen since I arrived.

"Four," Dr. Murphey said.

He offered no information. We stepped out.

"What sort of cancer is it, then?"

The corridor was deserted, night-lit, every third fixture burning, which gave the white walls and linoleum floor an air even more desolate than they should have had. The words seemed to echo.

"Uterine," he said quickly, matter of fact, glancing at the chart as if to remind himself. "Initially. All over now. Surprising she's lasted anyway, with her heart —"

"Her heart?"

"You didn't know?" He was triumphant. "It's been going on the last ten years. Palpitations. The usual. Then there was the minor attack two years ago, a couple after that."

"And the other?"

"What?"

"The cancer. How long?"

"Who knows. I found it when she had the first attack. Badly advanced already. Must have been painful. Nothing to do, really. You her son?"

"Stepson."

"Oh." He sounded disappointed. "Well, you don't have to worry then, I guess."

"How so?"

We had stopped at the nurses' station. He held up his hand to silence me and spoke briefly to the nurse. She disappeared down a different corridor.

"She'll check to see if you can see her."

"How so?" I insisted.

He looked at me quizzically, then recovered. "Oh, you know. Predisposition. Runs in families sometimes. Who knows with her, though. She doesn't like doctors much, or they haven't kept very good records. You can't figure what caused it. Bad genes. Bad abortions. Douching with Lysol. They used to do that, you know. She's had trouble down there for years anyway, from what she says. Dropped babies like . . ."

He stopped, his hand floating in midair. It was as if he expected me to hit him, as if he were baiting me so there would be a scene, so I would not see her, so he could call the police. I loathed him but smiled ironically.

"We owe a great deal to modern science."

The nurse returned. There was a muffled conference.

"This way," Dr. Murphey said.

We made the turn into one wing of the E-shaped building,

and I suddenly understood she was dying. It arrived a fact, breaching all exhaustion, nostalgia, and contempt, eradicating pettiness, shattering my self-control. I suddenly trembled all over, bit my cheeks hard and bunched my eyes to keep from crying in the gloomy hallway.

We stopped, and Dr. Murphey's hand brushed the knob. I touched his arm.

"There's little time left?"

It was absurdly formal, out of a costume drama. But the words softened him. The red-headed, red-hating brutishness flickered momentarily, and something like compassion flashed across his eyes.

"You're lucky to get here when you did."

The light inside was very bright. I squinted against the yellow of the walls, the furniture some awful army surplus, gray as a gun, a television squatting in one corner. There was a jumble of covers on the bed, but before my eyes could sort flesh from linen, there was the smell. Sweet. Rotten. Not unlike the singed reek more than three decades lost — but no, more like the marble slab at Everhardt's, sign of the Ellisons' damnation.

The doctor whipped out his handkerchief. "Don't faint," he said. The command — ridiculous — somehow worked. The bunched cotton filtered the air, and I saw her.

She was gone already, her skin a mysterious living glass over the body surrendered to death. She was a thousand years old, her whole self imploded, some dark star lost from the sky. Only, deep inside, the fire somehow reasonlessly kept alive by God or will. Her eyes, opening and closing at the dazzle of florescence, had faded from gray to no color at all, and her bony fingers plucked mechanically at the sheets. She was propped on pillows, her mouth slack with morphine for which I silently blessed the Legionnaire beside me. Her hospital gown was on backward, and her breasts dangled toward her waist like wilted flowers.

"Cover her, for God's sake!" I barked.

Murphey, caught off-guard, threw the seersucker robe crumpled at the foot of the bed over her.

"Mrs. Randall?" The querulous unbelievingness of a child denying. "Mrs. Randall."

Her eyes, still aflutter from the light, focused gradually through drug and disease, her shrunken mouth moving toward a word or smile.

"Mrs. Randall?"

Her hand, wrenched by an old, familiar voice from the opiated labor of touching, touching, touching a sheet imprinted "Franksville Memorial," reaching deliberately across air endless as life seems at seventeen and falling softly over my fingers, the dulled face brightening in revelation, smiling:

"There was a boy. A baby boy."

I cocked my head, patient as with a little girl who whispers some secret. "What? Mrs. Randall?"

"A baby boy."

She smiled wider, in recognition perhaps, her knuckles rubbing mine, repeating, soothing:

"Boy. A boy. A boy."

Her teeth showing now, as if she had imparted the wisdom of Solomon, some timeless truth.

"A baby boy."

Then her eyelids dropped, sudden as a shade, and she slipped toward some deadly, beatific sleep.

"Mrs. Randall!"

Her breath was shallow, like a beast's, exhausted, her fingers mindlessly caressing mine as her last dreams carried her beyond places living minds have leave to go. Perhaps already she had begun the trip down that dark tunnel which leads from one world to the next; had already glimpsed a light beside which the glow of kerosene, tungsten, mercury, the sun itself are as nothing.

"Mr. Stevenson."

It was Murphey.

"She's asleep now, Mr. Stevenson."

I took my hand away. Her own massaged the blanket, slower, slower. I was dizzy, and the smell, momentarily banished, suddenly was back.

"You should go now, Mr. Stevenson."

I staggered up, and there it was. On the nightstand, right where it had always been, though this was not her house, her room. The hope chest, its old wood polished, gleaming in the hospital's icy light. There beside her bed were the explanations, the means of understanding what she had always hidden, always meant. Was the cinder there? What else? What clues?

I picked it up.

"Mr. Stevenson," the doctor said.

I felt it in my hands, light but solid. Things rattled within it, the bones of her secrets awaiting only thoughtful reconstruction.

"Mr. Stevenson."

I shook my head to clear it. It seemed ghoulish, surely, to rob the corpse before it was a corpse at all. I set down the box. There would be time. Time for the rest of my life to sort through those talismans.

I smiled at the doctor. "It was her favorite thing in the whole world," I whispered by way of explanation. "She always kept it near her."

We had moved to the threshold. He held the door for me and switched off the light.

"No surprise to me," he said as we moved down the hall. "She's made everybody in the whole damn place promise to see it's buried with her."

I sat in the car, the last of my cigarettes half smoked, knowing where I would end up and what I would do. My watch had stopped, but it was surely three-thirty, four, the summer darkness cool and silent. Nothing would stir until the birds at dawn. But first it would grow blacker still. The stars I could see through the scented summer air would dim like the retreating promise of knowledge. I took a final drag on the cigarette and sent it pinwheeling through the night. I reached for the door handle.

As we crept down the corridor, I began to laugh, a choked, burbling noise I suspect Dr. Murphey took for sobbing. But then, I could no longer hold it back, and it leapt out full-throated, booming down the hall, ricocheting off the sterile walls, louder for the deadly silence.

"Mr. Gambit!" the doctor hissed. "Please!"

An orderly appeared, and the two of them hustled me to the nurses' station, one on each side, into a cubicle filled with cabinets of records and medicines.

"Mr. Gambit, get a grip on yourself!"

My head was as light as it was that evening at supper ("Hoppy did it! Hoppy! Hoppy did!"), and I felt my self slipping away from me, overflowing with grief and loss, appalled at the way the world worked. I would end up in bed again unspeaking, but this time no angel would come with a lamp to banish the darkness and smooth my path to escape.

"Mr. Gambit!"

He was shaking me hard by the shoulders, and suddenly my jaws clamped together and the laughter stopped. I was not a boy. There was no one now to help. I had seen enough of things not to assume life was full of mean surprises and mysteries never to be plumbed. The Legionnaire's face was flushed with effort and contempt. I leaned back in the chair.

"A cigarette, please, if you wouldn't mind. I'm afraid the traveling and her condition have all been too much."

He drew away from me. "I don't smoke."

"I do," I said, reaching inside my coat.

After that, I drove. There was no sleeping. Down past the stadium, its surviving half restored, a scoreboard installed. Past St. Peter and St. James, nearly consumed in ivy; in front of the cemetery; past the darkened depot, one end boarded up, no sign of recent paint. I saw the site of the high school, a city park now, and found its replacement set not far from where, as best I could determine, Pritchard III had stood. But there were no trees, nor any sign of a railroad siding; rather, streets and stop signs and a new subdevelopment stood where the piney woods and the Ellisons' place had been. I thought of calling Bobby, of trying to find Althea, as I drove aimlessly through the town, knowing where I was headed all along, wishing in the back of my head I might avoid the crime and certain I could not.

From the veranda, I could see the Cashes' neocolonial, ugly as Mrs. Randall had predicted, the inevitable black-faced lantern boy posted at the end of the drive. I slipped over the old boards, having forgotten which ones creaked. Or perhaps, with the years, some had healed while others had developed swells and rots, which made them now the noisiest. Each step I took seemed to shatter the calm, and yet I knew no one would wake. I stood by the French windows, beside which she had often sat when I spied on her when she had not even lived here.

I reached down and removed a shoe. Bunching my fist inside the heel, I shattered the pane of glass nearest the latch.

I was inside in an instant, inside the dark parlor, the only sound my heartbeat. I felt my way along the wall to the far end, to where the piano stood. There atop it, as before, was the candelabra. I struck a match and lit the three wicks one by one.

The room, this time, was the same as before, the same as that night I had dared all I could. Even the chairs sat before the fireplace at the angles I remembered. I might have switched on a lamp, but I knew it would be foolish, and too that electric light would explode the changelessness, show me new acquisitions or the rug threadbare now. Perversely, undeniably, I wanted the house in darkness.

I moved through the parlor, into the foyer, past Diana's cold marble, her breast warmed by the candlelight. Then, up the stairs, down the hall, quiet as breath. To my room.

I pushed against the door.

The furniture was draped, every piece shrouded: the outline of the bed, the bureau. No bearskin graced the floor, but, incongruously, the lamp sat naked on the desk. I moved toward it, then drew back. Better not to see if the tank was filled, if the wick was set; not to know if dust had settled over it or if the chimney showed the stain of recent soot.

I backed away.

To my father's room then. Shrouded too: the chifferobe, the full-length mirror, the bed, wide and long, grandly headboarded, covered as deep as Mr. Randall's years before.

And then her room. I entered. The chaise. The single bed. The nightstand, its second shelf empty where the hope chest should have been. All unchanged, alive, hers. Her make-up still in disarray upon the vanity; a nightgown thrown casually across the chair.

I stood there.

The air was sultry, stale, full of medications. But for me it was endless years before. There was cologne, rice powder, the scent of expectation. Pearls rattled, and silk and linen rustled. But she was not there. She had left a moment before. I went back into the hall.

Though there was no moon, there was a moon, and the light played through the rungs of the balcony rail, in through the windows, across the green carpet. I carried my candle bright up those stairs and out into the air, to the place she had always fled, where it was cool on the hottest day and the scent of mown grass and magnolias drifted lazily all summer. There, in the depths of the silence before dawn, I heard music. And at that instant, perhaps, the precise instant her ghost flew ascendant like the smoke of an afternoon thirty-five years lost, she appeared, her mystery intact, travertine, alive, above a world she detested and had made her own.

I would go back to Ravenna, eventually to Hollywood, then New York, London, retirement in Spain. But no moment after would be untouched by her, as no moment had been untouched before. The candelabra flickered, and I reached for her hand. Franksville shimmered below us, bejeweled, bereft, robbed, though unaware, of its most precious treasure.

She stood before me, fresh as when I first saw her, the naked marvel of love. And finally, in the stillness of that eternal summer night, we danced.

Epilogue

1972

THEIR VOICES MADE a murmur like wind in the August quiet, there before the church as they waited for the coffin. In the heat, he was glad he had refused the offered tie and jacket, even though it was a funeral. His cousins looked hurt when he said it; a little angry, too. He had seen them nod knowingly to one another as he turned away.

Others in the crowd peeled back their suits as much as was respectful, and he felt lucky for the tree he stood beside. Their faces were red, set on bullnecks redder still, near to apoplectic in the harsh, chalky glare. They were patient people. People made to wait. People who expected little more than waiting. Acquainted with a God who demanded, never asked, they fretted lazily, unconvinced themselves of their sincerity, as if their restiveness were as hopeless as railing against dying or the measles.

They snaked glances at him: curious, hard, and amused at once. There were other outsiders present, but with haircuts and suits at some time vaguely pressed. Even if they carried cameras or notebooks, they held them surreptitiously, with due respect. They were simply less obtrusive than he was.

He wiped his forehead and the back of his neck, his curls barely caught by a rubber band, regretting now the army tunic from the VFW thrift store: his grudging, last-minute compromise with formality. Perhaps he should not have come. Better to have made connections directly in New York, than to make this trip overland to places that once were his. Aunt Grace's death was the excuse for the visit, and though he had missed the funeral, it was only right — particularly by the lights of this redneck town — that he should pass through to pay his respects at her six-week-old grave. In the swelter of this early Sunday afternoon, he could smile that he had set down in Christina the very weekend of another burial, the interment of a man who had spent sixty years here, one who nobody really knew.

"Howdy, Nate."

Him, they did know, these neighbors, clerks, friends of his aunt's. Years meant very little in Christina, where they could tell you how it rained in fifty-two and snowed in thirty-four. Since the depression, they had lived a relative history, observing the world in the way of the very old. If they noted you could grow a mustache now; if they supposed you were not innocent anymore; if they guessed you'd seen, known, and tried things they had neither seen nor known nor tried — then they could accept it grudgingly, gracelessly, for you reminded them that time was a dimension, not an acquaintance that things happened to.

He shifted, set his shoulder against the tree, almost dreamy in the heat as he watched the ushers scurry to clear the doors and a path through the crowd to the waiting hearse. It would not be long now.

In those early years, taking the train down to pass a couple of weeks of summer away from those suburbs where he and his parents and brothers and sisters made their lives had been as exotic and magical as those recent months on the far side of the sea. Aunt Grace's house, the nearby woods and the lethargy of a town sliding slowly toward dissolution — these had lent the place enchantment in his child's eyes, much as those ancient churches and shady boulevards had touched him in his months abroad. Christina, with its borderland mix of Texas boasting, Sooner opportunism, and Southern laziness, seduced him. And now, after Europe, perhaps because of it, he had come back to touch his own past and found himself outside a church filled to capacity for the rites of another man passing through, who had not, and now never would, leave Christina.

They emerged suddenly: six pallbearers, all solemn and grieved as if they carried their brother in the casket, then six honorary pallbearers, older, frailer, not to be entrusted with a dead man's weight. All in black, the second half-dozen with their hands clasped before their flies as if in promise to abstain for a month beyond the burial. Nate almost laughed, but then Callan McAlpern appeared — almost ninety, gray-suited, with a satin armband, the preacher at his side — and to laugh was as unthinkable as swearing by his late aunt's grave.

Every summer that Nate saw him, Callan was elegant in white or gray linen with a pipe in his mouth. Aunt Grace always told him, "Callan McAlpern is the finest man, the most gentle man. A man of manners in a world of fools." Still, it had been hard to like Callan when he was ten, or six or nine, for that matter. Callan always treated boys as if they were men; girls he approached with the patronizing gallantry of a world long lost, of the world before women bobbed their hair, much less smoked or ran for public office. "Nate," Callan once said. "Nate. You should look that up in the dictionary." And he did. At eleven years old, he found that "nates" meant "buttocks." He begrudged Callan McAlpern the knowledge for years.

The procession shuffled, crowded, lurched into the street behind the moaning Cadillac hearse, moving slowly down the block, past the square and the courthouse and the statue of the queen almost featureless now for the rain and freeze and August sun. She had been ill-used, Nate thought as he passed her, a scraggly pigeon perched on her shoulder and a mass of old leaves peeping over her crown. He smiled, imagining what they must have said at Aranjuez or La Granja as they prepared the letter, displayed still in a gilt frame in the City Hall, thanking the citizenry of a far-off American town — which counted no more than a dozen Catholics and absolutely no one of Spanish descent in its entire population — for rechristening their community, formerly Indian Mound, in honor of Christina Marie Henriette Hapsburg de Bourbon, Queen Regent of Spain.

They made the turn toward the cemetery, behind that Cadillac like Victoria in mourning. Beside him, the buildings passed unchanged, squat brick and stone, some with dusty plate-glass windows, which reflected the procession. Then through the gates, up and down the hill, past sepulchers and cenotaphs: "Here lies . . ." "Rest in Peace." "In Memory of . . ." Dead of a fever. Lost at birth. Fallen on the Marne or on the Rhine, the Yalu, now the Mekong. One drowned at sea. "Honored." "Sainted." "Beloved." Old markers mixed with those of the recently departed, last week, last month, last year among us. Past the family plot. His aunt's grave; some cousin struck by a train long ago. On to the earth new-scabbed, to the pit that — even at eight o'clock, anxious to avoid the summer's heat — they must have sweated to prepare.

"I do not sweat," Callan McAlpern had told him once; and no, Nate thought, someone so old could have no sweating left. "In my work, in a basement, sweat is not required or permitted. Elsewhere, sweat is honorable, the badge of labor, the proof of manhood. But for me, to sweat would be . . . disrespectful."

The words came back to him as the procession stopped by the grave: Nate and the crowd and the Cadillac hearse. The preacher, aging but not aged, said the last words by the coffin. Then they lowered it noisily, clumsily, into the ground. Callan came forward, took the trowel, and scattered the first dust over the wood. The crowd pushed toward the front, and a couple of people cried. Some had flowers.

He glimpsed the casket, mottled with earth, and saw the gravediggers patient with their shovels beside the young trees nearby. A little shudder ran through him, almost as if he had looked into his own tomb. He turned away to follow the others. From the corner of his eye, he saw Callan motion.

Since they had patched the fan with cardboard, it had never been as good. She studied it in the shade of the porch, tracing the wicker with one finger till it touched the fraying smoothness of the paper. She had owned a wicker fan as long as she could remember, since the days when porches were verandas, when she, hidden the day long from the August sun, would sit at dusk all in white amid her family, watching the children at tag and crack-the-whip in the street and the young men passing by, tipping fedoras and bright-banded boaters. She had a fan the night Willie proposed, the last night of his leave, all starch and creases like the lot of them in uniform — Tommy Bob Milton and Morris Farrell and Carmichael, her brother; all so dashing they seemed ready to vanquish the Hun by the sheer virile beauty of their presence. She had touched the rough wicker to her nose to hide the blush she hoped had risen, murmuring about her father's consent. Willie agreed and assured her of the gravity of his intentions, that he asked for her not because the war had come but because he loved her.

"Besides," he said, only half jesting, "nobody around here should get married for fear of dying. They say Christina won't lose a soul as long as Revelation Sammy's above ground."

They laughed then, and he leaned to kiss her in that close evening turning to dark, and the wicker fan floated across his back like a flower petal on a still, green sea.

Nobody made wicker fans anymore. Her son had told her

that, and Mr. Minniman at the five and dime. They couldn't replace it so they had to fix it, but there was no one to weave the wicker. So they used a scrap of cardboard. It just showed what the world was coming to.

". . . It's indecent, like I said, just indecent to keep him around that long." The spring on the screen door sang, and her daughter-in-law thumped down beside her, mending in hand. "They could have just taken some pictures. They had pictures then. Or even if they didn't, they could have done it later. Long ago. It's indecent."

The old woman nodded. She smoothed her dress over her knee again and again, expunging an imaginary spot, rubbing the cotton violets threadbare. The smell of violets made her lightheaded, and she had never liked flowered dresses.

"Don't." Her daughter-in-law did not look up as she slapped her hand. "You'll ruin that pretty dress. If you ruin that dress I'll make Wilson put you in the Methodist Home in Rock Creek. We can't afford new dresses all the time."

She took up the fan again; stirred the air a bit, futilely, against the heat. There was no breeze, and the roses in the garden just below simmered red in the August still, as if they would burn if touched. The quiet was absolute and a little threatening, so perfect she could hear the whisper of thread through cloth as her daughter-in-law sewed. As she looked across the lawn, it seemed the air had turned to glass, that everything waited in awed and expectant silence, as if doomsday had come and gone and all that remained was the final judgment and the repopulation of the earth by the blest.

"I just can't understand it. McAlpern must be touched, and it's not just old age. He was a young man when he went into business. There's no excuse to have waited this long."

"Callan McAlpern is a fine man," the old woman said. "You mustn't say he isn't, Mattie Anne." She pictured him: natty, handsome if a little short, refined but never pretentious, certainly not the type you expect to be an undertaker.

"Well" — her daughter-in-law looped the thread and bit it through, then held the shirt up for inspection — "stand up for him if you want. Maybe it seems all right to keep a body around like that. Maybe that's how you did it in the old days. But the Pastor always said it was immoral. He always said it was a sin. If he'd had his way, people wouldn't have had anything to do with McAlpern."

"But he couldn't have his way."

Mattie Anne frowned. "He might have, if the Preacher had stood beside him."

"As long as I can remember, the Preacher and the Pastor have never agreed on anything."

"Well, you would think they might have put aside their differences just this once."

The old woman shook her head. She had warned Wilson against marrying a Baptist. Her daughter-in-law had never understood there was a difference between Baptists and Church of Christ, and even if she had, she would probably have inclined toward the Baptists. She had never really seen the light, and so she would go to hell. Of course, even if she were Church of Christ, she would probably go to hell anyway. The old woman really did not mind that very much.

"Callan McAlpern did the right thing, but it probably doesn't matter much now. Whatever kin might have come are probably all dead now."

"They were probably all dead thirty years ago." Her daughter-in-law jabbed the needle into a raveled sock. "He just made the town a laughingstock, that's all. After the order from the Board of Embalmers, well, they say the newspapers upstate are full of it. Myrtle Meister told me they've got three reporters put up at the Bedford Arms, and one of them said a carload was driving in today just for the funeral. Everybody'll think we're all just as crazy as McAlpern."

The old woman gazed beyond the street, toward the center of town where the steeples peeked over the trees. She had wanted to go to the funeral, and she thought Wilson might have taken her if Mattie Anne had not objected. "She'll get sunstroke," she had said. "She'll faint dead away or worse in this heat." But there was no need for her to go to the grave. It would have been enough to sit in church, where it was cool, hear the eulogy and pray the prayers. It simply seemed unjust, and somehow sinful, that she was not there to lay Revelation Sammy to rest.

"Well, I better put the carrots on." Her daughter-in-law stepped from the porch to the front walk and looked up and down the street. "I can't see why Wilson had to take Willie. He'll have nightmares for sure." She shook her head. "Should have put my foot down," she hissed, then mounted the steps and disappeared into the house.

The old woman heard the screen door slam, then went back to expunging the violets. There were always violets in spring-time, growing wild in May in the parks, the fields, in backyards and vacant lots. When they found Revelation Sammy, they smelled violets. His head was resting on a pillow of violets as she had leaned forward with Carmichael, her brother, to wake the man. Then Carmichael pushed her violently away, so she fell in the wet grass and soiled her dress. She might have cried, but Carmichael turned and shouted at her to run and get their father and Dr. Ellman and the preacher and Mr. Halliday, the special-guest revival preacher whom they had all come to hear. He told her too that the man was dead. She looked down on the cold and bloodless face, like stained ivory in a wreath of amethyst, and her heart beat very fast and she could barely breathe and she ran from there crying, "Papa! Papa!"

The man's hand covered hers and she heard his voice quiet,

calming: "Now, don't you do that, Mama. You'll get Mattie Anne mad at you."

Her knees were warm from rubbing as she smiled up at her son and her grandson beside him. They were both named Wilson. The eldest boys were always named Wilson in her husband's family, alternating Wilsons and Willies to keep the generations straight for as long as anyone could remember, since long before there was a President Wilson.

"Did you bury him?" she asked quietly.

"Oh, yeah, Mama. He's all buried now."

"Did the Preacher make the eulogy?"

Wilson smiled and patted her hand again, kneeling beside her chair. "Now, he made a real nice speech, Mama, about how Sammy was as much one of us as anybody, even though we never really —"

"Wilson? Wilson!" Mattie Anne's slippers smacked in the hall. "Wilson, is that you?" She appeared in the doorway, ladle in hand. She glanced at him, accusing, before she spoke. "Well?"

He nodded. "I was just telling Mama. They did it real nice. Had quite a crowd."

She sniffed derisively. "Grave-gawkers, the bunch of them. All the reporters from out of town."

"Now, there weren't that many people from away. Mostly town folks. And everybody was respectful."

"It's indecent, if you ask me. Waiting so long to bury him, and then doing it like it was somebody important who'd just passed on. As if anybody there knew or cared a hoot about him! And you, you're just as bad as the rest, and taking the boy along."

"Now, Mattie Anne . . ."

"He'll have nightmares for sure, but you had to take him." She thrust the door open. "Get in here, Willie. Get yourself upstairs and pick up your room."

The boy skittered past her. Mattie Anne brushed a stray lock of hair from her forehead, glared at her husband one final time, then vanished into the house.

Wilson stood for a moment, then settled into the chair beside his mother. He snuffed a laugh, embarrassed.

In the silence that followed, he looked at her, and could see, among the welter of tiny lines on her brow and cheek, that tension, anger, hurt, apparent only after years of knowing. He cocked his head as he had done when he was small, as he had seen his father do, and watched her with uneasy amusement.

She spoke finally, with concern in her voice, a soft and guarded urgency. "Was it proper, Wilson?"

He nodded slowly, only half to humor her. "Oh yeah, Mama. Like I said, there's quite a crowd really, and the Preacher gave a fine speech, and there were lots of flowers. The casket was closed, of course. In all these years . . ."

"Were there any violets?"

"No." He pursed his lips a moment. "No, Mama, I don't recollect any violets."

She sighed and almost smiled. "I would have thought Callan would have brought some. He was there, wasn't he?"

"Oh, sure. Sure. I guess you could say he was like the next of kin. He's the one who tossed in the first shovelful of dirt, anyhow."

"And was he sad?"

"Seemed to be." Wilson chuckled. "Of course, in his business, I guess you learn how to do that pretty good." His mother did not join in his laughter. It died in a cough. "I think he was sad, really sad, I mean. It must have been like losing family after so long."

"Yes," his mother said, agreeing, her eyes fixed straight ahead, toward the steeples, "like family."

They did not speak after that, the old woman gazing at the distant spires, her son sunk in embarrassed silence, almost afraid to make a sound for fear it would be the wrong one, and yet un-willing to leave his mother there in the thick noon stillness. He was almost glad when Mattie Anne appeared, scowling, to call them to eat.

"Oh, by the way," he said, jumping to his feet. "You remember the Potts boy?"

"Potts boy?"

"Grace Mellors's nephew. Used to come down to spend summers sometimes. Years ago."

Mattie Anne screwed up her face, first in effort and then in distaste. "Well, what about him?"

"He was out there at the church today."

"Now, that's real nice," she snorted. "Showing up here so he can go back wherever it is he lives now and tell all his fine friends what a bunch of hicks and heathens we are down here. A grave-gawker, just like the rest of you. Come to dinner." She threw open the screen to punctuate the command. The spring buzzed long after the smack of her departure.

Wilson turned to his mother. "Come on, Mama. Time to eat."

She did not hear him, eyes on the steeple, her hands moving slowly back and forth across her knees, over the white cloth and its purple flowers. Even when he touched her shoulder, she did not rise, did not even face him.

"You should have taken me with you, Wilson," she murmured. "You should have taken me to the funeral."

He held her arm to help her up and spoke, patronizing, but with a hint of contrition. "I know, Mama. I know."

It was not the sort of room you could forget. In his life, he had passed no more than a single cumulative afternoon there, always with his aunt, the last time years before, and yet now, Nate could recognize changes, a new settee and a moved spittoon, that any-place else would have begged ignoring. Nor had the room grown smaller, despite his growth since he last saw it, nor had the dark wood of its desk and panels lost the mellow half-translucence of the brandy decanted in crystal beside the jawless skull, which deserved cradling, a rueful and bemused "I knew him, Horatio." The prints in heavy frames upon the wall remained the slightly faded, innocent Greek mythic scenes. All this, unchanged, in that same summer light of afternoon streaming through the clear glass rims of the stained glass transoms, nimbusing like a halo the colors cast upon the carpet, gilding the room like morning haze, scented with old leather and good tobacco and the suggestion of some unnamable and all-inclusive flower.

Into the deep and golden quiet, that warm still, contemplative but not oppressive, came Callan's voice, soft and lazy as the light, sibilant but with an undercurrent of resonance like flowing water, rich and lost, cadenced even when the words possessed no cadence, rising out of that queer, small man in gray linen nestled in the chair behind the desk. In the years Nate had not seen him, he had grown no older, perhaps because he could age no more, all the folds and wrinkles having formed long before, spots flecked like chips of agate on his hands and neck. His hair, surely, had always been white, thrown back from his eyes like a lion's dreaming, and his mustache, which drooped, pensive, to the corners of his mouth, had always been rimmed where it touched his lip with a faint blond stain of nicotine. He held his hands as before, with the fingertips just touching, a gesture of thoughtfulness, of patience, like a magistrate or magus.

"I did not realize it had been so long — seven years is it? But then, long for me has become a very relative concept." He laughed softly. "When your aunt died, I thought you might have come then, but you were away, I recall your cousin said. I think he said you did not even know until after the funeral. In Italy, wasn't it? Italy where you were?"

"That's right." Nate nodded.

"Italy," he said, and picked up the pipe he more often held than smoked. "Of all the countries of Europe, Italy was my favorite, though when I was there it had only officially been Italy for a decade or so longer than you have been alive. But Italy is less a nation than an idea, as are all places, perhaps, though then Italy must be — as Hegel, I think, would have it — the antithesis to the idea that is Christina . . ."

And Callan continued, in that tireless voice which formed each syllable with the thoughtless love of someone for whom words taste. Nate imagined him with steamer trunks at fine hotels, this American less anomalous in Venice than in his own hometown. He wondered then what the story was, why Callan McAlpern had returned from that journey in the century's infancy, to set himself to undertaking, ferrying Christina's dead into the next world for nearly seventy years.

"But it's Sammy you want to hear about, I imagine," Callan said suddenly. "Sammy. Because you yourself have been to Italy and I cannot imagine the Italians, who had not changed much from the time of Seutonius to that of my visit, could have changed much from the time of my visit to yours. But Sammy, on the other hand, is a case that arises rarely, I think. And Sammy has little relation to Italy, except for the specific memory this moment draws up for me, when I spoke with a man, a gondolier, who in his youth had briefly been the lover of Arthur Symons before he — Symons — found the gondolier whom he loved for the rest of his life, in spite of being married and having a family, as both gondoliers were married and had families. But this gentleman, the Venetian boat rower, father and husband, told me over a bottle of cheap but somehow inspiring red wine, a chianti, I suppose, the story of his love for or with or whatever preposition serves Arthur Symons, to me, who was trying bravely to be continental and unshockable, told me because, he said, someone should know the story, but it was inexplicably but certainly wrong to tell it to another gondolier or to another Venetian. So he told it to me. And then he rowed me home and accepted my tip and disappeared down the canals to the arms of his wife and children. But . . ." His voice hovered for an instant, and Nate could almost hear the whir and wheeze of a mind recollecting like an old machine. "But, never mind . . . never mind." He eased out of the reverie, leaving a sigh unuttered in the air.

"Sammy." He smiled. "You'll need to settle in for Sammy's story. Get yourself some more brandy."

Nate poured another nip into his snifter and into Callan's, thinking as he did so that yes, that is what he had come for, to hear about Sammy, that because of the peculiar coincidence that had put him here at the time the order from the Board of Embalmers came down, at his cousins' house on his way back from Europe, he felt almost destined to hear about him. It made sense to him, what Callan had said about the Italian gondolier, about stories you tell to strangers and to no one else, made sense because he had been a stranger and had heard — at bars, on benches, in hotel rooms — all those "always did love"s, "never did hate"s, "don't know why I did"s, always opened, closed, parenthesized with "I never did tell him or her, but now I am telling you." So, if he were for Callan nothing more than a twenty-year-old vessel, an open ear trustable and foreign enough to be filled with something for no other reason than convenience, mere casual proximity, that was all right. Even so young, he was wise enough to know that that was all right.

"I suppose when you were a boy and summered here you heard about Sammy, because Sammy, friendless and anonymous, had the privilege of posthumous fame. Around here, they tell me, he became legend, particularly among small boys, a few of whom (the naughtier ones, I suspect, bullies maybe or more likely the friends of bullies) claimed to have seen him, though I can tell you that was impossible, because I carried the key to the padlock of the coffin where we kept him, and I myself, over the last forty years or so, saw him only occasionally, when I checked for decay. But that is really unimportant, because enough people said they had seen him over the years to begin to believe, as they grew older, that they actually might have seen him, had a picture so vivid in their minds they must have seen him sometime before they could really remember.

"But to understand, you must try to see him as I did, not that long after I had returned to Christina, the spring Mr. Halliday came to preach the revival. I had been undertaker then for perhaps five years, five years exactly, I think.

"They brought him in the late afternoon, Jackson Abbot and Charlie Farrell and Atkins the preacher and Mr. Halliday the revival preacher, from the very field where he, Halliday, had delivered even to my jaded and agnostic ears a fine and moving sermon on the Book of Revelation. And we, none of us, knew the dead man; had never seen his face before. He was not old, not more than thirty, likely younger, though he had on him the signs of dissipation, of too much raw whiskey and cheap tobacco, and too little rest and hope and greens. But still, he was handsome in his way, swarthy, with bushy hair not so long as yours but long for that time, and a collection of tattoos and scars collected probably all over the country if not the hemisphere. He looked peaceful when they brought him in, which is not unusual for the dead but is unusual for someone so young. The young often come to me with a look of hurt, as if they knew they had not lived long enough. But he seemed to accept what had happened, not exactly with joy, but with the look I hope I will have when the whole affair is ended finally.

"We would have buried him then. I would have prepared the body and we would have put in the county plot, but for something Mr. Halliday said, looking down on that dark face lighter for its bloodlessness, a sort of ivory color, with a wild violet or two clinging to that bush of hair.

" 'It is a sad thing,' he said, 'for a man to die all alone.'

"That was all. Certainly nothing so profound or beautifully worked as his glosses on the Apocalypse of St. John. I did not even realize then that I resolved not to bury him till someone came to tell us who he was and where he came from and why he arrived to die anonymous at a revival in Christina. It simply became unthinkable that someone should die pastless, without parents or brother or lover to see him to the grave, with no children to mourn him or friends to recall with a glass of whiskey who he was and what he had done or not done.

"So I embalmed him: stripped off those badly patched, sweat-rancid clothes he had fouled himself in the act of dying; drew out the blood that had served him for better or worse for the thirty-odd years of his life; prepared the tissue and organs and pickled him better than usual, prepared, I suppose, for a more than conventional wait; and dressed him in a suit, not just any one but one left me by my father, which had always been too large. And the sheriff then sent inquiries up and down the state and beyond, while the preacher, Atkins, moved perhaps by the same inexplicable compulsion I was, defended to his outraged congregation Sammy's presence among us, defended it so well as to convert them into the most vociferous champions of nonburial. Atkins, before his death, extracted from his heir, then a fresh-faced seminarian from eastern Carolina, the promise that he too would defend Sammy's right to a past, and defend me, the agnostic undertaker charged with the care of those slowly diminishing mortal remains. And he kept that promise, and today spoke the eulogy in the church and the prayers at the cemetery and told me after the ceremony that he and I and Atkins had done all that mortal man might be expected to, and though it appeared to have been in vain, we need not be certain, for God (as I have always suspected) works in mysterious ways."

He stopped, took a sip from the brandy which had sat through it all untouched, and then began to load his pipe. He dug into the marble-capped humidor, tamping the tobacco thoughtfully. He struck a match and disappeared momentarily in a sudden and magical squall. Then slowly, he emerged from the smoke, which made him seem even older, frailer, more wizardlike.

Nate shifted in his chair, chilled as something inexplicable moved through him.

"You know who he was, don't you, Callan?" he said unthinkingly, quietly.

Callan looked up slowly from the snifter, then set it gently on the desk, his hand steady as his gaze, which settled over Nate, warm and approving. "Who Sammy was? Who Revelation Sammy was? That's what the stone says, you know. Did you see it there? They won't set it till the grave settles, of course. 'Revelation Sammy.' People just started calling him that, on account of the sermon, I suppose."

"But you know who he was." Nate persisted, oddly determined and a little afraid.

"Yes and no." Callan emerged from the smoke again like the promise of comprehension. "Sammy. You must recall I lived with Sammy, though he was dead for more than two-thirds of my life. No one ever identified him, not one of those two dozen or so people who passed through for almost fifty years. I never knew what his name was, nor where he came from, nor what he did, except for the little I could tell from the tattoos: an American eagle and a dirty picture on the top of his thigh. I could read his scars, too, some of them. The one on his hand was from a slipped cable, I think, and one on his side from a knife fight he was lucky to survive. And the one on his belly? That one I don't know much about, except that it was old, very old, older than could be acquired at sea by anyone but a cabin boy."

"How do you know he'd been a sailor?"

Callan reached for his brandy and spoke gently, indulgently, with that peculiar softness which begs understanding of more than will be said: "You come to know about sailors. Their skin is different once they have been to sea. It's never the same for all the washings with water from rivers and lakes and creeks, somehow tougher and more pungent and less giving than the skin on anybody else, messenger boys or barbers or gondoliers . . ."

Nate drew in a breath too sharply, abashed as if he had glimpsed somebody naked or interrupted him at prayer. "Uh-huh." He nodded meaninglessly. He exhaled slowly, let the shiver of violation pass, then prodded softly: "So who was Sammy?"

Out of that haze of brandy and smoke in the dying afternoon, the voice came thin but purposeful: "Sammy was the one man one woman ever loved, one who came here and sat where you are sitting now, in a flowered dress, regal and gray-eyed, a woman who was still beautiful as you looked at her and imagined how much more beautiful she was years before you saw her. She sat there, after a dozen and a half people had come before her and another three or four were still to come, and asked to view the body. And somehow I realized even then that she knew him, that after twenty-five years in which I had tried, every year a bit more futilely, to stave off the transformation to dust of a stranger I first met on a marble slab, the effort was finally rewarded.

" 'Do you have some reason to believe that you know him?' I asked her. And she said, with the sort of assurance that men do not challenge, 'He may have been a friend of my brother's.' Then she gave me some name that she'd doubtless made up, and I said, 'I see,' and took her downstairs where we kept him. There was no weakness about her, though she was surely feminine. As we walked, her step was graceful but determined to the point of defiance, and she so interested or intimidated or disoriented me that I did not inquire — though I noticed it and it struck me as odd — why she laid her handbag on the sideboard in the hall."

Nate watched as memory enveloped him, watched as, for Callan, evocation ceased and instead became what it before re-created; heard the footfalls Callan felt and the breath of the woman there behind him.

"She had never seen an embalming room before, I could tell, but she followed me past the table and the racks of chemicals and the hoses. I reached for the key I always kept with those for the house in my right pants pocket. We went over to the corner of the cellar where it is especially dry and I snapped the lock and opened the lid.

"She held back at first, but then came forward and looked down on him, on that dark face lightly rouged but only lightly, and even after all that time, if you believed enough, it seemed that he was only sleeping, just as it had when he first arrived. And she looked, her fingers on the lip of the box straining as if she were falling off the edge of the world, but her face was seraphic.

" 'Open his eyes,' she said with no emotion at all, no more than she would have used to ask me to open the door.

"But I told her I did not think it wise. Suddenly, she clasped her hand to her breast and slumped against the coffin with a weakness I at first could not and then did not believe, and I took her arm, saying: 'What is it?' And she said: 'My head. It's so close in here.' 'Come along,' I said, "I'll help you.' 'No, no, my pills. In the study, in my pocketbook. Get it for me. Please . . .'

"So I ran out, up the stairs, with all the noise I could make. But I had seen where she laid her purse, and I caught it up and crept back, quietly, quietly down the steps. She was there over the body, looking hard, but not at his face. Lower down. And then I stomped and grunted to announce that I was coming, and when I approached she was standing by the casket, recovered.

" 'I'm so sorry,' she said. 'These spells come over me.' And then she smiled, that crafty smile women use when they invite your sympathy. I nodded and asked, 'Is this your brother's friend?' And she shook her head. "No. My brother didn't know this man.' She had a fine pride in saying that, something I have little doubt was true, but told me nothing except perhaps that her love for him was secret.

"I wanted to say to her then that I could tell, that I had watched recognitionless faces for twenty years and I had seen even before she viewed the body that she was as sure as I was that she knew him. But I didn't. She had the dignity of someone who was caught once in a lie, a lie tremendous and deathless, and she had learned the way to defy challenge.

"I said, 'I see.' Meaning I see, I comprehend, and won't you now trust me and tell me just exactly who this is, but she would not. I do not doubt she read my ambiguity as easily, more easily than I read hers. But she only smiled, a turn of her mouth so aware of its naturalness it became unnatural. I said, 'Very well,' and reached to close the coffin. Then I noticed that the clothes were mussed, that the vest was crooked and the shirt wasn't tight. I set them right, there in front of her so she would have to watch, asking without asking for her to tell me what she knew. But she stood there solid as resolution itself, and when I said, 'You're certain?' she said absolutely, confidently: 'This is not the man I knew.' "

He stopped, that declaration of truth not truth sounding in the utter quiet of the study; it was not a steady hand that now reached for the brandy, but one aquiver as it must have been that other afternoon, when a woman in a flowered dress stood before him and denied him the knowledge he had sought for near to thirty years and whose loss he would regret for forty more.

"She left then, with a fine 'Good day, Mr. McAlpern.' And had I been braver or less of a gentleman, I would have called after her, grabbed her, shaken the truth out of her. But I only watched. Watched her pass down the hall and push the screen open and disappear. And I wept then, all alone, of course, here in the study, quietly, as men are supposed to cry even as they confront lost empires, much less opportunities, as they confront death, much less life with continuation contingent upon the futile hope that someone will return sometime." He took a sip of brandy and closed his eyes. "And she did not, has not, and never will, so I can be sure only that someone did know Sammy once, loved him, though where and when, why and with what results, I cannot say, not even knowing who those lovers reunited, one live and one dead, really were."

Nate's voice was rough, raspy with an old man's hurt. "What did she look for?"

Callan smiled. "The scar. The scar that she knew for all the years would still show, which she had probably traced once or a hundred times as they lay together. Perhaps even as he slept she would pass her finger over it, just a paper's depth away so as not to wake him, the heel of Achilles that proved his humanity before all the other scars and an early death proved it all too well. Proved it surely when she did not know him anymore, after she had found some bright and respectable young professional to marry her and cherish her and fulfill punctually and competently his husband's duties. But from time to time, as she felt him upon her, her mind went back to some manic fraction of an hour when she battled, half unclothed, with a boy whose scar she loved more in that moment than man ever loved the wounds of God.

"Somehow, she heard. Cleaning a drawer one day, she read the public notice in the newspaper liner. Or some friend remarked after church there was a madman in Christina who had kept a corpse around for thirty years. Or perhaps she remembered one night in a fit of acted passion what they had said behind the counter that day as she penciled out a wire, something about a man of such a height and such a weight with this tattoo and that one and a scar that ran from his belly to his groin. And the cry she uttered among the feigned ones was not false, and her husband grabbed her harder in the sad illusion of his potency, and she let him, did not decide till next day or next year or five years after or after that husband was dead and gone that she was going on a trip, to escape for a while, a week or two, the pressures of drives and teas and charity balls."

"But, Callan" — Nate leaned forward with his elbows on his knees, shaking his head — "if all that were true, then why didn't she tell you? She could have made you swear and identified him forty years ago, and you could have buried him. If she knew him, then why . . ."

"Because she did not lie to me!" Callan said triumphantly. "Because it was not the man she knew, whom she last glimpsed probably in the dark after a single kiss as he left her, a man ten or more years younger than Sammy when he died, a man innocent, hardly a man at all, that had no more to do with a made-up and eviscerated corpse left to dry for twenty-five years than he had to do with the undertaker who preserved him. When she found that scar, her mind told her that Sammy was indeed the man she loved as one can only love for the first time: virginally and completely and certain that love comes but once, which is partially true, true for that kind of love.

"But her heart denied it, assured her an anonymous cadaver in a small town in decline could not be the man she had lost or who had lost her, reminded her that as long as she never found him that he was alive, that he was as beautiful as in that moment she last saw him, that his life was as bright, as golden as she chose to imagine it. And that he still, as long as he lived, loved her and only her, as she loved him and only him."

That ended it. Nate knew there was no more to tell, and felt oddly embarrassed before an old man spinning a romance quaint as the allegorical figures in the landscapes on the wall, the romance of a matron in a flowered dress and the remains of a man long dead. And ashamed, too, ashamed to be embarrassed, for Callan possessed, he understood, the imagination to transform the dust of a nameless sailor — likely a brawler and drunkard who took whores passionlessly, quickly, then went back downstairs to drink some more — into a small-town Romeo, denied even that last embrace in a Veronese crypt. He stroked his finger again and again across the stubble of his chin, regretting his doubts even as he weighed them, watching Callan McAlpern in gray linen with his white hair thrown back, with the grandeur of leonine grace and the faith that men matter, that they are each strange and wonderful and play out inevitably some great or minor tragedy that is uniquely and completely their own.

"Is all this true, Callan?"

The old man leaned across the desk, still intense but with the fine assurance of a man unburdened. "I believe it is. I believe it all is. Not only the part I saw, but also everything I said about Sammy and the woman who came to find him, about where she touched or almost touched him as he slept, about that last glimpse in the darkness. Everything. All of it is true, is real, because what we believe is more true, more real for our believing than what is."

It was getting toward sunset. The light flamed on the carpet through the transoms, bloodying even the blues and greens of the stained glass. In the misty silence of that unforgettable room, Nate sat unmoving, sat until Callan said: "You'd best get back to your cousins', Nate. They'll have to wait supper."

They went together to the front door, to the screen she had pushed aside in her flowered dress to disappear with her secret, with her love intact. Callan held it open, then followed Nate to the top of the steps, with a look on his face Nate recognized: a look of peace, a painless look, touched with a tired joy before a whole affair that has ended finally.

"I think you loved him more than she did, Callan."

"No." The old man shook his head. "No. She loved him enough to believe he had power over death. An undertaker can never love anyone that much."

They shook hands then in the late afternoon, with the finality of two friends, both of whom will soon proceed to new cities; one of whom surely will never return again.

She thought, grudgingly, Mattie Anne might have been right. Even as the sun dipped to the horizon, it was hot, and the hills, no matter how gentle, required all the breath she could muster and more. She should have stopped, rested from time to time, but she was afraid they had already discovered she was gone, had rung the sheriff's and taken off in the blue Pontiac, which she had always hated, which was Wilson's pride; he would be cruising up and down the streets while Mattie Anne stayed at home, fuming and sputtering and likely cursing too, determined now that the whole problem be settled by a trip to Rock Creek.

That kept her going, with a smile almost. The idea of Mattie Anne helling and damning her way to perdition gave her a satisfaction that took her mind from the ache in her legs and the loud, irregular pumping of her heart. Mixed with that giddiness borne of exertion and heat, it made her almost gay as she trekked, step after effortful step, toward the cemetery.

It had been years since she had made that walk, as she grew frailer and, too often, simply sent flowers or condolences as the last of her friends passed away. But before, she had known the route often in procession, in memoriam: for Carmichael her brother at the reinterment of 1919; six months later for Darlene, her sister, dead of the influenza. In twenty-eight, for her mother; twenty-nine, for her father. In thirty-two for Morris Farrell, struck by the train. And on down through the years — a still-born child, her best school friend, Preacher Atkins, her other sister, Lucy — to sixty-two, when Willie's heart failed and she had laid him down with the others, his retirement watch and war decorations with him in the coffin, the American Legion Post at attention and a boy scout playing taps.

She remembered them all as she passed through the gates in her violet-covered dress, with her handbag and pillbox hat, moving slowly up the path past the graves of her beloveds. It was almost as if they spoke to her, those dusty voices, beckoned her. Her funeral would be next, of that she was certain. She would sleep soon in that earth which had received them all, Christina's earth where her life had been made and then un-made as her children grew and those she had known since child-hood slipped quietly into memory.

She heard no one behind her, and she knew she could climb it, make the last hill and look down upon the hollow where the cemetery wandered, where the new graves were, because she had to see that Sammy was buried proper now that he had finally been laid to rest, and to place the violets she carried wilting in her hand on the fresh dirt, those for the memory of that day she and Carmichael had found Sammy so long ago, and to make up for what Callan, in his grief, she supposed, had for-gotten.

Her dizziness grew, but she toiled on, a whisper of disquiet in her heart as she remembered once again what she had recalled that morning, what usually came back to her only each Decora-tion Day, how they said Christina would never lose a soul as long as Revelation Sammy was above ground . . .

Striding down the sidewalk, he believed more than ever that what he had said was true. Callan loved Sammy. Loved him more than any gondolier, although or perhaps because he was dead. He had loved him enough to nurse what was past all nursing, to grant a cipher the unique celebrity of a constantly impending burial, to create a past from the visit of some matron making inquiries for her too-busy brother. And that legend sang of a love portrayed as greater than one that had endured half a century, an unreciprocated abnegation to a stranger, the penance of the amoral blade who awoke one morning with a sensuous Italian beside him, beneath the eyes of a small-town God whom he could not escape and who damned him then and there to Christina and her dead. And over the years, that God denied to Callan McAlpern even the recognition of his selflessness, nurturing in his mind the fable of a woman who loved this man no one, doubtless, had ever loved, who coincidentally passed away in Callan's venue, probably already fevered and scared into eternity by a brimstone lecture on the end of the world.

Nate did not miss the turn by accident. He continued, sweat bright at his temples. There was only one place he could go now; one final call he had to make.

He went through the new gate, into the divide with hills on either side where the graves were still raw and the epitaphs clear upon the stone. Through the young trees, the sunlight passed unchallenged, their shadows sharp and dark across the shallow. He passed the potted mums and gladioli, the remembrances of those for whom death was fresh enough to demand live flowers, moving on to the newest plots, the ugly, loamy scars, to Sammy's, beside it the flat oblong marker with a question mark and the current year.

In the silence, he squatted there, demanding from that which could not speak the vindication of Callan McAlpern, the thanksgiving of Revelation Sammy for the man who would not bury him till he had invented a true and immortal and moral love with which to send him to the grave. The sharp-etched words in stone beside him, Nate smiled, raising his eyes toward the crest of the hill, recalling that quiet room, the old man and the ridiculous lie about a woman who had come once and might come again to stand in her flowered dress,

with the handbag on her arm (was it the same as the one she hid on the sideboard for Callan to pass as he rushed to the study?), appalling in the sunset in age and hope over the one man she had ever loved, enough to journey to Christina, to the morbid palace of a small-town madman obsessed with the past of a stranger, to the basement, to stand over the corpse of the boy she had loved, and deny, deny unto death, that the man who bore the scar she had worshipped in some romantic and romanticized rendezvous was indeed her beloved; deny his death to keep her youth and innocence, so that even as she surveyed his long-delayed and ultimate rest, she could still reject with all her soul what her mind told her was true, transforming that long-dead lover to whom she paid tribute into a divinity immortal and forever young, a wanderer who would love her

. . . He did not die. In spite of the years, they could not put him in the ground, so now he knelt perplexed by the grave so long denied him, and could not see it as his own. He had not changed: his clothes and hair, in silhouette against the west, were scraggly, disheveled, as they were that day among the violets. If Willie were there, or Wilson or Carmichael or even Mattie Anne, to see he was immortal after all, that Christina might lose souls for all eternity, but that Sammy, lost and nameless, Sammy whom Callan had kept more alive than dead for sixty years, Sammy could not die. His soul could not be lost; remained free wandering forever, the good angel who protected them, who loved them all for Callan McAlpern's sacrifice, for the preacher and the new preacher, who refused the pastor the satisfaction of anonymous burial till Sammy be-pure as a fire and stronger than time over earth and sea forever, just as that madman imagined, as it might be told over a brandy or a cheap but inspiring chianti by one who knows too much to one who cannot yet see there are limits to knowing.

came celebrous in his own right, till he had earned a name. And even then he would not be still, but rose now, before the Judgment, rose as fresh as the day he died, to watch over them, to keep and comfort Church of Christ and Methodists, Episcopalians and Baptists, too, Catholics and Jews and unbelievers, until the end, until the repopulation of the world by the blest.

They gazed long, even as the sun sank low beyond them. Across the graveyard he saw her eternally faithful as she saw him immortal. Both greeted the other unspeaking, sublime, with the awe and respect that befits two specters, with the joy and wonder of perceived revelation.